The 40 Year Old Virgin

L D Raylene

Published by L D Raylene, 2024.

"Dimana bumi dipijak, disitu langit dijunjung" – an Indonesian proverbs, which means "When in Rome, do as the Romans do."

LGBTIQ may have been widely accepted globally, but it is not necessarily in Indonesia. There is a strong belief and religious value instilled in this beautiful multi cultural country. Respect is always the key to fostering a harmony of diversity.

Chapter One

Who would dislike Christmas time? It was a beautiful time when all the air on the street was filled with Christmas music carols and decorated with colourful Christmas garlands. The shops would be full of fancy stuff that would tempt anyone to buy them as gifts for their loved ones. It was also the time to meet up with your loved ones, a long overdue catch-up with some old friends and distant relatives. Furthermore, in Victoria, in fact, in all parts of Australia, Christmas was the time for enjoying the lovely sunny blue skies of the summer season and beaches.

Without the exemption, that also applied to Cassie. However, for her, Christmas time could be a dreadful time. It was the time that she would be grilled repeatedly with the same question, not only by her parents, aunts, uncles, sister, or cousins but even some of her childhood friends. The question on her age and when she would get herself hitched. After the new year, in ten months, she would be officially forty years old by Spring. Her biological body kept ticking, but it seemed love was still not on her side.

Cassie sighed while staring at the beautiful blue and green coastal scenery from the window car. Sitting next to the driver and witnessing such a fascinating view would be her only consolation. However, in a few hours, her miserable Christmas was forthcoming.

Despite that, she tried to count her blessings. Next to her, the driver was her handsome brother – Kieran. Born only twenty-two months earlier than her, he was not only her closest sibling but also her mate and perhaps her other half from another life. Unfortunately, they shared the same blood. Sometimes it made her wonder whether she would be happier if the man sitting next to her now were her boyfriend instead. They grew up together, inseparable even after they completed their year twelve.

At eighteen years old, Kieran moved to Melbourne to pursue his university degree. He did not mind paying extra rent for a spare bedroom in his apartment while waiting for her to complete college. He took more casual jobs while doing his study to cover the cost. Cassie had already started visiting him two years before entering her university. It was only about two hours drive to the city from their hometown in Wonthaggi. The only time they finally lived separately was when Kieran finally met his other half, the true one – Emily. Unfortunately, they only lasted for ten years.

The blasting music from the car's radio broke her reverie. The half-screamed singing tone from the back seats made her wince. However, her lips broke into an amusive grin. The children's Christmas songs had been their accompaniment since they started their journey this morning. This time the song played was their favourite.

Cassie the Koala Bear
Cassie with the fuzzy wuzzy hair
She likes to eat all the green gum leaves
From the eucalyptus trees in the bush
If you see my Cassie around, say hello .. 'G' Day, Cassie"
She'll be watching you from above, down below.

It was a song with her name all over it. It became the favourite song of her two nieces –Kieran's daughters. When Alicia and Ashleigh sang it, it sounded endearing. However, when sung by other people who wanted to mock her, it would be the opposite effect.

"Don't sing too loud, girls," reprimanded Cassie while glancing at her nieces, who were shaking their bodies in their car seats, following the upbeat music rhythm. Her hand stretched to the dashboard to lower the volume.

"We love the song, Aunt Cassie. That's your song," protested Ashleigh.

Cassie only smiled, and she caught a grin from her brother.

"Could you please repeat the song?" asked Alicia when the song finally ended. Cassie did not wish to deny the request as she pressed the reversed button, and the beat resonated in the car again.

The song was repeated three times before Kieran insisted on changing to another song. Cassie could not hide her hilarious laughter seeing the irritation in her brother's facial expression. She glanced at her two nieces from the centre mirror again and smiled when the girls did not protest and momentarily fell quiet.

Looking at her nieces only reminded Cassie of their mother. Welcoming this holiday season and recollecting her memory always brought a slight pinching pain.

The two girls inherited the curly blonde hair from Emily. If only Emily were still around, she would sit next to Kieran in this car instead of her. But, on the other hand, she would be in the back seat with the girls. They always had that routine every Christmas for ten years until Emily's life was taken away five years ago due to a car accident. Cassie believed even the two girls were now thinking about their mother.

However, life needed to go on. That was what Kieran and his two girls had been doing. The beautiful memory of Emily would stay in their hearts, together with the pain of losing her.

Inevitably Cassie took a deep breath, wishing to chase away a sudden tightness in her chest. However, it invited a curious look from her brother instead.

"Are you feeling anxious about seeing mum soon?"

Cassie chuckled. "Why should I?"

"You know her."

"Yeah, of course, I know."

There was almost no secret between them as siblings. Perhaps the only secret Kieran kept from her was his bedtime talk with Emily. Kieran knew exactly the negative feeling she always carried during Christmas when they visited their parents and met their relatives and friends. And this Christmas would be no exception or perhaps could get worse. Cassie was sure that her mother had not forgotten she was reaching forty by next year, with no single boyfriend throughout her life so far!

"Take it easy, sis." That were the only consoling words that her brother could offer. Cassie understood it as she could not expect more. After this visit, which was planned for a week, she would probably be in tears on their way back home.

They finally reached their parents' house half an hour later. The moment they arrived at the front yard, Ashleigh and Alicia jumped out of the car, called their Nana and Grandpa loudly and ran into the house. Soon after, there were only exchanges of greetings and warm hugs before they settled into their rooms.

It was still two days before Christmas, however, the ambience in her parent's house was full of Christmas spirit. The silver brown garlands hung on the mantlepiece, a Christmas tree with plenty of presents underneath it, and various Christmas snacks and drinks on the table. It was a tradition that Cassie knew her mother would not miss. In two days, this house would be full of people's chatter and laughter, which was not what Cassie looked forward to. But she knew she still had to go through it anyway.

Tonight was their family dinner. Cassie was helping with the food preparation, chopping some vegetables for roasting, when Tiffany – her younger sister by twelve years arrived with a handsome hunk on her side. Cassie recognised him as Tiffany's boyfriend of three years, and seeing them together always made her heart slightly sliced, though she tried to ward off the feeling afterwards.

"It's lovely to see you here, Tiffany!" exclaimed Janine Ferguson – their mother. She threw herself, giving her youngest kid a tight hug and warm smooches all over her face. When she arrived this morning, Cassie did not recall her mother giving her such a warm welcome. Quickly she shook her head, getting rid of her negative thinking of comparing unnecessary things.

Tiffany – her and Kieran's youngest sister- twelve years younger than her and fourteen years younger than Kieran, was like a diamond in the family. She was definitely Janine's favourite daughter, although her birth was probably unexpected. However, their parents welcomed the latest addition to their family elatedly. Cassie still remembered how her mother spent their annual holiday money on new baby stuff, including the latest pram model, baby cot, baby car seat, and new baby clothes. Janine did not even consider getting second-hand items instead. On the other hand, Cassie was still wearing the worn-out spiderman t-shirt passed down from Kieran.

However, perhaps all that lavish spendings were worthwhile. Cassie had to admit that Tiffany was a beautiful baby, born with a chubby cheek, shimmery dark eyes, and soft brunette hair. Growing up, everything about her little sister was flawless. From a solid academic brain, music talent to sports achievements. And she graduated from the university a cum laude. She also had a slender, lithe body, beautiful teeth, and a lovely smile. As a gorgeous twenty-eight-year-old medical registrar in one of the biggest state-run hospitals, she was a picture-perfect career woman. So when she got herself hitched by a handsome, intelligent IT Project Manager from one of the biggest FinTech companies in Australia, Cassie only shook her head in disbelief at how her sister's life could be so wonderfully perfect while she .....

"Cassie!" Tiffany threw herself at her. Cassie's lips drew a timid smile while returning the hug, and she waved her hands to Joshua. The moment their hug was released, something from Tiffany's hands flashed before her eyes. Her jaw dropped when her sister purposedly swayed her hands in front of her. Before she could utter any word, her mother's scream made her half jump.

"OH, MY GOD!"

It was a scream that made their father - Paul rush out of his room with a worried look written on his face, thinking something horrible had happened. However, Paul smiled in relief when the cry was followed by joyful squealing from Janine and Tiffany.

"Congratulations," murmured Cassie, giving her sister another hug after Janine. Her mother again landed a lot of smooches on her favourite daughter's face as if Tiffany had just won an AACTA award.

"Thank you," replied Tiffany with eyes welled with joyful tears. "I can't wait to share this great news with you guys! Oh, I must tell you how Joshua did it. It was so romantic," she added while giving a meaningful look to her fiancé, who returned it with a sheepish smile.

Yeah, right! It was something that Cassie would be able to guess anyway. If the marriage proposal was when they were only in the car, she was a hundred percent sure Tiffany would not accept it.

"Oh, I can't wait to hear it, my dear," squealed Janine while motioning Tiffany to the dining table. "Let's have a sit. I'm going to open the best bottle of wine for tonight. Such great news deserves a big celebration."

And for the next hour, before dinner was ready, Tiffany shared the story of her marriage proposal while holding hands with Joshua, who sat intimately behind her while placing his chin on her shoulder. Her parents and her two nieces listened to the story attentively while Cassie was still standing behind the kitchen bench, busy chopping a couple of vegetables for salad, checking the roast chicken inside the oven, and preparing the ingredients for the dessert. Occasionally, she would chime in into the conversation. Kieran did the same thing while grilling some prawns on the barbeque pit in the alfresco. For a couple of times, they exchanged glances with a laugh that threatened to sneak out from their lips, as if they understood each other how exciting this moment was for their little sister and mother.

"So, have you set the date?"

Cassie believed it was the question that could not wait to slip out from her mother's lips.

"We have," replied Tiffany. Her eyes glimmered with joy while she looked at each family member as if seeking approval. "We're thinking of Spring next year." She swallowed while giving Cassie a hesitant look. "We're thinking of the third Saturday in October. That is also your birthday, Cass."

If she was not shocked, perhaps it was an understatement. Cassie was flabbergasted. From fifty-two weekends a year, why did her little sister choose her birthday as the wedding day?

"Oh!" That was the only sound that inevitably slipped out of Cassie's throat. Her voice sounded flat. What confused her even more was that her reaction made the smile on her sister's lips wider.

"I know! It's amazing, isn't it?" Tiffany squealed.

Cassie sighed inwardly that it seemed her sister interpreted her reaction in a different meaning.

"It's going to be your fortieth birthday!" Tiffany jumped out from her seat to squeeze her hand. "I know you don't want to be reminded that you're reaching forty years old. So, that is why I think it is a perfect time to have my wedding. People's attention will be on the wedding. No one will bother you with questions about your age and why you are not with someone yet, bla..bla and bla...I know you despise those questions, especially on your birthday. So, my wedding will be your saviour."

Is it? Cassie was not even sure what to feel. Who was trying to steal the limelight here? She or Tiffany? She was unsure what her face looked like now, but she was speechless, with her lips parting. Her eyes glanced at Kieran, who returned her a concerned look. Perhaps only her brother truly understood the rippled waves in her heart at this moment.

"That's a good idea," Janine chimed in. "I am also tired of those questions. The wedding will be a good opportunity for you to have a little celebration, Cass. Otherwise, I'm sure you'll spend your birthday alone in your small apartment like you do every year."

"Well, that's not true," Kieran protested. "Me, the girls and Cass' best friend, ...ugghh..sorry, what's her name again, Cass?"

"Erin," added Cassie quickly, while she restrained herself from rolling her eyes that her brother forgot her housemate's name despite having met her several times.

"Yes! Erin! Your housemate. We always celebrate together. Right, girls?" Kieran darted a look at his daughters, seeking approval.

"We bought the cake for aunt Cassie on her recent birthday," said Ashleigh.

"Yeah, but the year before that, daddy was away for a business trip. So we were in grandma's house," added Alicia innocently. She referred to the night she spent in Emily's parent's house. "I remember we called aunt Cassie at that time, and she sounded like she just had a cold."

Cassie felt her heart slowly sinking to the bottom of nowhere, somewhere she even doubted she could reach. That was one of her birthday disasters when she only had herself to celebrate.

But perhaps it was her choice anyway. She felt like getting older but still not getting anywhere with her increasing age. Not only in terms of relationships but also career, which she even doubted that she even had one, and many others. Unfortunately, on her birthday two years ago, Kieran needed to be away for his business trip, leaving the girls with Emily's parents while Erin – her best friend and her housemate, was also away on a business trip. She could hang out with some of her colleagues and other friends, but somehow, she didn't have the mood to do so at that time.

"Well, she was unwell, I suppose," said Kieran with a half-defending tone. "You know when you're unwell. You're supposed to rest and not see anyone. Otherwise, you may spread your germs to someone else."

"I guess it's horrible to fall sick on your birthday," Paul added. Somehow her father's voice sounded soothing. Cassie swallowed as her father gave her a meaningful look with a twitch on the corner of his lips. It seemed her father also understood what she felt at this moment. "Why don't we ask Cassie how she wants to celebrate her fortieth birthday?"

"Oh, I have booked the venue," Tiffany interrupted innocently. "This place is fantastic! So I can't let it go. That is the only date available."

"Then you should not let it go!" approved Janine. It was the response that made Tiffany's face glow even further. Joshua, who was still unmoved from his seat, watching the exchanges in the family in silence, only smiled.

It was an obvious sign for Cassie that nothing could be changed. She had lost the battle. No one could defend her.

Hot tears threatened to well in her eyes. She swirled swiftly, pretending to check the roast chicken inside the oven, although the timer was not beeping yet.

A soft touch on her shoulder startled her. She managed to swallow her tears, seeing Tiffany standing just behind her.

"Thank you, Cass," said Tiffany while giving her another cuddle. "You're my best sister. I'm looking forward to celebrating your birthday on my wedding day."

"Oh, yeah. Sure!" stuttered Cassie while returning the hug. Quietly she was grateful that it seemed her sister did not see her disappointment. However, even if Tiffany could see it, her little sister always got what she wanted.

Cassie could catch another concerned look directed at her. This time not only from Kieran but also from her father.

One thing Cassie always loved when she visited her parents' house in Wonthaggi was strolling by the beach. That would be her daily routine, either in the morning or afternoon. Regardless, she did not want to miss the opportunity. It was her precious solitude time, away from her mother's scrutinisation, plus the Christmas disaster she had somehow foreseen.

After the bombshell news dropped by Tiffany last night, Cassie knew she desperately needed this walk. Luckily her parents' house was within walking distance to the beach. She quietly sneaked out of the house when everyone was still in their slumber or struggling to get off their beds. The summer daylight savings was an advantage as the dim morning sunshine was enough to illuminate her walk. The fresh morning air and the sound of the low tide waves were like calming music to her ear.

She could not deny that she slept with teary eyes last night, despite Ashleigh and Alicia sleeping in the same room. Kieran offered to take the girls to sleep with him, but both girls preferred cuddling up to their aunt. The request was a consolation prize for her, although she could not wait to find herself alone to shed tears. She was the favourite aunt, not Tiffany, though Tiffany never cared anyway. She took a quiet sigh inwardly, warding off her negative thought. She believed the girls loved Tiffany, too. However, although Tiffany lived not far from them in Melbourne for her work, she seldom had time to see the girls. Tiffany's high demanding job was the main excuse, regardless it was true or not. Ironically, they only had a chance to see each other for family occasions.

After reading the night story for the girls, she finally heard their soft snores and started to let her mind stray to her heart pain again. The tears started rolling down her cheeks, and she was unsure when she finally drifted to sleep.

She tried to have a self-introspection. What had caused her to be so upset with Tiffany's wedding news? Was it because the wedding date was also her birthday? She did not plan anything grand for her fortieth birthday anyway. It never crossed her mind. Perhaps that was her problem. She was not as outgoing as her sister. She liked to attend parties, but she was not a person who would bring herself out there, announcing to everyone her special day. That was also the reason for the last twenty years, she never bothered about how she was going to celebrate her birthday. However, she knew Kieran always tried his best not to miss celebrating her birthday. They only had a small dinner and birthday cake in the evening after work most of the time. It was their little tradition even after the girls were born. Her father sometimes asked her to come down to Wonthaggi on the weekend for another celebration, but sometimes it was impossible due to her work commitment. She was not complaining about such a simple celebration. It was enough to make her feel content and happy.

And for her next year's birthday, the big 40th birthday, she thought it would be just another birthday. However, it would be different when it was going to be Tiffany's wedding day too. Tiffany was probably right. If it were not for the wedding day, she would not have had a chance to celebrate her birthday with her parents. Her mother never really bothered to spend time with her on her birthday. However, that day would be remembered as Tiffany's wedding day, not her 40th birthday. Somehow she felt like being....*forgotten*. Being left out. That was probably the reason she was upset.

She took a deep breath while throwing her empty stare watching the rolling waves that finally splashed to the land and crawled to her bare feet. As the current swept the sand underneath her thinly, she felt her body sinking slightly. She hoped the tide had taken away the pain in her heart.

Letting things go would be her resolution as she strolled back to the house. Besides, there was a faint silver lining from all of these. She knew Tiffany always had what she wanted, and she did not plan to make it hard for her own sister to have the happiest day of her life.

Her heart felt much lighter afterwards, and she entered the house with a smile when she saw Kieran and her father in the kitchen having breakfast.

"Hey, sweetie," called Paul while giving her a light peck on the cheek. "You're always an early riser."

"Morning, dad," she responded. Her eyes caught her father and her brother's plain breakfast plate. There was only a slice of toast with vegemite on each plate, which made her chuckle. "I'll cook some eggs and bacon. I believe the girls would love it. Would you like some?"

The vigorous murmur and nods from both men in her life were what she expected. She released a soft laugh while taking the pan out of the kitchen cabinet.

Strangely, despite not living in this house for the last twenty years, she still remembered where all the kitchenware had been kept. Her mother never made any changes. Since their childhood, she would always like spending time in the kitchen, and her mother always let her do the job whenever she was there. Tiffany, on the other hand, seemed to hate cooking.

Soon afterwards, the atmosphere in the kitchen started getting more lively as, one by one, the rest of the house residents turned up with hungry, sleepy face the moment they smelt the food. It was the moment that Cassie would also enjoy, and somehow she was not bothered about Tiffany's wedding anymore. However, still, her Christmas disaster had not ended yet.

It was on 24th December. Usually, the day before Christmas would be filled with the time to buy last-minute pressies and cooking ingredients for Christmas day tomorrow. Then, they would go to church together in the evening for a short mass. It was not a tradition that Cassie despised at all. She was not looking forward to Christmas Day itself when most of their distant relatives would come over too. However, what she did not expect, her dreadful Christmas would also start today when Tiffany squealed in excitement when her two best friends paid a visit.

Ruby and Chelsea, childhood friends of Tiffany's. They grew up together in Wonthaggi and even went to university together in Melbourne. Their family already took these two girls, or perhaps Cassie should call them women now, as if they were part of the family. They also came back to spend Christmas with their families. So despite seeing Tiffany often in Melbourne, they would still be seeing each other throughout this holiday. Sometimes it made Cassie wonder how Joshua could stand them because she obviously could not.

"Hi, Koala."

It was a trademark greeting from Ruby and Chelsea for her. That was the reason Cassie sometimes hated the song that, ironically, her two nieces adored instead. The very same song was the source of mocking Ruby and Chelsea used towards her. It was rude, and Cassie remembered that Kieran was not hesitant to reprimand them for calling her that nickname. However, those bitches and Tiffany only responded with a sheepish smile and never took it seriously. They kept calling her by that nickname, but this time they intentionally did it quietly, only within her earshot, and when her parents or Kieran were not nearby.

"Hi," Cassie replied, but her smile was tight. She sometimes wondered why these two women liked to mock her, even though she was much older than them. The only reason she could stand them was because of Tiffany. Sometimes she wondered too why she had to be called Koala. Perhaps her face was slightly chubby, and she did not have a slender body like Tiffany's or theirs, but she was not fat. She understood they were just bullies, making her wonder whether Tiffany grew up as one too.

"You're getting cuter and cuter, Koala," smiled Ruby, followed by Chelsea's giggle. "I heard you'll be forty years old next year."

Cassie decided to interpret it as a compliment. "Thanks."

"So, are you seeing someone already?" Chelsea raised her eyebrow. "If not, maybe I can introduce you to someone."

Cassie swallowed. She knew where this conversation was going. It was not new that even Tiffany's friends knew about her difficulty in finding someone for a romantic relationship. It was just another laughable topic for them.

"Thanks for your concern. But I'm fine."

"Oh, come on, Koala." Ruby's face turned into a comical pity look, her lips pursed and her brow knitted. "It's going to be Tiffany's wedding day. Are you saying you are coming to the wedding alone?"

"Yeah, even though we don't have boyfriends yet, we will have fun with the groomsmen. We know that Joshua has some cute friends for us that day," winked Chelsea. "But how about you?"

"Is coming to the wedding with a partner a requisite?" Cassie raised her eyebrow.

Ruby and Chelsea's laughter erupted.

"So, you'll be dancing alone on the day? On your birthday?"

Cassie felt sick, but she tried to keep her cool. "Dancing is also not the only thing you can do on your birthday or wedding day."

As she had expected, there was another roar of laughter and giggles. She knew whatever she said, these two silly women would laugh at her anyway.

"Poor you, Koala." Chelsea rubbed her hand softly on Cassie's forearm as if trying to soothe her. "I think Tiffany's decision to choose her wedding day on your birthday is right. Otherwise, it will be pathetic for you to spend your birthday alone."

"Well, thanks again for your concern. But I don't feel pathetic," retorted Cassie while taking a huff. "Having a birthday is the time to be grateful for another year of your life. It's not the time to simply throw your life for a party," she added curtly with a lifted chin.

14

The shrieking voice of Ashleigh and Alicia saved her. The girls must had an argument and need to be mediated. She used it as an excuse to leave. She left with rolled eyes while taking a relieved sigh that at least she could escape from those two bullies.

Tomorrow, Christmas Day would be another day for her to fight.

Chapter Two

"Is she for real?"

It was three weeks after Christmas. Cassie returned to the tiny two-bedroom apartment she shared with her housemate Erin last night. Together with her brother and nieces, they reached Melbourne in the evening, and after a quick dinner and shower, the girls finally went to bed. That was the only time Cassie felt at ease leaving her brother's house. It was a weird feeling, as if she was the girls' mother, despite Kieran was more than capable of taking care of his daughters. However, it had been her habit every time they returned from a trip together, especially after Emily's passing.

Erin also just returned from visiting her family in Brisbane today. The moment her housemate reached the apartment, they agreed to order some takeaway pizza while sharing their Christmas holiday stories, relaxing for the last weekend before returning to work tomorrow. The story of Tiffany's wedding plan was inevitably the first thing Cassie announced, and Erin's reaction was something she had expected.

Cassie restrained herself from badmouthing her sister, and she had not, as far as she remembered. She was proud of Tiffany's achievements, but it did not stop Erin from disliking her sister. So far, perhaps Erin had only met Tiffany a couple of times, although Erin had been her housemate for the past two years.

"Your sister is so self-entitled!"

Cassie could not help but wince at that comment.

Erin threw a guilty look afterwards and quickly added, "Sorry, I know she's your sister. But I can't stand her sometimes!"

"You don't see her often," murmured Cassie. "In fact, we don't see her often."

"Precisely! But from your story and the way she behaves, jeez..." Erin shook her head. "I still can not forgive her for choosing to date her boyfriend instead of going for a short dinner with you on your birthday."

Erin referred to Cassie's birthday two years ago, the birthday disaster, which, unfortunately, Erin and Kieran could not be around due to business trips. Cassie called her sister three days prior and asked her out for dinner. However, Tiffany excused herself because she had a date with Joshua. Cassie even offered that the dinner invitation was extended to Joshua as well. However, Tiffany still insisted that she preferred to have a date with Joshua alone. Cassie thought her sister probably needed a private moment with her boyfriend and did not want to press further. However, deep inside, she was disappointed by the rejection. Tiffany did not even call to wish her a happy birthday.

"She's young," Cassie muttered while biting her pizza.

"She's twenty-eight years old, but she behaves like a teenager," sighed Erin. "Just because you're going to be forty years old, then you think everyone else is much younger than you, Cass. I think it's just her personality. I could gather that your mother spoils her from your stories."

"Well, she's smart and beautiful. I am not surprised if she is my mother's favourite."

And it was true. Cassie understood why Tiffany was the source of pride for her mother. Janine also boasted about Kieran on how handsome and charming her brother became. Meanwhile, she, as a middle child...Cassie took a sigh inwardly. Perhaps it was the curse of a middle child. She was just average in everything. From academics and sports, career to physical appearance. Those were probably the reasons she became 'invisible' in her mother's eyes.

"And her friends too!" Erin's continued her grumble. "If I were there, I would slap them, Cass. They are just bullies. Have you ever told your sister that her friends are horrible?"

Cassie shrugged. "I think Tiffany knows."

"And she did not try to stop them? What kind of sister is she?"

"They are her best friends."

"A good friend will not bully your family."

Cassie winced. "I guess Tiffany thinks they are just joking around with me."

Erin shot her a stern look. "I think the line between being rude and joking is pretty clear here. But I'm not surprised for such self-entitled people like your sister and her friends, they will not know the difference."

Cassie cringed. She could see that Erin was consumed with her annoyance in this matter. Nevertheless, she only drew a solemn smile on her lips, assuring her friend that she was fine.

Erin was actually about the same age as Tiffany, and if Cassie remembered correctly, Erin was already in her early thirties. They met when Erin had just landed her first job in the same company where Cassie worked. She was actually a mentor for Erin as an IT helpdesk. After five years of working together, Erin secured a better role and career as a project manager in a fintech company.

On the other hand, Cassie was stuck in her role for the last twenty years as IT customer service in a small local bank - not one of the big four banks - in Melbourne. She felt content and happy with her job and did not think much about pursuing a great career. She had to admit she always longed to find someone right to build a family, but ironically, she never even met any guy and had a relationship. Since her work field in IT, she had many male colleagues and buddies, but most were already family men. She was sure one of the culprits was her unattractive appearance. Apart from that, she was probably too late, only started looking now when she was approaching 40 years old.

Meanwhile, she found Erin was an attractive woman, rewarded with over the shoulder smooth, wavey blonde hair, blue eyes, slender body and curvy boobs. Cassie also had to admit that Erin knew how to dress up nicely. Even though her attire was only from local brands, Erin seemed proficient in soft makeup, enhancing the glow on her face.

As far as Cassie could remember, Erin always became the centre of male attention whenever they went out together. She could not count how many guys her housemate had brought home. Every time she accidentally found a naked hunk appearing in the living room when she went to the loo in the middle of the night, her cheek would blush. She pretended to see anywhere else but the person. She never asked Erin who they were unless Erin told her.

"So, how's your holiday?" asked Cassie, wishing to change their conversation topic away from Tiffany. "Are your family well?"

"Yeah, all great," replied Erin with a chuckle. Cassie could interpret that was not exactly a positive reaction. Erin gave her a weak smile knowing she should speak more. "My ex-boyfriend, Craig, is going to have a baby soon. With my childhood friend." She rolled her eyes. "What a cliché."

"Oh, I'm sorry to hear that."

Erin waved her hands dismissively. "That's alright. I'm okay with it. But you know men!" She took an exaggerated sigh. "I thought we could go back together again, but apparently, he had moved on."

Cassie tried to sound diplomatic. "Well, I guess it's hard to build a long-distance relationship."

"Yeah, you're right." Erin took another sigh and seemed defeated. She threw herself onto the sofa. "How's your brother and his girls? Did they have a good time during Christmas?"

Cassie nodded. "Of course. The girls had a lot of fun. I think they miss you." She did not lie. Ashleigh and Alicia had been regular visitors to their apartment. Cassie knew that the girls loved to play with Erin, too, and her housemate was great with kids despite not having nieces or nephews from her siblings yet.

Erin's grin broke. "Do they? Awww..I miss them too. Is it still a school holiday now?"

"Yes, the school starts in February."

"I can take them to the museum or the zoo tomorrow."

Cassie furrowed her brow. "You have work."

"No, I am taking another extra day of leave tomorrow. I was thinking of having an extra day for rest. But I don't mind taking the girls. What is their plan tomorrow?"

Cassie shrugged. "I think Kieran is working from home tomorrow. I know the girls will be with Emily's parents some of the days next week."

"Then, tell your brother I'll take the girls tomorrow so he can focus on his work."

"That's very sweet of you, Erin. Are you sure? Tomorrow is supposed to be your rest day."

Erin's lips spread a convincing smile. "Spending time with them will be my relaxing day." She jumped out from the sofa, heading to her bedroom. "I'm taking a shower now. Don't forget to tell your brother about this. If he doesn't mind, can I have his number?"

Cassie swallowed nervously. "Yeah, sure," she responded while watching Erin disappear to her room. Guilt immediately struck her, recalling that even Kieran did not remember her housemate's name. However, she was determined to ensure Kieran had Erin's number on his mobile phone this time.

Taking most of the summer in Melbourne, plus the daylight savings, was crucial for Cassie. She took the opportunity to carry her running attire every day to work, so she could have a chance to jog in Flagstaff park after work. The sun was still glaring fiercely, though fortunately, some cool breeze started blowing in, making her feel more energetic to start her run.

It was a perfect day for a run. Not only because of the adrenaline that pumped into her afterwards but because of seeing the lovely scenery around her. Some people were doing gym fitness, couples were pushing the baby pram, and children were playing on the grass. It was such a blissful moment that she felt no one should take it for granted, knowing all the worldwide wars, poverty, natural disasters, and famine. Life could be short and fragile. She was sure if Emily was still around, her sister-in-law would also choose to be in this world, spending her time as much as possible with her daughters.

She strolled to calm her heartbeat and let her sweat dry by the breeze. She planned to return to her apartment, shower, and visit Kieran's house. Today Erin executed her promise to take the girls to the zoo, and they agreed to meet for dinner at Kieran's place.

Luckily Kieran's house was not far from the city. In fact, Kieran purposedly bought his current house because of its close location to Cassie's apartment and because of its reputable state school. It would be much easier for Cassie to pay a visit and help with the kids' errands, like taking Ashleigh and Alicia for their ballet, swimming and netball lessons. Being involved heavily with her nieces' activities had been her life since Emily passed away. In other words, she had become their second mother.

Fortunately, Emily's parents also lived not far from them and shared the kids' errand duties with her. This little 'teamwork' made Cassie feel grateful. It reminded her how important to have families around. Kieran echoed the same thought but occasionally reminded her to think about her own life, too, focusing on finding someone to be with. It was something that Cassie definitely wanted too, but what else could she do? Was there something wrong with her social life?

She did hang out with her friends, sometimes even joining in with Erin and her other friends. Occasionally, she also hung out with her colleagues for a drink on Friday nights. Apart from her work, nieces and friends, she was even involved in volunteer activities in the local community and sometimes even in overseas projects. Thinking of overseas volunteer project, her mobile phone suddenly rang, and she smiled to see the caller.

"Hello there! Happy new year!" greeted the caller, a friendly tone of voice that Cassie loved to hear. Sometimes she wished the person on the other line could be her boyfriend instead.

"Hi, Chandra. How are you?" she greeted back.

Chandra was her Indonesian friend who had lived in Australia for twenty years. He came to Melbourne as a university student, in the same courses with her for four years, and they have stayed in touch since then. Occasionally they met for a catch-up, and Cassie admitted that she liked him as a friend. However, if they could be more than friends, she definitely would welcome the idea. But it seemed Chandra did not think likewise.

Or perhaps she should be the one who made a move?

Perhaps.

Regardless, she knew the purpose of Chandra's call today. Definitely not for asking her out for a date.

"I'm great. How are you?"

"Yeah, same old, same old."

Chandra's crisp laughter was like a piece of music to her ear. She smiled as a result, wishing she could see him in person instead. They talked briefly about their Christmas holiday until they came to the point of the primary purpose of Chandra's call. Knowing he had just returned from his hometown in Jakarta, Cassie knew he wanted to talk about their upcoming overseas volunteer project. Chandra was the project manager as he worked for a non for profit organisation in Melbourne.

"The plan is teaching the poor, vulnerable kids here. We plan to have you in Jakarta in March. The reason we choose March is that it is past raining season. Usually, Jakarta is prone to floods at the beginning of the year. Although this is your first overseas volunteering experience, I do not recommend you plunge yourself into a town that could become like Venice during the rainy season," explained Chandra.

"Venice doesn't sound bad," Cassie chuckled.

Chandra laughed. "Yeah, right. But unlike Venice, the flood water comes from the drainage. It doesn't smell pleasant, and it could make you sick instead. I don't think you want to get sick there when you're supposed to be helping out. So, are you in?"

"Hundred percent," answered Cassie enthusiastically.

"Shall I book for you a flight ticket? Oh, hang on! When is your sister's wedding?"

Cassie almost wanted to reply that it was on her birthday. But again, with her quiet nature, she did not inform everyone of her birthday. Despite their twenty years of friendship, perhaps Chandra had no idea when her birthday was. "It's still in October. So, there is no clash."

"Great! Remember to book your leave, then."

"For sure."

"There will be a couple of other people coming too. Some are my colleagues, some are volunteers like you. So, you'll meet new people. Isn't that exciting?"

"Yeah, of course." It was a statement that made Cassie furrow her brow. She wondered whether it was a hint from Chandra that she should keep her eyes open if any of those people could be someone for her. It made her wince, wishing he would be the one for her instead. She showed her interest in volunteering because she wished to get closer to him. However, it seemed he did not get the hint.

Or, perhaps, not yet.

Their phone conversation ended soon afterwards with a promise to have a catch-up drink next week. As usual, after their conversation, Cassie sighed, realising that they were just still friends. Somehow it shook her thoughts from her dream.

She continued her stroll, following the pathway that would take her to the street leading to her tram stop, passing through the playground and a basketball court. Suddenly a basketball rolled towards her and slowly landed on her feet. She picked it up and looked around, wondering who the owner was.

She saw someone on the basketball court. A tall man who looked like a serious basketball player. It seemed he was the only one playing, and definitely, it was his ball. However, he did not seem to miss it. His back was on her, with two hands on his waist, he looked down at his feet. Cassie guessed perhaps he did not realise that his ball had rolled out, so she walked into the court, approaching him.

"Hi, mate!" she greeted.

The man turned around, and Cassie had to admit that she found him dashingly handsome as she could see his face closer now. Dark hair, sharp brown eyes, and a strong jaw. There was some dark aura from his appearance. Despite that, Cassie swallowed, admiring his athletic muscles prominently shown by his basketball singlet.

She wondered whether she would be lost for words if she were a twenty-year-old girl. But now, in her late thirties, having spent her life seeing different people, she felt her libido was more mature and under control.

"I suppose this is your ball," she made a sound while extending her hand to give away the ball. "It was rolling to outside the court."

The man only looked at the ball in her hand, took it and walked away.

If she was not flabbergasted, she was probably a robot without any feelings. Or perhaps he was the robot? No single word was uttered from him, not even a short 'thank you'. And what amazed her more, the man started dribbling his ball as if she was not even there!

What an attitude! Well, perhaps that was what most handsome people did anyway. 'Self-entitled', as Erin said. Cassie rolled her eyes and decided to ward off her annoying feeling. Then, without looking back, she continued her pace leaving the court as soon as possible.

The delicious smell from the kitchen immediately made Cassie's tummy grumble the moment she stepped into Kieran's house. She had restrained herself from snacking on the way here, despite her tram journey shaking her tummy quite violently. Hence, once she was in the kitchen, she could not wait to tug in; however, the vision before her made her forget her protesting gut.

It was a sight worth to behold. It brought a lively, warm feeling into the house since Emily passed away. Kieran was in the kitchen, chopping some vegetables on the chopping board. Ashleigh and Alicia were washing some salad in front of the sink, and Erin...As far as Cassie remembered, Erin never touched the kitchen in their small apartment. What she understood was that her roommate did not like cooking. This was definitely the first time she saw Erin wearing an apron, standing behind the stoves, boiling some water while pouring some spaghetti into it.

"Aunt Cassie!" squealed Ashleigh and Alicia at the same time. "You're finally here!"

"Yes!" Cassie ran into her nieces and cuddled them. "And where's my dinner?" She turned around to catch a sheepish smile from her housemate, to which she returned with a smirk. "I don't know that you can cook, Erin."

"I don't. Kieran does most of the things. I can only boil water," Erin said with a blush.

"Well, Erin has been nice taking the kids to the zoo. I insisted that she sit down and relax," said Kieran while giving his sister a light peck on the cheek. "How's your day, sis?"

"Great! Oh, before I forget, I need to let you know that I'm going to Jakarta in March for three weeks."

Erin and Kieran looked at her with furrowed brows which was a reaction that almost made Cassie laugh. She only realised now how her housemate and brother could look comically similar.

"I'm joining a volunteer project there with Chandra."

"Oh?" Kieran's lips broke into a grin. "Your Indonesian friend? That sounds like going to be a great holiday."

Cassie chuckled. "I'm going to work there, not exactly a holiday. But it's going to be a great experience."

"I bet so," Erin chimed in. "I know you always love helping people, Cass. I'm glad you're going with someone from the local area. The safety there is quite a concern. It's also a good time to get to know him more," she said while playing her eyebrows up and down.

Cassie knew the meaning of all the teasings. Inwardly, she was hoping that would be the case for her and Chandra.

"Yeah, but I'm sorry I can't help with the girls' errands while I'm away," she said while giving her brother an apologetic look. "I'll check with Amanda and John whether they could cover some days." She was referring to Emily's parents.

"I can help," Erin quickly piped in. It was unexpected as Cassie and Kieran gave her a bewildered look.

"Oh no, no, no...." Kieran shook his head. "I don't want to trouble you. You just told me about your upcoming work project. You'll be busy at that time. Besides, it's okay if the girls miss some of the activities for three weeks. It's no biggie."

"But I don't want to miss my ballet practice." Ashleigh's innocent voice interrupted. "There's a concert in Easter, and we'll be performing."

"That's true," added Alicia. "I also do not want to miss my swimming practice. I'm getting better with my freestyle."

"I will make it up to you, girls," sighed Kieran. "Daddy promise."

Cassie felt a huge pang of guilt hitting her chest. When planning this trip, she did not take into account that some of her responsibilities would be neglected. It was true that this was perhaps her first overseas holiday trip since Emily passed away. However, she totally forgot how her nieces' schedules depended on her too.

"You know what? I might cancel the trip," she muttered. The words immediately made Kieran and Erin squeal simultaneously, making her body half jump. She did not expect her words would make such a reaction.

"I'll manage this, alright, Cass?" Kieran darted her a stern look. "Don't you dare to cancel your trip!"

"That's right, Cass. Let us talk with Amanda and John to see if they could cover up some of the schedules. If not, I can help out," Erin quickly added. Knowing Kieran wanted to interrupt her, she raised her hand to stop him and raised her eyebrow at him. "I don't mind at all helping out, Kieran. As long as you trust me."

Cassie wasn't sure whether it was only her who felt the tension between her housemate and her brother. Erin and Kieran looked at each other for quite a while without uttering any words, as if their eyes did the talking instead of their lips. Cassie raised her eyebrow while glancing at her nieces, who seemed to have a hint of a playful grin on their faces. Did she miss something?

"Alright, Cass? Don't you dare cancel your trip plan!" Finally, Erin broke the trance. "We still have plenty of time to organise something. I can plan my project schedule so I can still help out without affecting my work. At the end of the day is about good planning, isn't it?"

Kieran took a quiet sigh, seemed defeated and nodded weakly. Cassie only followed with a repressed smile on her lips.

"Time management. That's definitely your forte, Erin," she said. Both of them exchange smiles before getting back to preparing for dinner.

The rest of the night went through uneventfully. It was full of chatter and laughter. It had been a while since the last time this house had such an atmosphere. In fact, it reminded Cassie of when Emily was still around. This was probably the first time Erin joined them for dinner. While observing her brother and her housemate with the two girls, Cassie felt something tinglingly warm within her. Something that she could not put a finger on.

Chapter Three

"Hi, Cass! I'm glad you're here!"

Cassie quietly felt relieved to see Tiffany herself who opened the door and welcomed her. Her sister threw her arms around her shoulder as they exchanged cuddles and a brief peck on the cheeks. When Tiffany motioned her to enter her apartment further, Cassie recognised the uncomfortable feeling creeping in when her eyes caught Ruby and Chelsea.

It was Tiffany's birthday. That was why Cassie ended up in her sister's apartment after work tonight. Otherwise, she might be in Kieran's house, preparing dinner for her nieces. Tiffany asked her to join a celebration party in her apartment that she shared with Ruby and Chelsea. The same offer was extended to Kieran, who regrettably had to decline as no one could mind the girls. Kieran offered to celebrate at his house instead, but it seemed celebrating her birthday with the kids was not on Tiffany's agenda at all. They planned to visit their parents on the weekend, though. It was a tradition as their mother would never miss preparing a grand party for her favourite daughter.

"Hi, Cass," greeted Joshua, to which Cassie returned politely.

"Coming alone, Cass? As usual?" smirked Ruby.

Cassie only responded with a tight smile. She had to admit that everyone seemed to be dressing up at their best for the night. Ruby and Chelsea were in their low-neck sack dress, prominently showing their curvy body. Tiffany was in her low deep V-neck white gown, revealing the pale skin of her cleavage and her back, which conveniently gave an opportunity for Joshua to rub his knuckle on it. Meanwhile, Cassie came straight from work. She had a last-minute request from a manager to solve his computer problem, so she did not have time to return home for a change. Hence she just turned up with her blouse and jeans.

"Any drink, Cass?"

Another relieved sigh as Joshua stood beside her, while Tiffany was already busy with other guests, as Cassie expected. There were probably about twenty of them in the apartment, all around Tiffany's age. Cassie noticed Ruby and Chelsea were talking seductively towards some blokes, probably Joshua's friends. It was somehow a standard and expected sight she would see here.

She chatted with Joshua briefly before her future brother-in-law was distracted by another bloke who motioned him for a drink on the balcony. For men's talk, perhaps, as Cassie noticed, some of the blokes were gathering outdoors. Luckily, it was quite a big balcony, and this apartment was just on the second level.

Tiffany's place was a three-bedroom apartment in an old heritage building in South Yarra, only a few kilometres away from the city. Cassie liked that this apartment was well maintained and had a shady garden with mature gum and oak trees. The tram's bell could sometimes be heard from a distance, adding the Melbourne life atmosphere to the apartment.

Cassie knew if she came here, she would know no one. Initially, she was reluctant to come, but Kieran pushed her to go. Her brother said she should spend her time socialising more, meeting various people, not only from work. Kieran also did not want her always to spend time helping him with the girls after work every night, not because he did not like to see her, but because he felt it was unfair to her. Managing the house and the kids were his responsibility, not hers, even though he understood she did it happily without complaints.

An idea to ask Amanda and John to mind the kids for a few hours popped up in her mind so Kieran could come as well. However, Kieran rejected the idea as he felt such a last-minute arrangement was unfair to his parents-in-law. Tiffany's party plan was indeed a bit impromptu. They thought they agreed to have it with their parents in Wonthaggi at the weekend. However, it seemed Tiffany did not want to let her actual birthday be missed.

Another idea for asking Erin's help was also in her mind, which Kieran also rejected. What surprised her when hearing the panic in Kieran's voice when she offered the idea over the phone. She understood if her brother was not comfortable bothering someone outside their family.

So here she was now. While observing people around, she wandered alone at the party, entertaining herself by nibbling some tapas that Tiffanny ordered for the night. She looked at the time. It was still 6 o'clock. She promised herself that she would excuse herself to leave by 9 o'clock. Three hours of agony was enough.

"I heard you're going away for a holiday soon, Cass." Joshua was suddenly behind her. Cassie turned around to see Tiffany come towards them and land in her fiance's arms. "I think your dad mentioned it when we spoke with your mother on the phone last week."

"Oh yeah!" Tiffany jumped in enthusiastically. "Where are you going?"

"It's not really a holiday. I am going for volunteer work in Jakarta," replied Cassie while sipping her cider.

"Oh? With your Indonesian friend? What's his name again?"

"Chandra."

"That fat man with the glasses?"

It was probably the ugliest voice Cassie wished she did not need to hear tonight. It belonged to Chelsea. The laughter from Ruby followed afterwards. Cassie wondered what attracted them to join in their conversation.

Cassie could not remember when Ruby and Chelsea had seen Chandra before. She furrowed her brow, questioning the unpleasant comment.

"We saw both of you when you had a date with him in one of the pubs in Southbank," said Ruby as she read Cassie's expression.

Ah, yes! Now Cassie remembered that night. It was actually a great night that she spent with Chandra. After almost a month of losing contact, they caught up as Chandra had just returned from his overseas charity project. No kissing, no touching whatsoever. However, still, they talked for hours. She just seemed to click with him.

Chandra was not fat like Chelsea said. Not that fat, in her opinion. He probably did not have a muscular, well-toned, six-pack male body. Still, he was taller than her, with black wavey hair that Cassie liked because it seemed he always trimmed it regularly. He had an alkaline nose, small lips, and black almond eyes behind his spectacles. Regardless, Chelsea liked him not solely because of his looks but because she always felt comfortable around him. Perhaps the first feeling she ever had with any male species, apart from her brother and father.

"It was not a date. We just had a drink." Cassie restrained herself from rolling her eyes while sipping her cider again.

"So, you're going for a holiday with him?"

Ruby whistled. "What an improvement, Cass. I hope he's great in bed, though."

"If he knows what to do in bed!" laughed Chelsea. "He looks like someone who only knows how to play video games."

"Perhaps he plays porn video games," added Tiffany.

Cassie was perplexed hearing her sister's words adding fuel to the jokes. She knew it was only a jest, but she wished they would stop talking about *her* Chandra.

"Let us know if the thing doesn't work out after you return from holiday, Cass." Ruby gave her a pretend pity look with a downturned mouth. "Perhaps it's time for you to consider joining a reality show to find a hot guy."

"Bachelor in Paradise?" Tiffany laughed. "You can get famous, Cass."

"No, no, no...." Chelsea put her finger on her lips, drawing everyone's attention to her, watching her in anticipation. "Perhaps she should join 'Too Hot To Handle'. She certainly could win!"

A burst of laughter exploded in the room. Cassie winced while hiding her face behind her bottle. She probably did not care about Ruby and Chelsea, but somehow, her chest was tight when she watched Tiffany also laugh hysterically as she had just watched the best comedy ever in her life.

"Unfortunately, you're reaching forty soon, Cass." Ruby's lips twitched, mocking her. "I don't think any TV producer will let you join the show."

Another laughter erupted again. Cassie was not sure what her face looked like. She did not even chuckle or smile. On the other hand, she pursed her lips while watching everyone around her keep laughing. Her eyes caught Joshua's guilt-ridden eyes, but unfortunately, Tiffany did not notice.

A call from one of Tiffany's work colleagues perhaps was her saviour. Tiffany and Joshua went away, attended and started talking with other friends. However, Cassie could not take a relief sigh yet as the two people she wanted to avoid the most were still lingering around.

"Come, Koala." Suddenly Chelsea's pulled her hand gently. Cassie furrowed her brow while catching an exchange of glances between Ruby and Chelsea. "I want to help you because you're Tiffany's sister. Perhaps I know what you need."

Hesitantly Cassie let herself be pulled away. Where else these two women could take her in such a small apartment? Chelsea was still holding her hand, leading the way to one of the rooms, occasionally looking at her with a mischievous smile on her lips. Ruby was walking behind her to ensure that she would not run away.

Though her heart began to race, Cassie quietly swallowed, thinking about what the worst things these two women could do to her.

They entered the room Cassie guessed was either Ruby's or Chelsea's room. She had visited this apartment before but only went to Tiffany's room. This room was messy, with many posters of celebrities and heaps of photos almost on every inch of the wall. There were even some dirty clothes and lingeries on the floor. Definitely, it was far from Tiffany's neat, white, beautiful princessy room. It made Cassie wonder how her sister could stand to live together with these women.

What made her mouth hang open even more was when she realised two other women were on the bed. The two women were naked, with only the lower half of their bodies covered under the blanket. Cassie immediately felt her cheek warm and twirled around as she did not wish to intrude on someone's privacy. However, Ruby blocked her way out.

"It's alright, Koala. They are here for you," said Chelsea.

Cassie slowly turned her head around with a furrowed brow.

Chelsea laughed. "I know you've never been in a relationship. I suppose you're still a virgin, and Tiffany confirms it. That's exactly why you need our help because I think I know what you need."

"I..." Cassie couldn't help but stutter. "I don't understand." She gulped, realising Tiffany was telling all her friends about her pathetic sex life. She had never shared her story with her sister before. Perhaps it was pretty obvious anyway.

That was true that she had never been in a relationship or had intimate physical interaction with anyone. However, was having it as a joke necessary? It was her choice as she had not yet found someone she felt comfortable with to have a sexual relationship with. People could accuse her of being choosy or mocking her as weird. She did not care. She just wanted to do it when she felt it was right.

"Come, Koala. Come over." Chelsea's sweet voice was heard again. Cassie was unsure why she let Chelsea pull her hand again to get closer to the bed. Or Ruby also nudged her from the back? Before she opened her mouth again to protest, Chelsea signalled the couple on the bed to uncover themselves. Her jaw dropped to witness the bare bodies of the two women. And not only that. They started to touch each other private parts and mauled each other mouths as if there was no one else.

Cassie was not that naïve. She had watched porn before, regardless of same-sex or not. However, she had to admit that seeing them right before her eyes, than watching them from the screen, was vividly different. Her body went stiff as she stared at the couple with tight lips.

What the hell?

"This could be good practice for you, Koala, before you have it with your Indonesian boyfriend," Chelsea's seductive voice was now in her ear. Cassie flinched to realise how close Chelsea stood behind her. "Just look at them." Chelsea gripped her chin and turned her face to the couple on the bed. "And let yourself be aroused."

Cassie gulped nervously. She did not understand why this was happening. But she went numb, and not only her brain but also her body. Seeing the couple on the bed touching each other passionately did arouse something within her. Something was buzzing between her thighs. Then, without realising it, her breath became shuddering as Chelsea's small hand opened the button of her jeans and gently went inside her undies. A soft moan inevitably escaped from her lips.

"You're wet, Koala," whispered Chelsea. Cassie closed her eyes, feeling the warm breath on her cheek as Chelsea's soft lips were now caressing her. "We can do it too."

The words somehow snapped something inside Cassie's head. Now she understood the meaning of all these. Instinctively, she pulled herself away, hastily buttoning up her jeans again while breathing heavily, realising what trap she almost fell into.

"I don't want this." Cassie was surprised to hear her own hoarse voice.

"Are you sure?" Chelsea grinned. "You seem to be enjoying it earlier."

"Not with you," Cassie hissed with gritted teeth. She knew now what game Chelsea and Ruby were playing. It was not the first time Tiffany's best friends mocked her. She would not let herself fall into their trap. They must have planned all this to perhaps videotape her naked.

However, Cassie did not expect when Chelsea returned her look with a half-opened mouth and squished brow. There was a flash of pain in her eyes. Did her words hurt her? However, Cassie chose to harden her heart. There was no way she would fall into any of these women's acts.

"I know what you're trying to do." Cassie lifted her chin while smoothing her wrinkled blouse. "And I'm not going to fall into your trap." Then, without bothering to hear any other words, she twirled around and strode towards the door, pushing Ruby away from blocking her way in the process. She appeared again in the living room to find that everyone was preparing to sing 'Happy Birthday' to Tiffany. She quietly took another deep breath, joined the crowd and was too scared to look back to see if Ruby and Chelsea were following her.

Chapter Four

Cassie gazed blankly through the wide window of the Airport bus, watching the moving trees and shrubs along Tullamarine Freeway. She was on her way to Melbourne airport to catch her flight to Jakarta. She had been longing for this trip, and it was a relief to successfully organise the schedule of Alicia and Ashleigh's errands while she was away for three weeks.

She did not breathe a word to anyone about what had happened at Tiffany's birthday party. She wondered whether Tiffany was aware of what her friends had done. There was a glimpse of pride within her that she did not fall into the trap set up by Ruby and Chelsea that night. Otherwise, by now, perhaps her naked video would be on social media, and she would be the whole of Melbourne's laughing stock.

Fortunately, no other occasions afterwards allow them to meet. In fact, she had not been talking to and seeing Tiffany since then. She managed to put on her indifference mask before her brother, who seemed not to sense anything amiss. She did not wish to let Kieran know what happened. Somehow recalling the flash of hurt in Chelsea's eyes tickled something within her, telling her something was not right. She did not understand what, though.

She had organised Amanda and John to help out with the girls' errands while she was away. To which Kieran reluctantly agreed, Erin would also take over some days.

Erin sent her off from Southern Cross station with a big wide grin on her face. Cassie knew her housemate was excited for her. However, she felt what made Erin more excited was because of the opportunity to spend more time with Alicia and Ashleigh. Erin handed her a thin square box, beautifully wrapped with a pink ribbon, when she stood at the bus door's steps. She squished her eyebrows to read the writing on the box.

Victoria Secret.

Cassie felt her cheek warm as she gave her friend a bewildered look.

"You might need it later. Who knows, perhaps you'll come back from this trip with a ring on your finger," giggled Erin.

"It's a work volunteer trip! It's not a honeymoon!" hissed Cassie, trying to keep her voice volume in check.

Erin laughed. "I know. Regardless, something might happen. You want to look your best ...." She wiggled her eyebrows. "If he makes a move."

Fortunately, there were not many passengers on the bus. The bus driver was in his seat, and Cassie wasn't sure whether he was listening to their cheeky conversation.

"Come on, Cass. You are open to the possibility, aren't you?" Erin shot her a severe look. "Why are you panicking? I suppose it's not the first time you've done it."

It was the question that made Cassie even more embarrassed. Erin saw her blushing cheek, and her housemate's hand immediately flew to her lips, and her eyes widened.

"You must be joking! How old are you???"

Cassie rolled her eyes. She knew this kind of reaction was expected. "Thank you, my friend. I'm almost forty years old."

"How about a kiss?"

Cassie winced as she squeezed her brain. It was a good question, as she could not recall when was the last time she had a kiss. Would a brief smooch from one of her childhood friends in high school count? Perhaps she had a kiss with her dance partner on prom night. Apparently, it was not impressive since she could not even recall it.

"Why, Cass?" Erin was now the one with the furrowed brow.

Cassie liked her friend's reaction, which contained a genuine curiosity, not a concern, pity or mocking hint she usually received when people found out about her virginity. She chuckled, giving her usual answer, "Because I feel I haven't found someone right yet. I can't just do casual or a one-night stand." Inwardly, she hoped Erin was not offended by what she said, knowing that Erin perhaps had one nightstand a couple of times.

"Oh.." Erin's mouth bobbed like a fish. Something seemed struck within her that made her go into deep thought for a moment. "Is Kieran also like that?"

Cassie was taken aback by the question. How did her virginity relate to her brother?

"What do you mean 'like that'?" she returned the question with a furrowed brow.

Erin blinked her eyes several times as she had just awakened from her dream. "Nay, nothing. Just my silly question. Yeah, of course, you must be comfortable having sex with someone. So, do you think Chandra could be the one?"

Cassie shrugged. "I am comfortable spending time with him. I click with him. But I'm not sure what he thinks about me."

"Luckily, you have this pressie." Erin was back in her teasing grin as her brows wiggled at the *Victoria Secret* box. "I believe it's going to be useful. You have to give it a go, Cass."

Cassie chuckled. "Thank you, Erin."

They exchanged cuddles before Cassie went inside the bus. Erin waited until the bus moved and sent her off with her goodbye waves.

The journey to the airport was smooth. Within half an hour, Cassie was already in the waiting line at the check-in counter. While humming and tapping her feet to the rhythm of music played on her mobile phone through her earphone, she could not wait to be on the plane and land in Jakarta soon. The beautiful, friendly smile that belonged to Chandra filled her mind.

Unfortunately, Chandra could not join her on the same flight, as he had to be in the field a week earlier. Chandra had mentioned some volunteers would join in from Melbourne, perhaps on the same flight with her. Unfortunately, he forgot to share the contacts with her, and Cassie assumed he was busy. Though she was slightly disappointed that she had to go through this eight-hour journey alone, she took a positive side by promising herself to enjoy the flight entertainment as much as possible.

When it was her turn, and she successfully pushed her luggage to the airport conveyor belt, the check-in lady passed her boarding ticket with the warmest smile matching her light spirit.

"We have upgraded your seat to business class, Miss Ferguson."

Cassie's face lit up. "Oh? Really?"

"There are some overbooking errors in the economy class, so you're one of the lucky ones that we upgrade to business class."

How could she complain about that? Eight hours flight journey in a more spacious seat and perhaps better food and alcoholic drinks. How could she reject that? The fortune ball definitely was on her side today.

"That's fantastic! Thank you."

Cassie took her boarding pass with a broad smile and bounced on her feet while dragging her cabin luggage to the boarding gate. Within the next forty minutes, she was already inside the plane and placing her cabin luggage in her top compartment. She almost squealed excitedly to see her spacious seat next to the window. This definitely would be a perfect journey.

While waiting for other passengers to settle down, she smiled, recalling Erin's question on why she had not had any sexual relationship before. It was probably her choice because she simply wanted to have it when she felt sure and comfortable with someone. But why was it so difficult to have such a person? Why could Erin do it easily?

She did a self-introspection whether she had a problem socialising with people. But she felt she had no issue getting along with people since school and even now in her working life. Perhaps she was not aggressive enough to make the first move. However, reaching forty years old soon, she felt she had more courage and confidence. She wanted to initiate it with Chandra, and if things did not work out, she could be mature enough to stay as friends. She believed Chandra would think likewise. The thought of him made her smile even wider.

When she realised the person who would sit next to her was coming, she lifted her head and put on her congenial smile. Her would-be neighbour was a tall male in his smart casual shirt and jeans. He seemed not to see her, busy placing his luggage in the compartment and getting his seat belt on. Cassie kept watching him, wishing he would look at her and they could at least exchange greetings. However, he immediately opened his sleek laptop and started typing without even taking a glimpse of her.

Though she was slightly disappointed that it seemed the passenger next to her was not friendly, she tried to ignore it and chose to start enjoying the entertainment on the screen. However, her eyes became tired within the next thirty minutes, and she drifted to sleep.

I t was perhaps the most beautiful place that Cassie had ever seen. The white sand spread ahead of her and ended with the beach's crystal blue water. The warm sun and the cool breeze made the coconut trees on the shore dance elegantly. She was lying on her tummy, without any layer of clothes. Her eyes closed, savouring the smooth massaging on her back. She had longed to do this, and having it in a grand resort on a beautiful tropical island was a dream come true. The gentle massages on her back by the firm, steady hands belonging to Chandra made this holiday complete. Now and then, he also landed a kiss on her back, adoring every inch of her body, and slowly moved up to her hair and nibbled on her neck.

His hands slowly moved to one of her breasts, kneading gently while his other hand started to travel to the area between her thighs. The stimulation made her body hum for more. The tension between her thighs pushed a moan out from her lips. She arched her back as Chandra's firm lips mauled her passionately. When they gasped for air, he gazed at her tenderly while saying...

"What food would you like, ma'am?"

That was not how Chandra sounded like. Even though it sounded like Chandra's English accent, it was a soft female voice.

Cassie's eyes slowly fluttered open. With a loud thud in her chest, she jerked up and quickly straightened herself up. Her eyes panickily stared at the stewardess. The latter stood on the aisle, looking at her with a knitted brow and downside lips.

Where were Chandra and the massage?

"Excuse me, ma'am. Chicken or Beef?" The stewardess repeated the question. She seemed annoyed because Cassie only stared at her with her mouth hanging open.

"She's asking you what you want for the meal. " The man next to her suddenly spoke. His deep baritone voice sounded stern. "The option is either Chicken Fried Rice or Beef steak with some vegetables."

"Oh!" Now her brain finally woke up. Cassie realised she was still on the plane on her journey to Jakarta, and it was still a few hours away from seeing Chandra. Chuckling nervously while feeling the heat creep to her cheek, she nodded.

"So, chicken or beef, ma'am?" The stewardess's voice became impatient.

"Chicken!" answered Cassie quickly. "Chicken, please. Thank you."

The stewardess snatched the tray table open with a grumpy face and placed her food on the tray. However, when she asked the man next to Cassie the same question, her tone changed three hundred and sixty degrees. It was polite and gentle. Cassie wondered if the different treatment was because she was just a lucky economy passenger who got upgraded to business class.

She opened her food though she did not feel hungry yet. While trying to calm her racing heartbeat, realising the wetness from her undies only made her blush more. What was the dream about again? Was she moaning earlier? And did the man next to her hear it? Oh, that was embarrassing! While munching her food, she purposedly maintained her gaze on the window or the screen and did not even dare to look at the man next to her.

"I think she did not know that you were sleeping."

Cassie jerked up as the firm baritone voice next to her was heard again. She hesitantly turned to him but found his eyes fixed on his food as he was slicing his beef. It made her wonder whether he was talking to her or if it was just a voice in her head?

"You must be dreaming of something pleasant earlier," he continued, still with his eyes focused on his food.

Cassie squished her eyebrow while watching him for a couple of seconds. He finished slicing the beef, pierced it with his fork and placed it into his mouth. And yet his eyes were still unmoved. Was he talking to her?

For a moment, Cassie thought that he was probably blind. It was a pity if that was the case, because she quietly admired his face from the side. He had a well-defined solid nose, a concrete jaw and soft stubble. She just realised that the pleasant earthly masculine scent she had drunkenly breathed in since she boarded the plane belonged to his cologne. She tried to look into his eyes again. It seemed his pupil's eye blinked like normal, and his gaze was not a blank stare. She did not notice that he had come with a guiding stick earlier. Besides, the way he sliced his food was so precise. It was impossible for a blind man to do it!

Feeling awkward and unsure, Cassie kept quiet, threw her gaze away to the window, and finished her food in silence.

Half an hour later, the stewardess returned and collected the empty dirty food trays. Cassie cursed inwardly, realising she had been drinking too much, and now her full bladder started to kick in. She looked up to see the sign of lavatories was green, which was great, but that meant she had to get herself past the man next to her to get out of her seat.

Fortunately, she was in business class. The leg space in between was quite spacious. She was sure she could pass him without even touching his knees.

"Excuse me," she murmured. "I need to pass through."

He did not reply or look at her even after Cassie had stood up. His eyes were fixed on the laptop screen on his lap. Cassie knew there was plenty of space anyway, and he did not need to move away from his seat to let her pass. Quietly she swallowed and told herself to move on anyway.

The lavatory trip was quite refreshing since she had been sitting too long. She looked at the time on her mobile phone, and it seemed the journey so far was only halfway. She sighed quietly. It seemed this was the longest journey she had ever had.

She had not done much overseas holiday. In fact, after almost forty years of her life, this could be just her third. She went to Auckland and Fiji before with some of her friends, and if she was not mistaken, Erin was on one of the trips. The rest were mostly just within Victoria or interstate trips. Kieran arranged those holidays during the school holidays to please Alicia and Ashleigh.

The pilot's voice echoed, announcing that some turbulence was coming and advising everyone to return to their seats. Reluctantly Cassie walked back to her seat to find that the man on the next seat was still unmoved, typing on his laptop.

"Excuse me," she murmured again as her polite gesture, and as she expected, he ignored her. The plane started shaking, and she quickly moved forward to reach her seat soon. However, she did not take into account that the turbulence became slightly more violent at the wrong time. While she was just in front of him, she lost her balance and landed on him and his laptop instead.

If Cassie could re-enact the whole scene, perhaps when she told this embarrassing incident to Erin or Kieran later, her face probably be as pink as a crab. Her brain was screaming, 'crap!'. This would be the last thing she would wish to happen, especially with this uncongenial cold-blooded man sitting next to her. She landed on him on her side as her breast conveniently landed on his face. Her fall also caused his laptop accidentally close and hit his hands.

"Bloody hell!" The cursing from his lips was full of disdain for sure.

Cassie apologised profusely, quickly gaining her balance and getting herself seated. "I am really sorry." She did not know how many times she had been repeating the words. She was too embarrassed to look at him, though she sneaked a glance a couple of times, trying to gauge whether he was still angry. However, again, he did not even look at her. Instead, he opened his laptop again while his lips were still cursing before finally standing up rather abruptly.

A man in a black uniform who seemed to be one of the cabin captains approached him, and Cassie watched the whole thing unfold before her with a mouth hanging open. The tall man murmured a few words to the captain while his eyes stared at the floor. Still, the captain listened to him attentively and nodded his head a couple of times as if agreeing with something from him.

A few minutes later, Cassie's 'neighbour' moved to another seat at the front, a few rows away, the one with extra leg space. Cassie assumed he must be such an important person that even the airline crew bowed their heads toward him. Cassie did not give a damn about whoever he was as long as he would not sue her for that silly accident. Now she understood why he did not even bother to look at her for one split second.

She chose to enjoy the rest of the flight journey by flipping through all the in-flight entertainment.

T he announcement from the pilot that the plane would be landing soon was like music to Cassie's ear. It was something that she had been dreading to hear. The local time showed 7 o'clock in the evening, and after the incident with an obviously filthy rich, arrogant guy who sat next to her, she could not wait to see a charming, congenial smile belonging to Chandra. It would help her forget this horrible journey and enjoy the rest of the trip! She was absolutely fine if she only had an economy seat for her return trip. She had enough of high-class self-entitled people in her life.

Fortunately, she was the first in line to exit the plane. At least she did not need to see that man's face again, whoever he was. Cassie was certain he must be somewhere behind her while queueing in the immigration line. She tried to focus and kept reminding herself that the exciting volunteer holiday had just begun. She just had to leave the unpleasant things behind. She decided to admire the airport building architecture decorated with traditional crafting, Javanese puppets and paintings of Indonesian women in their traditional attire.

Once she collected her luggage, her heart pounded with excitement. She could not wait to see Chandra soon and looked forward to the activities they would do together. Her eyes wandered around, trying to find the familiar face she longed to see. When finally her eyes caught a familiar figure of Chandra waiving at her, she was probably half running towards him. Chandra opened his arm wide to her, and she crushed herself into him and swung in the air.

"Welcome to Jakarta!" he exclaimed.

Cassie felt like she was in heaven and laughed her heart out while savouring the warmth of his embrace.

"How's your trip?" asked Chandra once he put her down safely back to earth.

"Yeah, alright," she chuckled nervously. Her eyes suddenly caught a man standing behind Chandra, watching them with a sheepish smile. The man was probably slightly taller than Chandra, with blonde curly hair and a long skinny face. Cassie knitted her brow, wondering whether this person was coming with Chandra.

"Let me introduce you to my colleague, Cass."

Yeah, right! Of course, Chandra would be coming with his colleague. Wasn't this trip about his work too? Instantly Cassie extended her hand for a handshake when Tom introduced himself.

"Oh, there is one more person that I need to pick up too." Chandra craned his neck while his eyes searched through the crowd. "He should be on the same flight with you."

"Really?"

"Yeah, sorry I forgot to tell you about him. Otherwise, you guys could have known each other on the plane. His coming is unexpected. Initially, he said he couldn't make it."

"Ah.."

"Here he is."

Chandra's eyes stared through to something behind her, and he walked passing her. Tom quickly followed him afterwards, making Cassie knit her brow while turning her head around. Her eyes could not see the person mentioned as Chandra, and Tom blocked her view. They seemed to shake hands formally before finally turning back.

As the three of them walked back towards her, Cassie could finally have a better view of Chandra's special guest. Her jaw dropped, and she probably forgot to breathe for a few seconds. She couldn't believe her eyes, but it seemed her eyes did not lie to her.

The person now walking with Chandra and Tom was the same man she wished she could forget that she had met him.

Chapter Five

His name was Brad. Cassie did not know exactly what he was doing in this volunteer project, but it seemed he held an important role from the way Chandra and Tom spoke and behaved formally towards him.

Darn! It seemed this trip would not be as fun as she thought. Cassie quickly shook her head and warded off that negative thought. *Remember, Cassie. You're also here for Chandra!* She was determined that she would focus on her goal.

When the three men finally landed before her, Cassie took a deep breath, lifted her head high, and felt ready to face that man more than ever. In rewinding on what happened earlier on the plane, she did nothing wrong with that embarrassing incident. She had apologised! He was the one who arrogantly ignored her.

"Hi Cass, this is Brad. Brad, this is Cassie. Do you guys realise you have been on the same plane?" said Chandra.

"Yeah, I do realise that," responded Cassie, raising her eyebrow with a smirk. "We sat next to each other."

"Far out!' Chandra exclaimed in surprise, glancing between them curiously.

"I was lucky to get upgraded to business class. And yeah, Brad sat just next to me." Cassie extended her hand for a handshake. "Nice to finally know your name, Brad. I am Cassie."

Brad looked at her hand hesitantly before taking it. "Nice to meet you too, Cassie."

Cassie did not expect him to take her hand. On the other hand, she guessed he would arrogantly reject it. However, she noticed his eyes were not looking at her but at her hand. He did not lift his eyes at her even after they pulled back their hands. Instead, he turned to Tom and murmured something to him.

"You guys must be tired. Let us head to the hotel," said Chandra while taking Cassie's luggage and motioning her to the exit door. His gentle touch on her small back was enough to send a shiver down her spine as she inwardly giggled.

They were all placed in the same hotel, same floors. However, Cassie's room was in the middle. Meanwhile, Tom and Brad's rooms were next to each other at the end of the corridor. Chandra stayed in his parent's house and took this trip as an opportunity to be close to his loved ones as much as possible.

After Brad and Tom entered their room, Cassie felt her heart flutter as she was the last person Chandra wished to speak to.

"I'm thrilled you're here, Cass," he said with his soft, intense gaze.

"Me too," chuckled Cassie nervously. She could feel her cheek become warm.

"Oh, you haven't told me how your plane journey was. I suppose it was pleasant since you had a free upgrade to business class. Did you have a chance to have a chat with Brad while on the plane?"

Cassie swallowed nervously. If it was not because Brad was also in this volunteer project, perhaps she would tell Chandra what happened on the plane. Perhaps she would one day, but definitely not now.

"A bit. I think he was busy with his work. He was on his laptop most of the time."

"Yeah, he's a busy man. But I'm glad he can join in. His expertise will be a great help to this project."

Cassie squished her eyebrow as her curiosity started to rise. "What is his role in this project? Is he going to teach too?"

She had been informed that her volunteer role was mainly to assist the poor and underprivileged primary students in learning Math and English as well as teaching them hygiene and well-being. Cassie was excited to work closely and, in a way, pretty much hands-on with these students.

Chandra shook his head. "No, he will help with the school's IT Infrastructure. He's also one of the main benefactors of this project."

"Oh! Will he be here for three weeks?"

Chandra nodded. "That's the plan. Let us see. As I said, he's a busy man. I'm afraid he could only be here for a week." He shrugged. "Anyway, it's getting late. Have a good rest, Cass. Tomorrow is going to be a big day. I'll see you at breakfast."

"Yeah, sure." Cassie smiled sheepishly as Chandra lowered his head and gave her a light peck on her cheek. He whispered good night before waving his hands and walking away. She was still standing at her room door for a couple of minutes until he disappeared into the lift. Then she closed the door and leaned on it while smiling to herself.

She felt her heart flying. Perhaps this was called falling in love. She could not recall whether she had this kind of feeling before. It made her feel silly for acting like a teenager when she was almost forty years old. But this was getting real. What she felt was not what those teenagers thought. Chandra was an adult, mature, and stable man. She was sure he would be ready to commit to a long-term relationship if they were together.

She had to admit that it had been a long day. Fatigue started to creep in, so she decided to freshen up herself with a shower. When she was already in her bathrobe, suddenly, her doorbell rang. She peeped through the door hole and was surprised to see the person outside the door.

"Hi!" she greeted once the door flew open.

Brad seemed taken aback to see her appearance. Cassie wondered whether she looked that horrible. She admitted that she had not had a chance to get her over-the-shoulder hair dried yet with a hairdryer. She had let them down, uncombed and frizzy.

"I'm sorry to interrupt your rest," he muttered. His adam's apple bobbed down before he continued, "I may need your help to speak with the staff here. " He shoved his hair with a sour look, pacing back and forth. "The showerhead in my room is not working. I need to change to a different room. I called them, but it seems they cannot understand me."

While he was speaking, she noticed that his eyes stared at the floor instead of looking at her. He spoke pretty fast, like babbling. It was not surprising if the locals could not catch his meaning. He also looked agitated as his breathing was rapid, and he clenched and unclenched his hands a couple of times. Cassie assumed he must be someone who always got what he wanted, and when he did not get it, he was frustrated.

As much as she was still annoyed with their silly incident on the plane, Cassie reminded herself that they would work together on this volunteer project. Hence they would see each other quite often. She reluctantly let her door open wider to let him in. But he stayed outside. Cassie ignored him, reached for the phone on the bedside table, and dialled the operator.

"Selamat Malam," she greeted 'Good Evening' in Indonesian once a welcome voice was heard on the other side. Then she continued to speak in her broken Indonesian, mixed with a couple of English words she intentionally spoke as slowly and clearly as possible. Once she hung up the phone, she turned to see him still standing outside the door. The tension on his face slowly dissipated.

"They are coming soon." Cassie sauntered towards the door. "I'll stay around until they are here."

"Thank you," he murmured. "I really appreciate that."

"No problem." Cassie tried to catch his eyes, and there was a split second he finally looked at her before his gaze was back to the floor.

"Is Tom not in his room?" she asked

He shook his head. "I knocked, but there was no answer."

Cassie knitted her brow. Where could Tom be? The time already showed 10 o'clock at night. For someone like Tom, perhaps the night was still too young. He was probably having a drink in the lounge lobby downstairs.

She was thinking of grabbing her mobile phone number and calling Chandra. However, the hotel staff arrived. Most of the time, she spoke in English to explain what had happened. Brad stood beside her without uttering any word, letting her speak most of the time. Finally, they agreed to move Brad's room to another one, coincidentally just next to her.

"Thank you once again for your help," he muttered after the hotel staff finished moving his luggage. "I wish you a good rest tonight. I'll see you tomorrow."

Cassie returned it with a tight smile. "No worries."

Though his gratitude was genuine, he delivered it stiffly, and she was bothered by the fact that he did not even look at her while speaking. In her communication dictionary, eye contact was crucial. Of course, if someone had a vision problem, that would be another story. She was unsure whether Brad did it intentionally or not. However, after the incident on the plane today, she had interpreted his lack of eye communication as part of his arrogance.

Unfortunately, it was something that she probably had to bear for the next three weeks.

Chapter Six

The hotel Chandra had booked for them was a four-star local chain hotel, located in one of the most crowded suburban areas in northern Jakarta. Actually, perhaps every part of Jakarta was crowded and highly populated. While they were on the *Grab Car* – Indonesian Uber-style type - from the airport to the hotel, Cassie could see people on almost every street corner. The motorcyclists, cars, hawkers, public transport of various sizes, plus the traffic jams. The city was stunningly alive with the blinking lights throughout the street, from the banner advertisement to the shops, department stores and houses. It was a totally different ambience than Melbourne city.

The motor and horn clamour from the street outside the hotel woke her up in the morning. Despite the room window being closed tightly, it did not stop the noise from coming through. She still had a good sleep, though. She practically slept soon after Brad moved to his new room and after she texted a message to Erin and Kieran that she had arrived safely. She looked at the time and knew it was her wake-up time, as Chandra had told her what time she had to be in the lobby for breakfast.

Feeling refreshed after changing her clothes, she came out of the room to bump into Brad, who had also just come out of his room.

"Good day," she greeted.

"Good morning," he greeted back.

Again, she was annoyed that there was no eye contact even though he returned her greeting. Worst, he just walked past her as if she was not there!

Cassie restrained herself from rolling her eyes and scoffing. She joined him to the lift, and an awkward silence unavoidable fell while they were inside the lift for a couple of minutes until they reached the ground floor. She tried to ward off her unhappy mood and drew her biggest smile when she saw Chandra waiting for them in the lobby with Tom beside him.

"Good morning! How are we? I hope both of you had a good rest last night!" Chandra's gleeful voice welcomed them. He approached her and landed a light peck on her cheek, with both his hands squeezing her forearms gently. It was a moment that Cassie had been looking forward to.

"Yeah, I had a good rest," replied Cassie. "I helped Brad last night moving into his new room. Now his room is just next to mine."

Chandra and Tom looked surprised.

"Oh? Is everything alright, Brad?" asked Tom with concern. "You should have called me."

"I did. I knocked on your door, but it seemed you were not in the room," replied Brad.

"Yeah, where were you last night?" Cassie chimed in. "It was about 10 o'clock last night when Brad had issues with his room. Were you downstairs?"

Tom looked blushed and stuttered. "Oh, yeah, I was downstairs to buy some snacks. If you notice, there is a small 24-hour grocery shop in the corner." He pointed his fingers to the mentioned shop in the far-left corner of the hotel check-in counter. "They sell plenty of good snacks there."

"Oh yeah, good to know there is such a shop," commented Cassie. However, her critical brain was running. Her gut feeling told her that Tom was hiding something. Last night's issues took almost an hour before Brad finally settled into his new room. What did Tom do for one hour in that grocery shop?

"Let us go for the brekky." Chandra's voice severed the conversation. He motioned them to the hotel restaurant.

While having breakfast, Chandra introduced them to some local volunteers. Cassie guessed about three people would be teaching like her, and all of them were young women, definitely younger than her, perhaps in their twenties. Seeing them made Cassie feel slightly intimidated, thinking that maybe any of these women were probably close with Chandra too. She quickly warded off her negative thoughts and focused on enjoying herself.

A woman with long curly hair, fair skin, with a sweet smile drawn on her lips, and almond eyes similar to Chandra's suddenly took a seat beside her. Cassie could sense that she wanted to initiate a conversation with her.

"Hi, my name is Helda. I'm Chandra's cousin."

"Hi, Helda" Cassie quickly offered her hand for a handshake which Helda accepted. "I'm Cassie."

"Yeah, I know who you are."

Cassie repressed her smile. Helda gave her a sheepish grin.

"Chandra speaks a lot about you."

Cassie felt her heart flutter. "Does he?"

"He said you were the first friend he met when he stepped foot in Melbourne. He said you're such an angel, helping him settle down in Melbourne."

Cassie could feel her cheek getting warm. They talked briefly about how it was Cassie's first year in Melbourne too, but at least she was lucky that she had Kieran helping her to settle down. Cassie remembered how Chandra struggled in his study because of the language and cultural differences, and she helped him catch up. She sometimes wondered why she had never thought of having more than a friend relationship with him at that time. Perhaps what they needed was time to be on their side finally. Hopefully, since they were approaching forty years old, they could finally see each other in a different light.

"So, have you been joining Chandra's volunteer project often?" asked Cassie. She noticed that Chandra's eyes were smiling at her, sighting she and Helda were talking. Unfortunately, he sat at the other end of the table, close to Tom, Brad, and other volunteers.

"Yes." Helda nodded. "It's been my passion."

"Have you been teaching the kids as well?"

Helda nodded while munching her food. "They are great kids. Seeing a foreigner like you, they'll love you."

Cassie chuckled. She sneaked another glance at Chandra, who unfortunately seemed to fall into serious talk with Tom and Brad.

"Is this the first time you are in Jakarta?" asked Helda.

"Yes, it's my first time."

"Did Chandra ask you to come?"

Cassie caught Helda's lips upturn into a teasing smile. She tried to guess the direction of the question.

"Well, we had a catch-up, and he mentioned this volunteer project. So, I decide to sign up."

"When he told me that you're coming, he was so excited."

Cassie chuckled as she lowered her face, trying to hide the blush on her cheek.

"I think he will introduce you to his mother," added Helda.

Cassie felt her heart skip a beat for that second.

"You're one of his best friends in Melbourne. Unfortunately, his mother hates travelling on the plane and has never been to Melbourne ever since Chandra lives there. She always wants to know with whom Chandra is mingling with."

"Right." Cassie smiled sheepishly.

Their conversation then severed when Chandra signalled everyone that it was time to leave and start their work. Cassie felt her heart fluttering again when Chandra approached her and sat on her side when they were on the minibus to the school.

"How's your breakfast, Cass?" he asked.

"Wonderful," she replied. She referred more to the conversation she had with Helda than the food.

"How do you find the food? What did you have?"

Darn! She did not remember it. She ate local food that she had no idea its name. It was a yellow soup with glass noodles, chicken, and bitternut crackers. It was flavoursome, and she loved it, though perhaps the soup was too hot for the humid weather in Jakarta. But certainly, she did not want to miss tasting the local food.

"It was *Soto Ayam*." A voice piped in. Cassie turned her head to find Helda smiling at her.

"Great! That's my favourite food too." Chandra clucked his tongue. "I will not miss it every time I am here."

What was the name of the food again? It sounded to her like *ottoyam*. However, they had reached their destination before Cassie popped up the question.

The location of the school was not far from the hotel, separated by a small drainage river and another block of houses. But it looked small and rusty, hidden behind the glamorous tall buildings. Yet ironically, it took them a twenty-minute bus ride, including the morning peak hours, to reach it.

"This school is not exactly a state-acknowledged school." Chandra motioned her to enter the school. Cassie liked the way he put his hand on her small back. "All the students here, either do not have a mother or a father and are very poor. They need to pay a minimum school fee, even for a government school. Bear in mind there's some cost for the books, stationery and uniform as well."

"How many students are here?" asked Cassie quietly as they walked further inside. She noticed that there were perhaps only a couple of classrooms, and each classroom was full of students. Moreover, the students in each room seemed varied and not from the same age group.

"About a hundred, but we only have three classrooms here. If there's enough funding, we're thinking of finding a bigger building."

"I suppose not all grades classes are available here."

"You're right. We don't have enough teachers and resources. We are fortunate to have some volunteers like yourself." He gave her his soft gaze and smile, which was enough to make Cassie's heart beat faster.

"How about the funding to pay full-time qualified teachers?"

"Yeah, we are talking about that too. But this is just the beginning."

Cassie nodded understandably, and at the same time, her eyes caught Brad, who walked inside the school as if he owned it. Tom and Helda were behind him and occasionally spoke to him as if explaining something. Chandra turned around to see where her eyes were going, and he chuckled.

"Yeah, it's supposed to be my job to take Brad around. Excuse me." He was about to walk away but stopped and turned to her again. "I'll get Helda to help you around, so you can start settling down with the students."

"No problem, I'll be fine." Cassie winked. She quietly grumbled that they did not have much time to talk yet. She took a breath reminding herself that she had to take it easy. It was just their first day. Everyone needed to settle down, though she wondered what Brad's role was in this project. Because it seemed he was treated as a VIP by Chandra and Tom.

When she stepped into one of the classrooms, the echo of gasps from the students welcomed her. She was probably the only volunteer with a foreigner look. However, one female student, who was probably in grade one, uttered her disappointment that she was not blonde.

"Oh, you can understand her?" asked Nina, one of the local volunteers.

Cassie nodded in her laughter. "Yeah, I learned Indonesian when I was in primary school. So I can remember some words."

The student looked embarrassed and giggled with the rest of her friends.

Cassie was then assigned to assist Tita, another local volunteer, in teaching grade one Reading and Math. There were probably thirty kids in the class, and all of the students looked excited to speak with her, even though in their broken English.

Cassie did not expect it would be a busy day. She was hoping to catch Chandra even for a brief during lunchtime. However, it was impossible. Chandra seemed to be in back-to-back meetings with Brad and Tom most of the time, while Tita pulled her to discuss the teaching plan for the rest of the day. Before she realised it, it was already two o'clock in the afternoon, and the class was dismissed. All the students bid them goodbye before they left the school.

"Are their homes nearby?" asked Cassie when she noticed that most of the kids were leaving the school without any sight of the parents picking them up.

"Some of them live quite nearby, perhaps only three minutes walk. Some of them may need to walk for five to ten minutes," answered Tita while tidying up the books and cleaning the whiteboard.

"I'm surprised they walk home by themselves, and I don't see any of their parents."

"Their parents are out for work. So they won't have time to drop off and pick up the kids."

Which is tough, Cassie thought. Even though she grew up in a regional area, as far as she remembered, her father and mother always took turns to ensure she went and came back from school, accompanied by either of them. If they could not make it, some close neighbours would help out. The only time their parents finally let them go by themselves was when Tiffany was born, and obviously, her mother was too busy to do the drop-off and pick-up with a newborn.

"You did great today," said Tita while taking a broom and started sweeping the floor. "The kids love you."

Cassie chuckled. "Is there any foreigner volunteer like me before?"

Tita shook her head. "No. You're the first. I guess you're special. That's why Chandra brought you here."

Cassie was unsure whether it was just her feeling, but it seemed to her that Tita smiled at her mischievously.

"Do you have any kids?" asked Tita.

"No. But I have two nieces."

"Now I understand why you are a natural with children."

"They are beautiful children. It's not hard at all to be with them. Do you have any kids, Tita?"

Tita shook her head. "If I have my own kids, perhaps I won't have time to do this volunteer work."

There was a blitz moment her curiosity crept in. However, Cassie felt relieved that she still could hold her tongue. She had observed that all the volunteers, apart from Helda, were beautiful young women. Perhaps they were in their twenties only. She wondered whether any of these women might have a heart interest in Chandra.

Since it was still daylight, Cassie could clearly see the properties and the street surrounding the school. Her eyes immediately recognised the tall hotel building that she lived in. It looked close, however, the more she observed it, it was pretty far, perhaps about ten kilometres. Some of the buildings near the hotel were not as tall as the hotel. In fact, the rest were just single-storey simple houses.

She walked further outside the school's small concrete front yard, which was probably only five metres before the gate. The school did not have a backyard, so the front yard was the only space that the students had for taking a break earlier. There was no sports court, park, or small playground. It was far from the ideal school in Melbourne.

Her curiosity was tickling as her body itched to explore the area.

"Tita, do you mind if I take a walk outside? Do you still need any help?"

"No!" Tita answered from inside. " Just be careful."

"Sure, I will."

Cassie was fully aware that she did not look like a local. Even though her hair was not blonde, her facial feature was different from being Asiatic. Nevertheless, she felt proud, wearing a brown colour dress with designs similar to the famous Indonesian craft 'batik'. She bought it from Kmart, but she planned to get the original batik from here once she had a chance to shop.

As the thought of shopping came into mind, her eyes caught another tall building at the end of the road. It looked like a clothes shop since she could see the mannequins on the window display. Strolling further approaching the building, she noticed a couple of old houses and shops along the way. But she was put to a halt when she saw a couple of rotten houses near the river. Realising the stinky smell from the river that was almost entirely covered by rubbish, she held her breath.

"Miss Fergie!"

A girl came up from one of the rotten houses and ran toward her with panic spread across her face. Cassie recognised her from one of the students today. She had told the students to address her as Miss Fergie instead of Miss Ferguson.

"Rini?"

"Miss Fergie, kenapa di sini *(What are you doing here)*?" Rini asked.

"I just have a walk."

"Anda tersesat? *(Are you lost?)* Ayo, saya bawa Miss Fergie balik. *(Let me take you back)*."

Cassie did not catch the last sentences, but she let Rini take her hand and half dragged her towards the school.

"I'm okay, Rini."

But Rini did not listen as she kept pulling her hand. It attracted the attention of the passing people who stared at them with squished eyebrows.

"Londo cantik dari mana, Rin?" (*Where is this beautiful foreigner coming from?*)" asked one of the young men, who was smoking in a nearby hut. Cassie heard the word 'cantik' and understood its meaning. She smiled shyly at the man, who winked at her, but Rini kept dragging her.

"Jangan pedulikan dia, Miss Fergie. Kak Chandra pasti khawatir mencari Miss Fergie." (*Ignore him, Miss Fergie. Brother Chandra must be worried looking for you).*"

Cassie knew that it was useless to argue. She did not expect that the small hand belonged to a little skinny girl like Rini was that strong. Once they reached the school, Cassie practically almost lost her breath. However, what surprised her even more, Rini was right. Chandra rushed out from inside with a blanched expression.

"Where have you been? Are you alright?" Chandra grabbed both of her forearms, scanning up and down from her head to her toes.

"I'm fine." Cassie felt thrilled seeing his worried look. "Relax, Chandra. I'm alright."

"Where have you been?" he asked again frantically.

"I just went for a stroll. I only went along this street. I guess I walked up to Rini's house, and then she dragged me back here."

Chandra's face became relaxed. Cassie repressed her smile, felt the tingling warmth in her heart, realising that he was worried for her. However, seeing Tom's darkened face, her breath hitched as he hissed angrily at her.

"So irresponsible."

Her jaw dropped, not expecting the fiery in Tom's eyes directed at her.

"Where do you think you are now? Do you think this is your country?"

"It's okay, Tom. She's fine," Chandra interrupted calmly. He raised his hand and stood between her and Tom as if trying to protect her. Cassie squished her eyebrow, questioning the anger directed at her.

"Look at your face, mate." This time Tom darted a glare at Chandra. "You almost fainted when you could not find her."

"She's my friend, Tom!"

"Perhaps you should *fuck* her now!"

"Cut it out, Tom!"

Cassie watched the quarrel between the two men before her with a half-open mouth for a couple of seconds. Both men had a heated argument as if there was no one else, despite Nina, Helda, Tita, and Brad stood not far from them. And what made Cassie unable to understand why Tom looked furious, that even his face reddened. His head snapped back to her, and he shot her a sharp glare. Chandra held him back, stopping him from coming closer.

"You'd better behave, Miss Ferguson." Tom was practically gritting his teeth at her.

Being intimidated that way made her hands wet with nerves. However, Cassie lifted her chin while squeezing the side of her dress. "I'm a grown-up, Tom."

"Do you realise what trouble you will give us if something happens to you here?" He narrowed his eyes with a flare of anger from his nostrils.

Cassie pursed her lips. Now she had a glimpse of understanding the reason for Tom's reaction. She did not think that her action to have a stroll was reckless. Quietly she swallowed and took a breath.

"I'm sorry," she murmured.

A sarcastic snort was heard as Tom strode away while banging a door along the way. Seeing him leave somehow made everyone take a quiet, relieved breath almost simultaneously.

Cassie shoved her hair as a punch of guilt hit her for causing such a scene. "I'm sorry, Chandra. I'm..."

Chandra gently touched her shoulder. If it was not because the rest of the people were still watching them, Cassie perhaps would throw herself into his arm.

"It's okay, Cass. I'm glad you're alright. But promise me, don't go by yourself alone here. Jakarta is not a safe city, especially for a foreigner like you."

Cassie only nodded and felt relieved as Chandra threw his arm around her shoulder and motioned her back to the classroom. She wished they would have more time together for the rest of the day. Unfortunately, that was not the case. Chandra apologised for not accompanying her for dinner, so she ended up eating at the hotel restaurant alone.

Chapter Seven

For the next four days, Cassie did not have a chance to see Chandra at all. Instead, Helda, Nina, and Tita accompanied her for breakfast and then took her to school every morning. Sometimes the ladies also accompanied her for shopping and dinner, then took her back to the hotel. She did not see Tom and Brad often, and Helda explained that they were away for meetings at the head office.

"Do you know Brad's and Tom's roles in this project?" asked Cassie one day while they were on lunch break. The students were out having a break, and today she assisted Helda.

Helda shook her head. "I am not sure. I guess they are from the management team where Chandra works."

"I know Tom is Chandra's colleague. That's what Chandra told me. But I don't think Brad is," commented Cassie.

Cassie had no idea what Helda was eating. It looked like it was rice with some chicken covered full of chillies. Cassie felt her tongue hot the moment she looked at the food. Luckily, Helda had bought her another non-spicy food wrapped in brown paper.

"I was terrified seeing Tom the other day. I thought he probably would hit you. I was practically shaking," said Helda while munching her lunch.

Cassie understood that Helda was referring to the quarrel the other day. She was shocked too by Tom's reaction. She had been trying to get him, wishing they could have another good talk about it. But it seemed Tom was avoiding her. She knocked on his room several times, but there was no answer. She guessed he was not in the room. Where could he be? He could not be in the meeting all day. He still needed his room to sleep.

"I did not expect he would react that way, too," murmured Cassie. "Well, I was at fault too."

"Luckily, *kak* Chandra was around," sighed Helda.

Soon after they finished their lunch, the students returned from their break. Cassie felt seeing the kids was like another fresh air to her. She was disappointed that this trip was unlike what she had envisioned because she did not have much time with Chandra as she had hoped. Still, she felt content to join this volunteer work.

While sitting on the ceramic floor of the classroom, preparing to do the story for the students, Rini approached her and took her hand.

"Kenapa Miss Fergie sedih?" (Why do you look so sad, Miss Fergie?)

Cassie smiled. She could not deny that she was partly in low spirits because of Chandra.

"I'm alright, Rini. Thank you."

"Miss Fergie rindu kak Chandra?" (Do you miss brother Chandra?)

Cassie chuckled. She glanced at Helda, wishing her not overheard this conversation. Luck was on her side as Helda was giving instructions to other students for the math lesson she was teaching that day.

"How do you say 'I love you' in Indonesian, Rini?" she asked almost in a whisper.

Rini giggled at hearing that. "Saya suka kamu." (I like you).

Cassie digested the word carefully and stored it in her memory brain. Hopefully, she would remember the words the next time she needed to say them again.

Time flies away quickly. It was because Cassie also enjoyed her teaching time. When the bell rang as a sign of school dismissal, Cassie felt slightly dejected. She was not looking forward to spending the rest of her weekend alone in the hotel. She wished she could see Chandra, but unfortunately, he had not replied to her text message.

It seemed to stay that way. Even until dinner time, she still did not receive any reply from Chandra. Partly annoyed, she tried to call him, but to no avail. There was no answer. She started feeling agitated and was thinking of leaving the hotel alone. However, when she just came out of her room, Brad returned.

Cassie quietly took a sigh. From all the people she was familiar with on this trip, Brad would be the last person she had in mind.

"Hi, Brad," she greeted. Of course, she would expect him to ignore her as usual. But she was baffled when he stopped.

"How are you, Cassie?"

"Uh..oh.." She did not understand why she was the one who became stuttered. "I'm fine." Then she remembered perhaps she could find some information about Chandra from him. "Did you just have a meeting with Chandra?"

"Not really. Our last meeting ended around 3 o'clock in the afternoon today."

"Do you know where he went afterwards?"

Brad shook his head. "No idea."

"And what about Tom? Did you have a meeting with him too?"

"Yes. Both of them left the meeting together."

"Right."

Cassie took another disappointed sigh. Her eyes followed when Brad had moved towards his room door as if her interrogation had ended. Then, in a spur of the moment, perhaps because she was desperate and bored, she blurted out, "Do you have something on tonight?"

He seemed puzzled and glanced at her briefly before he lowered his eyes again. "No."

"Shall we have dinner together?" She tried to make it sound casual, like a mate. That was her real intention. There was no way that this arrogant guy was interested in her anyway. But, perhaps he already had another plan. For a handsome and possibly still single man like him, she would not be surprised if he was hooked by pretty ladies here. "If you don't mind, of course," she added quickly.

There was no immediate answer. He seemed to fall into his deep thought for a moment before he made a faint head nod.

Since no words were uttered from him, Cassie was flabbergasted as he walked past her. However, suddenly he stopped and turned his head.

"Shall we?"

"Oh!" She jerked up and rushed to match his pace. She did not want to complain about his behaviour. It was better to bear with it temporarily rather than lose a companion for dinner!

Brad took her to a restaurant outside the hotel. To Cassie's surprise, apparently, he had a personal Uber driver, a local man with well-spoken English who was always available whenever he needed a ride. Cassie remembered that Chandra mentioned that Brad held a crucial role in the project, but she did not have a chance to ask further. She would assume he would be one of the management team in the project; hence he was mainly involved with meetings.

They hopped into the car, and the driver – Budi, recommended him a restaurant with good local food. Unfortunately, since it was Friday evening, it seemed everyone was going out, so their car was trapped in the traffic jam for almost half an hour.

Cassie realised there had been no conversation between them since they entered the car. Somehow, she was also engrossed in seeing the hustle-bustle of Jakarta's road, full of various vehicles, cars with different models and brands, and the local public transport. Even there were multiple types and sizes of buses. The most interesting one was the motorcycle covered with a red hut and a passenger seat at the back that could fit three or four people. She remembered Helda mentioned to her the name of it, but she had forgotten.

"What's that vehicle called again?" she giggled as their car seemed to be racing side by side with the red motorcycle.

"*Bajay*," replied Brad.

Cassie did not expect Brad would reply. She was expecting Budi would be the one who responded instead.

"Yeah, you're right!" She turned to him, and as usual, he only glanced at her briefly before throwing his gaze to the window. "How do you remember? Have you been to Jakarta before this?"

" A couple of times," he answered. He did not move his gaze from the window.

"Right. Do you like this city?"

He shrugged. "It's alright."

Sensing his lack of interest in a chat, there was a slight regret of asking him out for dinner. But Cassie tried to see the positive side of it. At least Brad took her out of the hotel, so she had a chance to see other parts of Jakarta, other than her hotel room and the school!

Cassie chose to stay optimistic. Perhaps this dinner would not be that bad. *Just enjoy the food, Cassie!* Her heart leapt when they arrived at their destination. The restaurant looked decent and not overly fancy. After they were seated on the upper floor, on the outdoor balcony, Cassie felt excited to see the view from upstairs despite what she could hear only the traffic noises and car horns. Various people were walking on the streets, blended with colourful lights from the traffic and hawker carts on the street side. It was a view that would be enough to occupy their dining time.

She smiled, looking at the menu written in Indonesian. Hiding her face behind the menu, she wondered whether Brad knew how to read it.

"Are you allergic to peanuts?" he asked.

She shook her head. "No."

"Good. All the food here contains peanuts."

"I guess most Indonesian food contains peanuts," commented Cassie. She read the word 'Gado Gado' from the menu list and knew it was the traditional Indonesian salad with peanut sauce. It was one of her favourite Indonesian food that she usually found in Melbourne.

The waiter approached them, and Cassie was surprised that he had already recognised Brad.

"Just get me the usual," said Brad. The waiter nodded, made a note on his small notepad, and looked at Cassie expectantly.

"What are you ordering, Brad?" Cassie asked curiously.

"Satay and rice."

"Good choice," smiled Cassie. She also loved satay. Chandra took her to one of the Indonesian restaurants in Melbourne before to eat the food. However, he said it was not as authentic as in Indonesia.

"I'll have the same, too," said Cassie, which the waiter acknowledged with his nod. She turned to Brad again. "Shall we share some dishes too?" She remembered that Chandra recommended some other Indonesian food the last time they visited an Indonesian restaurant in Melbourne. "How about some soup?" She lifted the menu book to the waiter and pointed. "How do you say it? Is this soup spicy?"

"It's *Lodeh*. Like a chicken curry soup," replied the waiter.

"Go ahead. I'm fine with anything," said Brad.

Cassie felt her spirit lift up. Her appetite seemed to have returned. After these few days, she had been losing it.

While waiting for their food order, they fell into silence again. Brad looked at his mobile phone screen most of the time while her eyes wandered around. She just wanted to enjoy herself tonight, having some fresh air outside. The restaurant had some other visitors. However, it was not crowded, unlike the last time Helda took her to the food court centre in a nearby shopping mall.

"May I know what you guys have discussed in the meeting?"

She cursed inwardly for being unable to hold her tongue and curiosity. She was supposed to ignore him like he had been ignoring her.

Brad did not lift his eyes from his mobile phone screen as she had expected. He did not answer straight away and seemed to be thinking to find the right words.

"I understand if you prefer to keep it confidential." Cassie restrained from rolling her eyes.

"We are just discussing what we plan to do moving forward," he finally said. "We are thinking of expanding the school premises, to provide more facilities for the children. We are expecting more children would be beneficial from this project."

"That's for sure. So how are you going to expand?"

"That's still in discussion. We are considering another location."

"Other location? But the current students are living nearby."

"That's true. But the new location might also provide them with a new home for living."

"Right." Cassie leaned back and crossed her arms while staring at the man in front of her with squished eyebrows. "Do you think they will be open to the idea of moving to the new area?"

Brad seemed taken aback. He briefly lifted his eyes to her before returning to his mobile phone screen. "We think so. It's a better life for them."

"Yes, that's how we see it. But what if their source of living is close to their current house? An example is Rini. I know her mother is a cleaner for residential houses. Most of her customers are from the surrounding suburbs. Is the new location far from the current location?"

"Yeah, a bit."

"I guess it's something that the management needs to think through."

Brad nodded. "You're right. You bring up a valid point."

Cassie inwardly groaned. Despite their -not so short- discussion, perhaps he only looked at her for a second. *What is his problem?* They fell into another silence before she cleared her throat, trying to get his attention. But he seemed unaffected.

"Do you always do that?" she blurted.

"Do what?" His eyes still did not move from his mobile phone screen.

"When you talk with someone, do you not even bother to look at them?"

He did not respond, but Cassie could see that he pursed his lips and clenched his hand. His body looked tense.

"Do you do that because you think they are less important than you?"

His adam's apple bobbed nervously. Cassie smirked as she felt she had the upper hand in this conversation.

"No," he answered with a deep low voice.

"Then, is it so hard to look at the person's eyes when you talk to them?"

"It's not my intention to offend anyone. Besides, you talk with your lips, not your eyes."

Cassie scoffed. "Well, that's true. But it's not only about talking. It's about communication. You convey your message through words and facial expressions, especially eye contact. I'm pretty sure your eyes are perfectly fine. Of course, if you're blind, that's another story."

He did not respond, and they went for another silence. However, Cassie believed he could feel her stern gaze as she was still waiting for him to speak.

"Why don't you give it a go?" she broke the silence. "Unless you do think I'm less important than you."

He took a deep breath. "If I think that way, I will not take you here for dinner."

"Great! I feel appreciated." Cassie snapped her finger. "Then, could you please look at me when we talk?"

His adam's apple moved up and down again. Cassie repressed her smile, watching him. She did not plan this little revenge to make him feel cornered. However, she still remembered his reaction to the silly incident on the plane that made her feel embarrassed. The accident was out of her control, but he arrogantly ignored her apology.

For a moment, there were only hushed sounds of other guests chatting as she watched him seem to struggle to retaliate against her words. He shifted uncomfortably and clenched his hands tightly until Cassie could see the bulge of his forearm. She had to admit that he was a good-looking man with his strong jaw feature and great athletic body shaped nicely with a tight-fit casual shirt and jeans. Cassie also guessed he must have a good role in his job, whatever it was, making people look up to him. He had every reason to be proud of himself, but she had enough of his superior attitude.

She folded her arms, put them on the table, and leaned forward while still giving him an unwavering gaze. She was sure he knew what she was doing. Finally, after it seemed like his hundreds of swallowing, he slowly lifted up his face. His eyes were initially down before slowly moving to her hand, and finally....it seemed like they were heavy, his eyes slowly up to meet hers.

Cassie felt her heart seem to stop beating at that moment. Something was captivating her. His eyes were definitely the culprit.

He had one of the most beautiful eyes she had ever seen. Gazing at them brought her into something profound and serene. They were opalescent brown, with a hint of amber, surrounded by brownish eyelashes. Then now, she could also see his face clearly. He had a perfectly straight nose, firm curvy lips and a heart face shape. She wasn't even sure for how long she had held her breath before finally taking a shuddered exhale. She could not believe herself staring at this gorgeous man before her with her mouth half-open in awe. She must look silly, and he must had thought she was admiring him!

The interruption from the waiter as their food arrived saved her. Cassie felt relieved that it gave her time to calm her pounding heart. She threw her sights anywhere but him and pretended to be excited to tug in soon by looking at the food. However, this time she was the one being stared at! She could feel the heat of his intense gaze on her. *Damn!* He obviously wanted to get back at her.

Once the waiter left their table, she gathered her courage to look at him. Her breath hitched that he was still unmoved. He looked stiff without any hint of a smile on his face. *Is he angry?* Cassie had no idea. But she lifted her chin and smirked, pretending to be brave.

"So, that's not hard, isn't it, Brad?"

Chapter Eight

The sound of the noisy car horns and traffic from outside her hotel room window was the one that made Cassie sluggishly open her eyes. Despite the blackout blind, some of the morning sunshine still managed to pierce through. Cassie knew it was a sign for her to get up.

It was Saturday morning, and there was no school today. It was her first weekend in Jakarta, and ironically she had no idea what to do. Initially, she thought Chandra would be on her side most of the time, and they would spend plenty of time together. However, it seemed everything did not always go according to plan. She should have taken into account that Chandra came here for work, unlike her. However, what made her feel disappointed further was that even on the weekend, it seemed Chandra still had to work. She had sent him a text, and he only responded with a short message that he was at work.

She thought he cared about her safety, but she seemed to have no choice but to explore the city alone. Perhaps Brad could join in if he was not working too. Though she was unsure that would be a great idea.

Thinking about Brad, her mind went to last night. After the bravado of forcing him to maintain eye contact, she felt annoyed afterwards. He started to stare down again, but he did look at her every time they talked. They ate their meal while conversing about family and the weather. They returned to the hotel afterwards and went straight into their rooms, although the night was still young.

She did not know why she had to feel annoyed, perhaps because his eyes were captivating. Although he did have eye contact while talking, she felt he was overdoing it. Definitely, she could not lick her own words anymore.

Spiritlessly, she pushed her body up from the bed and opened the window drapes to see the scenery of the busy metropolitan city of Jakarta. The vibrating from her mobile phone startled her, and she smiled to see the incoming video call.

"Wakey, wakey!" Erin appeared on the phone screen.

"Good day!" laughed Cassie while shoving her messy hair.

It was four hours difference between Jakarta and Melbourne due to daylight savings in Melbourne. Cassie glanced at the clock to realise it was already noon in Melbourne.

"How are things going there?" asked Erin. Cassie noticed that Erin seemed not to be in their apartment. In fact, the wallpaper background behind Erin looked familiar.

"I'm in your brother's house." Erin seemed like she could read her mind. "Today is my turn to take the girls for their ballet lesson in the morning. We just came back, and now I am cooking their lunch."

Erin had offered help to do errands for Ashleigh and Alicia while she was away, but Cassie could no longer remember which day Erin was on duty.

"Where's Kieran?" she asked curiously.

"He is not awake yet. He came back from work very late last night."

Cassie squished her eyebrows. "So, you were there too last night?"

Erin nodded. "Yes, he had an urgent request to accompany a big client. So, he called for help."

"Oh, no!" Cassie slapped her forehead. It was one of those days that Kieran would desperately need help to mind the girls. She felt bad she could not be there. "I'm sorry for troubling you, Erin."

"Not at all, Cass! Don't be silly! I'm happy to do it. I had nothing to do anyway."

"So you slept there?"

Erin chuckled. "You said it as if I slept with your brother."

Cassie bulged her eyes, which made Erin giggle sheepishly.

"The girls are in Ashleigh's room, luckily."

The joke somehow tickled something within Cassie. The thought of her brother sleeping with her roommate was slightly .....*intriguing*. She must find time to think it through again. Erin is an attractive woman, and Kieran is charming. If they were together, wouldn't that be great? However, something made her doubtful that it would work. It seemed Kieran and Erin had different lifestyles and life perspectives. Perhaps she was wrong.

"So, how's the thing there? Give me an update on how you are going with your prince."

Cassie saw Erin chopping some vegetables, which distracted her from the question. "What are you cooking this time for the girls?"

"Pizza." Erin lifted a package of Coles' pizza base to the screen. "I found this in the pantry. And there is plenty of leftover ham and cheese. So, that's all I can think of."

"You're a genius! The girls will love it. Since when you're so good at cooking?"

Erin laughed. "I used to cook before I'm too busy working, Cass."

"Aren't you now still busy working?"

"Yeah, but most of the time, you've done the cooking when I get home."

Cassie chuckled. It was true that whenever she got a chance to cook, she always cooked extra for Erin.

"You're a saviour, Erin. Kieran and I owe you a lot."

"Don't mention it, Cass! I love to be with the girls."

Then the sound of noisy running steps overtook their audio. It sounded like a hurricane was about to strike. Erin winced before her face on the screen was replaced by Ashleigh and Alicia.

"Hi, Aunt Cassie!" screamed the girls. "We miss you!"

Kieran appeared behind the girls, shirtless with his messy wake-up hair, waving at her.

Cassie's eyes widen. Didn't he realise that Erin was there? She caught a hint of pink blush on Erin's face as her roommate threw her sight to anywhere else except Kieran. Cassie hated to admit that her brother had a well-toned body, so she would not be surprised if he were proud to show it off.

"Hi, Cass. How are you there?" asked Kieran. Erin shifted her mobile phone screen showing him taking a juice bottle from the fridge.

"I'm alright here, bro," Cassie replied.

The doorbell sound was suddenly heard, making them knit their brows.

"That doesn't sound like our house's doorbell," said Alicia.

"Yeah, you're right, sweetie," commented Kieran.

When the bell rang again, Cassie realised it was her room doorbell.

"Oh, that's my room doorbell. Let me check who's outside." She went to the door and peeped from the door hole to see Brad outside. Without thinking, she opened the door, forgetting she was still on a video call.

"Hi, Brad. What's up?" She thought that he might need help again speaking with the hotel staff. Perhaps something happened with his room.

Brad was startled by her appearance. His surprised look made Cassie realise that she was still in her pyjamas and her 'wake up', uncombed hair.

"I am just.." he stuttered. "I'm just thinking whether you would like to have breakfast together."

"Oh!" Cassie could not hide her surprised tone. She did not expect that now he would become so friendly toward her after last night. But, since she had a companion, how could she reject it? "Sure! Give me a minute."

Cassie did not realise that while she was talking with Brad, her mobile phone was still in her hand in an upright position. The moment she closed the door, she was startled by the sound from the video call.

"Who's that hunk?"

She cursed inwardly, realising Erin was still on the other line. Worse, when she saw the screen, it was not only Erin, but also Kieran, Ashleigh and Alicia staring at her curiously.

"He's one of the volunteers," she lied, wishing to save the trouble of explaining.

"Right. I always think Chandra is an Asian," commented Kieran.

"Oh, how are you going with Chandra, by the way?" asked Erin.

Cassie took a sigh. She wanted to share her story, but definitely not when the girls were also around. Furthermore, she still remembered that Brad was still waiting outside.

"I'm going for breakfast first. We'll talk again later, alright?"

"Alrighty."

She could see Erin and Kieran repressing their smiles. Ashleigh and Alicia waved goodbye, and after a couple of seconds, finally, she pressed the end call button. Once the phone hung up, she quickly changed her pyjama into a t-shirt and shorts. She assumed they would just go for breakfast at the hotel restaurant downstairs, however when she came out and followed Brad to the lobby, he kept walking.

"Where are we going?"

It was a question that put Brad to a halt.

"I want to take you to another place for breakfast. I suppose you're already bored with the breakfast here."

Cassie's eyes widened. "Where are you taking me to?"

"You'll see."

She blinked a couple of times, could not believe what she had just seen. Did she see a ghost of a smile on his lips? He continued his steps and opened the car door for her. Feeling curious and anxious, she quickly hopped in and did not wish to make him wait.

Their car journey only took about fifteen minutes, which was great because Cassie started feeling starving and dizzy. She did not want to be a hangry person. She had no idea, though, where Brad had taken her into. It looked like a big area with hawker sellers and plenty of tables and chairs in the middle. It was like a food centre but in an outdoor setting. She felt a jolt of excitement within her, seeing plenty of food selections and variety that she could choose.

"How do you know this place?" she asked while they were seated down. Immediately a couple of people pushed their restaurant menu cards to them. Cassie giggled while reading the menu.

"A friend told me about this place. I know what I want. The local coconut rice wrapped in banana leaf from stall number three is my favourite."

"Can you order one for me as well, please?"

"Yeah, sure."

In the next fifteen minutes, their order arrived. Brad also ordered the local coffee for both of them so she could give it a try. She laughed out loud when she drank it as it was different from what she used to have in Melbourne. She could not say if she liked it, but Brad seemed used to the taste.

There was a bizarre feeling within her as she gazed at Brad sipping his coffee. She experienced this local ambience with Brad instead of Chandra as she had hoped for. She quietly took a sigh as her mind drifted to Chandra. Until now, there was still no single reply from him despite the fact she had sent another text message last night.

"What's your plan today?" asked Brad.

Cassie shrugged. "I have no idea. I tried to contact Chandra, but he is ignoring me."

"I suppose he's working."

"It's Saturday!"

"Some office workers here still work until Saturday afternoon," stated Brad solemnly.

"But Chandra is employed by an Australian organisation," argued Cassie. Then she furrowed her brow. "How about you? If Chandra is still working, are you going to work too?"

"Perhaps."

"Are you going to go to the head office and see Chandra? Don't tell me you guys are having a meeting."

Brad shook his head. "No. I am not working on this project today. What I mean is my own work."

"Oh. What do you do, Brad?" It was a question that she had wanted to ask but kept forgetting.

"I develop apps."

"For?"

"Various organisations. Mainly finance companies."

"Right. Chandra mentioned to me before, that your expertise is needed for this project. Are you going to develop some apps for this project too?"

"That's the plan."

Cassie noticed that he tried maintaining eye contact with her whenever she spoke. He looked like he was struggling initially, but he seemed to be doing it naturally the more they talked.

The sudden vibration from Cassie's mobile distracted her. Her breath hitched, seeing a new incoming message. She prayed hopefully it was from Chandra. However, when she saw the sender, she had a mixed feelings between disappointment and excitement.

It was from Helda, asking her to join them for lunch. But what sent a loud thud in her chest was that Chandra's mother invited her for lunch.

It was probably perfect timing. Brad dropped her back to her hotel room, and he planned to bury himself in his work for the rest of the afternoon. Cassie did not mention the lunch invite by Chandra's mother. She felt it was unnecessary to let him know. She only mentioned that Helda was the one going to take her out for lunch.

"That's good. At least you're not alone spending this weekend," commented Brad.

Cassie only smiled sheepishly. She thought likewise. It seemed Brad also could sense that she felt lonely. This trip was supposed to be her holiday too. She should go out more and have fun. She should not depend on Chandra to take her out.

She quickly got herself showered. The humid weather made her sweat easily. She did not want to look like a filthy woman when she would potentially see her future mother-in-law. She giggled, thinking about it, hushing off her thought. Chandra had not given her any green signal. Likewise, she had not made any move.

But why did Chandra's mother seem interested to see her? Regardless, she had to look her best. Luckily she brought some of her best dresses. Before Helda came to pick her up in the lobby, she went out of her room, wearing her over-the-knee-length lime flowery summer v-neck dress. It was a perfect coincidence as Brad also came out of his room when she locked her room door.

He seemed startled. His eyes travelled from her top to bottom before resting his eyes back on the floor.

"Hi, Brad," Cassie greeted casually.

"Hi," he replied without looking at her, making her slightly annoyed that he had returned to his old habit.

"Are you going out?" she asked while walking towards the lift. He followed behind her.

"Yeah, thinking of catching some fresh air before returning to work."

They entered the lift together and went silent for a few seconds before his soft voice was finally heard.

"You look great."

Cassie did not expect the compliment. "Thanks!" she turned to him with a big broad smile, but as she had expected, his eyes stared at the floor.

"Is Helda coming to pick you up?"

"Yes." She looked at the time on her mobile phone. "She should be here by now."

They reached the ground floor, and the lift door opened. Cassie felt her limb was light and stepped out of the lift, full of energy. Helda was already in the lobby waiting for her as she had expected. However, she noticed another woman behind Helda, whom Cassie guessed was perhaps about the same age as her mother. Cassie felt her heart beating fast as she realised the lady was probably Chandra's mother. She did not expect to see her here. She thought she would see her later in the restaurant.

"Hi, Cass. This is Chandra's mother. You can call her aunt Yuli," said Helda after they exchanged a brief cuddle.

Cassie immediately offered her hand for a handshake with a shy smile, and a sudden nervousness hit her. "Hi, aunt Yuli. Nice to meet you."

She did not realise that Brad was still standing behind her. Cassie noticed Helda's widened eyes go beyond her. She turned around with a soft gasp, finding Brad had probably heard their conversation. She was not sure why, but she felt awkward.

"Oh, tante Yuli, ini juga temen kantornya kak Chandra *(Aunt Yuli, this is also Chandra's work colleague)*," said Helda to her aunt while pulling her forearm gently. "Hi, Brad, how are you? I'm taking Cassie for lunch. Since you're here, let me introduce you to Chandra's mother. Aunt Yuli."

Brad hesitantly also offered his handshake without much comment. Cassie sighed slightly relieved when he quickly excused himself after the introduction. Helda then motioned them to get into the car.

The journey into the restaurant took perhaps half an hour. However, the time was easily passed by as Helda and aunt Yuli filled up the conversation most of the time. Aunt Yuli was a soft-spoken lady. Cassie could see the similarity between her and Chandra, not only from their fair skin, but also from their almond eyes, chubby cheek, spectacles and even the way they spoke and smiled. Cassie immediately felt comfortable talking to her.

The lunch was in an elegant oriental-decorated building full of Chinese calligraphy and paintings. Cassie felt being transported into China instead of Indonesia, despite everyone, including the staff speaking in fluent Indonesian. Some guests spoke in a Chinese dialect that Cassie could not recognise. But being here reminded her of being one of Melbourne's Chinatown restaurants where she usually had *yum cha*.

Aunt Yuli had reserved a private room for them. The room had three big round tables, which Cassie guessed could fit ten people at each table. She furrowed her brow, wondering whether the three of them needed such a massive space.

Her confusion became more evident as several people around aunt Yuli's age arrived.

"Cassie, please come over," aunt Yuli called her. "This is my brother and his wife. They are Chandra's uncle and aunt."

"Nice to meet you all," greeted Cassie politely while offering her handshake. She noticed that the new visitors giggled at each other in Indonesian, and somehow Cassie could catch some of the meaning.

Did they say that she was not too bad? Helda reprimanded them for the possibility she could understand them.

"Is this a family lunch?" Cassie whispered to Helda when she had a chance while the rest were busy talking to each other.

"Sort of," Helda replied, also in a hush.

"Why are you inviting me to your family lunch?" Cassie squished her eyebrows. Something did not feel right.

"Because *kak* Chandra is here. You know, he lives in Melbourne most of the time. So since he's here, so this lunch is meant for catch-up between families."

"Alright." Cassie started to feel the moisture in her hands. "And why are you inviting me too?"

"I told you before. Aunt Yuli always wants to get to know *kak* Chandra's friends from Melbourne."

"Am I the only Chandra's friend here?"

Before Helda could answer, they were distracted by the presence of the same person that they had just talked about. Chandra entered the room with his congenial smile, the smile Cassie always liked and missed. However, slowly his smile faded when his eyes caught her presence. He blinked a couple of times and seemed in disbelief to see her. Cassie felt her chest tight, realising he had no idea she would be here.

"Cass?"

Cassie broke a weak nervous smile. She felt something was not right and felt uneasy seeing Chandra's blanched facade while he stuttered, "What....?"

"Kak Chandra, Helda yang bawa Cassie ke sini. Yiyi Yuli yang minta *(Brother Chandra, I am the one who brought Cassie here. It's aunt Yuli's idea)*," Helda interrupted.

Chandra glared at his cousin, and before Cassie could open her mouth, he grabbed Helda's forearm and dragged her to the corner, away from others. However, even though it was only a few steps away and they spoke in Indonesian, Cassie still could overhear some of their conversations. She knew Chandra reprimanded his cousin for bringing her here without telling him.

After a few minutes she stood like a statue, watching Chandra and Helda's argument, Cassie was startled when aunt Yuli suddenly touched her forearm gently.

"Let's sit down, Cassie. I would like you to sit beside me, so you can tell me lots of stories about what Chandra does in Melbourne."

Cassie was speechless, and Aunt Yuli pulled her hand before she could think of any excuse. Cassie turned her head to Chandra in panic, but it was too late. She finally sat down at the table, treated like a special guest, sitting next to the queen and grilled with many questions about Chandra and Melbourne. At one point, she sneaked a glance at Chandra, who sat on his mother's right-hand side, giving her a guilty look while she returned it with a sheepish smile.

Chapter Nine

"I am really sorry."

It seemed like the hundredth time Chandra had been apologising.

The lunch finished around 3 pm, and that was because Chandra made an excuse to leave first while the rest of the family stayed back for another karaoke session in the room. Cassie was amazed to see how the dining room was converted easily into a disco room. The initial chandelier light was turned off, the downlights were dimmed, and the colourful blinking lights slowly took over. Chandra grabbed her forearm gently and stood on her side most of the time while bidding goodbye to everyone. They went back to the hotel straight away with a Grab.

The journey was rather awkward. Cassie stole a glance at him with a sheepish smile a couple of times, but he seemed to be falling into his own deep thought. Until, at one time, he let out a deep exhale and said his first apology word.

"It's alright, Chandra. Your family means well." That's all Cassie could say to console him. But his face looked grave, as if someone had died. Was it that bad if she was his girlfriend?

"Helda should not take you there," he murmured. They took the lift, and Cassie could feel her heart leaping as he accompanied her back to her room.

"She said your mother is curious about your life in Melbourne. You never tell her anything, do you?"

"I do. But you know, like any mother, she is just curious with whom I have been mingling with."

Cassie chuckled. "Think it on a positive side. It's good to have someone who cares about your life. Unfortunately, my mother never cares about what I've been doing. I'm not her favourite child."

"I'm the only child, Cass." Chandra chuckled. "At this stage, I prefer to be ignored, like you."

Cassie laughed at hearing that. If Tiffany had never been born, perhaps her mother would pay more attention to her. But she quickly warded off that thought, reminding her that reality spoke differently.

They stopped outside her room and lingered there for a moment as if no one wanted to say goodbye first.

"I'm sorry that I was busy last week. I meant to ask you how you went with the teaching."

Cassie felt her heart fluttering that at least he wanted to speak longer with her. "It was great. I enjoy the interaction with the kids. They are such amazing kids! Independent, mature with strong resilience too. I guess life's hardship teaches them a lot about life."

"I agree. Perhaps we should be the one that learns about life from them."

He gazed at her softly, something that was enough to make her feel the butterflies in her stomach. Would this be their opportunity?

"I've finished my report, so I'll be around most days next week. After that, I'll have more time to accompany you for lunch or perhaps shopping. Since you're here, I want to ensure you've seen plenty of things in Jakarta."

Cassie's eyes lit up. "That would be fantastic. Can I take it as a deal?"

Chandra lifted up his pinky finger, which Cassie tangled with hers enthusiastically.

"It's a deal. I'm sorry for being such a lousy host. But I'll make it up next week. Also, by the end of next week, there will be a surprise for you."

Seeing the flicker in his almond eyes with his twitched lips, Cassie felt her pulse beating faster. What surprise did he mean here? Would there be something special? A date, perhaps?

"I am sorry today I can't accompany you. If you want to go out, I suggest contacting this Uber driver." He took out a card from his shirt pocket. "He's reliable. At least I know you are going with a trusted person."

Cassie read the name on the card and immediately recognised it. "Oh? Is this the driver that Brad also uses?"

Chandra looked stunned. "How do you know?"

"Well, Brad and I went for dinner last Friday, and he introduced me to this driver."

"Oh? Do you often go out with him? I thought both of you..."

Cassie wondered whether he was jealous. His unfinished sentences made her curious. Had she said anything bad about Brad to him before? Despite her unpleasant first encounter with Brad, she did not recall sharing the story with Chandra.

"Well, great to know you get along well with him," he continued. "I'm glad you could have his companion at least sometimes."

"Yeah, but he works most of the time," she added, unsure why she had to add that statement. Looking back, Brad had taken her out for a meal twice. Chandra had not taken her out since she stepped foot in his hometown. She felt her heart slightly sinking, seeing Chandra's neutral facial expression.

"Look, just contact the driver. He can take you anywhere you want. I believe he can recommend some good places here too." He sounded casual, almost like she meant nothing to him. She did not understand why he was frantic the last time she walked alone outside the school.

"See you on Monday, Cass." Then he lowered his head and planted a light peck on her cheek. Breathing in his earthly masculine scent, at least, something that always lifted the spirit within her. Cassie smiled while returning his goodbye wave to her.

Chapter Ten

Despite a quiet weekend, Cassie looked forward to the week. It was not only because Chandra would be in the school more often, but Cassie always felt her spirit lifted when she met the kids.

Chandra took her out for lunch and accompanied her for dinner for a couple of days in the week, but they never had a chance to be alone. Brad and Tom often joined in. Every time Chandra spoke with her, the kids would giggle with teasing looks in their eyes. It was something that made both herself and Chandra smile sheepishly.

As the time was approaching the end of the week, Chandra paid a visit in the afternoon after school had been dismissed. Cassie tidied up the class with Nina and Helda when he came in. His face was beaming with an excited smile drawn on his face. Brad and Tom came in after him.

"Remember I mentioned a surprise by the end of the week, Cass?"

Cassie's eyes lit up, and her smile slowly broke. Her heart pounded as she was curious about what the surprise would be.

"We're going for a short getaway in Bandung this weekend. We are departing this evening," announced Chandra.

Helda and Nina immediately squealed. Seeing their reaction, Cassie knew it must be exciting though she had no idea where Bandung was.

"Bandung was just two hours' drive from here," explained Chandra. "The board thinks you guys deserve this little treat after your hard work."

"Sounds great," responded Cassie. "What are we going to do there?"

"We'll stay in one of the best hotel resorts there. There are plenty of team activities organised, but the main intention is for you to relax." Chandra winked. "I've arranged that you get one of the best rooms."

Cassie smiled sheepishly, feeling her heart seem to float. This trip sounded fun, and perhaps something more exciting would come between her and Chandra.

Within the next few hours, they were already sitting in the minibus, hired for them to have a journey together in one vehicle. Unfortunately, Chandra did not sit next to her as she expected. Instead, he sat next to Tom and had a chat with Brad. Meanwhile, she sat together with Helda, Nina and Tita. It seemed like the males and females made their own group.

Once they checked into their room, they agreed to have a brief rest before meeting up in the lobby restaurant for dinner. Cassie almost could not believe finding herself in such a big spacious room with a huge outdoor balcony. Helda, Nina and Tita shared a room since Helda claimed she disliked sleeping alone. Meanwhile, the males' rooms were not far from them. All their rooms were on the same floor.

While Cassie got herself to freshen up, her mobile phone rang—an incoming video call from Erin.

"Hello there! How are things going?"

Erin's friendly face somehow made her feel a bit homesick. She had told Erin about the lunch with Chandra's family through their chat messages. Erin sounded excited hearing that story.

"So, it seems you've already had a seal of approval from his family. That's a good sign."

Cassie chuckled. "Yeah, so it seems. But still, there's nothing between us."

"Well, Cass. After being your housemate for two years, I have no idea about your love life. My apologies for being such a lousy housemate."

Cassie squished her eyebrow. She could see Erin looked nervous.

"I wonder whether you ever liked someone before," continued Erin. "When you told me you never had sex before, and you're reaching forty soon, I wonder why. I mean, whether you've been brokenhearted or had a traumatic relationship."

"I've never been in a relationship," Cassie cut in solemnly.

"Yeah, Kieran told me."

"Did he?" Cassie arched her eyebrow. Her brother seemed to have so much time to talk with her housemate. She was sure Kieran could remember Erin's name by now.

"But have you been in love before?"

Good question! Cassie went silent for a moment, reflecting on the past nearly forty years of her life. Well, perhaps the first eighteen years of her life were not counted.

Everything seemed blurry now. Perhaps this was a sign of ageing. During eighteen years of schooling, her focus was mainly on school, maybe there were a few crushes during her teenage years. Still, she never had the courage to make a move or even show herself more. She was practically under the shelter of Kieran's protective brother's love.

After moving out of her parent's house, she felt her social life was pretty average. She hung out with her friends, although most of the time, she always followed Kieran wherever he went until her brother got hitched by his late wife.

When Kieran and Emily got married, she was already thirty years old. Alicia was born a year later, and she was excited to be the dotting aunt. Ashleigh was born eighteen months apart, adding joy and hectic life to her brother's life. Though Emily's parents live not far, babysitting a toddler and a baby was too much of a handful for them. Cassie did not mind being the first person that Emily would rely on.

Unfortunately, things did not get better. The tragic car accident took the precious life of a loving mother, leaving behind two toddlers in the hand of her brother. Kieran was almost a wreck, and Cassie knew she had to step in to help. She moved to her brother's house, became like a second mother to the girls, and worked reduced hours so Kieran could focus on his full-time job. It was a tough life for her brother, and Cassie knew she just had to be there for him.

She finally moved out of her brother's house only two years ago. It was not by her initiative. It was a push from Kieran, encouraging her to have her own life too.

The rest was just history. But it made her realise the possible causes of her singlehood so far. She only opened her heart to the men who cared for her – her father and brother. Perhaps she was too idealistic, but both her father and brother had been her benchmark. Furthermore, she never found herself attractive and was not surprised if anyone was not interested in her.

But now, she was almost forty years old. Perhaps her age and maturity gave her the courage to take the initiative and be the first to make a move.

"Perhaps," she answered. "But I never made a move. The other party did not too. Well, I am not an attractive woman."

"How could you say that?" squealed Erin. "You are special, Cass. You are the most loving, selfless person I have ever met. I understand how your brother and his girls love you dearly. If Emily were still around, she would say the same thing I'm telling you now."

"Thanks, Erin."

"Anyway, back to you and Chandra, if you like him, you must tell him. I'm pretty sure your feeling will be reciprocated."

"You reckon so?"

Erin nodded her head vigorously. "He's stupid if he let you slip away from his life. So what makes you like him?"

"We just click, I guess. I enjoy my time with him. It seems easy and smooth." But, when she said those words, she suddenly realised that she had hardly spent time with Chandra the past few weeks.

"Then, I guess it's not hard to express your intention to him," commented Erin. "Can you imagine having sex with him?"

Cassie burst into laughter hearing that.

"I'm serious, Cass." Erin gave her a stern look. "If you like someone, surely you have some desire to sleep with that person too."

Cassie could feel her cheek getting warm. She could not believe she was having this conversation with Erin. After two years of being housemates, they finally talked heart-to-heart about their love life. Perhaps Erin had shared more about her romantic life than her because she simply did not have any!

"I ..." she couldn't help but stutter. "I have not thought that far yet!"

Erin was the one laughing now. "Alright. I will let you reflect on it. Where are you now? That doesn't seem like your usual hotel room."

Cassie moved her mobile phone camera lens around to show her new spacious, luxurious hotel room. "I'm in one of the best resort hotels in Bandung. It's a city two hours away from Jakarta. It's a weekend getaway, perks given by the organisation I volunteer for."

Erin whistled. "Your room is massive! Wow! So, is Chandra coming too?"

Cassie nodded. "Yes. He already told me last week that there would be a surprise for me. So, this is the surprise. Oh, you should see this place." She showed the rice paddle scenery laid before her from the wall-to-wall room glass window. "Beautiful, isn't it?"

"Yes, it is! Oh, I should go there too one day."

"Yeah, I don't mind coming here again one day."

"There is a possibility, isn't there? When you are together with Chandra?"

Cassie only responded with a laugh. "Alright, I have to get ready." She looked at the time on her mobile phone. "We agreed to meet in the lobby for dinner in fifteen minutes."

Erin's eyes lit up. "Oh? Is that a date?"

"No. There are others too. Other volunteers are here, too."

"What a shame!"

Cassie's head threw back again with her laughter.

"Alright. I'll let you go. But I am looking forward to hearing something from this getaway." Erin's eyebrows were dancing up and down. "Don't forget the little gift that I gave you. You probably need it soon."

Cassie could imagine that her face blushed. Quickly she waved her hands. "Ciao!" It was enough to clue the end of the call.

Their conversation did make Cassie think. She went to wash her face, and when she saw her reflection in the mirror, inevitably, she observed herself closely.

She never thought of herself as someone strikingly beautiful, unlike Tiffany or Kieran. Both of her siblings had blonde wavy hair inherited from their mother and captivating blue eyes from their father. They were the best combination of traits from their parents' genetics. Meanwhile, she was the only one with frizzy brunette hair, brown eyes, a button nose, and thin lips. Her father said she looked more like her grandmother when she was young.

Hence, she understood if she had never been the centre of attention in school, while both Kieran and Tiffany were popular kids. Not only because of their physical look but also their academic and sports achievements. Meanwhile, she was just average. She did not wish to be under the shadow of her siblings, and she was not bothered that she looked different from them.

But now she is approaching 40 years old. She could see some traces of wrinkle lines around her eyes. She had no idea where all her youth life had gone. Regardless, she never regretted it. Perhaps she would never taste sex her whole life, which did not matter to her. Somehow, she still felt content. Was there something wrong with her? Was she weird?

She shook her head, warding off her thoughts. Then, after a deliberate exhale, she smoothed out her dress and hair before striding to the door.

This time she was wearing her V-neck sleeveless crème floral midi dress. It was one of her favourite dresses. Erin's words resonated again about having something special with Chandra from this getaway. She smiled, admitting she wished likewise, too.

She met with the ladies in the lift while Chandra, Tom and Brad were already in the lobby. She noticed Chandra's eyes seemed to light up when they met, and her heart fluttered.

"Don't you think Cassie looks beautiful tonight, *kak* Chandra?" teased Helda. Chandra only chuckled sheepishly in response.

They took the minibus to the restaurant outside the hotel. It was a lovely local restaurant with the calm flowing water sound from the small pond added to the ambience. There were some big colourful fish in the pond, which the waiter explained as the famous and expensive koi fish. The food was Sundanese, the local authentic of Bandung. Cassie felt she would never get bored being in this country for its variety of food.

One of the dishes they ordered was grilled fish with spicy dipping sauce. By the look of it, Cassie's tongue felt like dancing. However, seeing Nina, Helda and Tita eating it with high enthusiasm, she did not want to give it a miss. As a result, the moment a piece of the fish meat touched her tongue, she choked.

"Are you alright?" Brad gave her a concerned look. Obviously, she could not answer him as she was struggling to breathe.

Chandra, who sat at the end of the table, quickly approached her and rubbed her back, soothing her. Brad snapped his finger calling the waiter to get her a glass of warm milk. Cold chocolate milk packed in a long-life small carton came instead.

"Good thinking, Brad. I did not even think about that," commented Chandra. "How are you feeling, Cass? You're okay?"

Cassie felt silly, trying to hide her embarrassed smile by lowering her head. When she felt much better and had the courage to lift her head, her eyes clashed with a glare from Tom. It was like a jab pierced her heart.

She sensed Tom disliked her. It must be because of the incident when she was wandering alone outside the school. She had been planning to have a good talk with him. However, it seemed he had been avoiding her. Perhaps she should try to catch him alone during this getaway.

They returned to the hotel after dinner. Nina, Helda and Tita went straight to their room, but Helda gave her a wink seeing Chandra walk beside her. Tom and Brad seemed to have a serious conversation about the project and walked further behind them. Cassie felt this could be an excellent opportunity to be alone with Chandra. Chandra also seemed to understand her meaning as they entered the lift together to their room floor and arrived outside Chandra's room first.

"Is this your room?" asked Cassie. "It seems you have a bigger room," she commented, seeing the double door.

Chandra laughed. "I'm lucky. I got a free upgrade to a premier suite."

"Wow!"

He opened his room door and gestured his head. "Do you want to have a look?"

"Sure!"

Without hesitation and more of curiosity, she entered the room with excitement. As she expected, the room was much bigger than hers, with an additional small lounge and meal area. Best of all, there was a small balcony facing the hotel's best scenery. Unfortunately, the sky was dark, though the night air was crisp and cool. However, they only could hear the sound of grasshoppers filling the air.

"This is great. I guess the view from here in the morning would be fantastic," commented Cassie while they were standing on the balcony. She inhaled the night air deeply, filling her lungs and giving lightness to her head and chest. On her side, Chandra had also done the same thing. Somehow she felt this moment could be a good time for them to speak.

"So, Chandra, what does your family think about me?" That was the first question that came into her mind. Although, at the end of the day, it was about them, like it or not, Cassie believed that the family's opinion was also important.

An earnest smile spread on Chandra's lips. "Of course, they like you."

"And, how about you? What do you think about me?" Her voice was slightly raspy, and she swallowed hard.

"You know I like you, Cass," he replied with twitching lips. It gave her enough butterflies in her stomach. Her heart swelled as the apprehension within her increased. At least she knew her feeling was reciprocated. She looked at him again, wishing to see his eyes. Instead, he threw his gaze on the scenery before them.

Was he actually shy? Should she make a move first?

While taking a shuddering breath, she gathered her courage. Her right hand slowly crept to his hand on the balcony railing bar. He was slightly startled, not expecting the touch, but did not pull back his hand. Instead, it made his eyes turn to her. Seeing his soft gaze and congenial smile, Cassie took it as a green signal. She moved forward and captured his lips.

It was her first kiss, and Cassie had to admit it felt weird to press her lips on someone else. But before her brain described the feeling on her lips, her forearms were grabbed and pushed away within a second. Her gasp was matched by his bewildered eyes.

"Cass.." He looked grave as he briefly closed his eyes before giving her a guilt-ridden look.

Cassie immediately felt her heart shrinking. From his blanched facial expression, she could interpret that he did not expect this.

He did not want this.

An unnatural, awkward silence fell, and they were frozen in place. His hands slowly dropped from her forearm with a deep heavy sigh that perhaps she had ever heard from him. His head and shoulder were down as he shut his eyes in agony.

Cassie quietly exhaled after it seemed like an eternity she had been holding up her breathing. Feeling absolutely like trash, perhaps her face even crumpled, she strode towards the door.

"Cass, I'm sorry. Please..."

His voice was like a passing wind only. She just wanted to get away from here as soon as possible. Unfortunately, luck was not on her side. The moment she opened the door, familiar eyes landed on them. Cassie wished she had Harry Potter's invisible cloak at this particular moment to make her disappear in this instant!

"Ah, are we disturbing you guys? We are just passing by," teased Helda innocently. However, Cassie caught her sparkling eyes and a repressed mischievous smile on her lips.

Oh, my, this is embarrassing! She wished they knew what exactly happened inside and stopped the teasing.

What intensified her apprehension further was seeing Tom's reaction. His eyes almost bulged out, and his face reddened. His body looked tensed with the engorged vein on his neck. Cassie pursed her lips, anticipating that he would explode soon.

However, what happened next was just awkward silence. While she was having heart palpitations, Cassie's brain was racing, thinking about how to escape from this. If she just ran away, it would create more questions. Helda, Nina and Tita were looking at each other confused. In contrast, she tried to interpret Brad's staring. Was it a pity look?

"What a coincidence to have all of you here!" Cassie had to compliment herself to make a fake gleeful sound finally. "You should see Chandra's amazing room. He just showed me around. His room has a private balcony! Have you guys seen it?" Her question was directed more to the ladies.

Helda, Nina and Tita nodded hesitantly.

"*Kak* Chandra showed it to us when we arrived," acknowledged Helda.

"Great!" Cassie snapped her finger. Now she felt like a performer. Perhaps her face now looked like a clown. She glanced at Chandra, who stood beside her at the door, wishing he could say something. But his face looked stressed, and a glimpse of guilt hit her. She wanted to let him know she was totally fine with their earlier incident.

Was she alright? She was unsure. Definitely, she was disappointed.

"There's live music downstairs, in the ground floor's lounge," announced Brad. His voice sounded flat as if he was reading the news, but it gave relief to Cassie that at least someone talked. "We are about to go down to watch it. Do you want to join in?"

"Sure!" she replied with fake enthusiasm. It was an excellent excuse to escape from the tension. Brad extended his hand, gesturing for her to lead the way. She immediately strode to the lift.

The ladies were joining them, but Tom and Chandra were not.

"Chandra said he would join in later with Tom," said Nina.

Quietly Cassie felt relieved that was the case. After what happened a few minutes ago, she could not imagine what she would do to face him.

There was only silence in the lift, which Cassie used as an opportunity to gain her composure. Once the door lift opened, she briskly stepped out, assuming the rest would follow. Her mind was still hazy, and she had no idea where they were heading. But Brad's gentle touch on her small back gave her some relief as he guided her to the lounge.

The waiter gave them a couch outdoors on the balcony, the best spot to enjoy the live music performance. They ordered some cocktails without much chatting while listening to live music. Cassie knew that the girls were whispering to each other, and she chose not to join in. Her eyes were straight to the stage, as if she was enjoying the performance, while her mind was whirling around.

What the hell just happened? What have I done? She tried to rewind what had happened earlier and her interactions with Chandra throughout their acquaintance. They were naturally getting along well, and he said he liked her. But why did he never make a move, and when she initiated the move, why did he seem stressed about it?

She took a heavy breath while sipping her drink. Perhaps he never thought to like her more than friends. They had been friends for twenty years! Her initiative earlier was a stupid move and could potentially ruin their friendship instead. She should have thought about this. She did not wish because of what happened earlier, they became awkward towards each other. Inevitably she closed her eyes in agony. No one seemed to notice, thanks to the dim light in their sitting area.

A soft touch landed on her hands. Her eyes flew open, and she found Brad's hands on top of her hand. Was she dreaming that she saw a ghost of a warm smile on his face? Feeling the warmth of his hands on her somehow consoling. A warm feeling that she did not expect.

"Shall we have a dance?" His deep baritone voice whispered to her ear against the loud music.

She smiled weakly with a shuddering breath.

There was a dance floor near the stage performance, and some couples were already swinging when the singer started playing some slow oldies jazz songs. Cassie had no idea whose music was that, but the melancholy tune described her sinking heart well at this moment.

She was unsure whether she had given any response but obligingly followed when Brad took her hand to stand up and walk to the dance floor.

There was a floating sensation as he took her right hand and placed his hand on her small back. She placed her hand on his shoulder and conveniently sniffed his aftershave cologne. It was a fresh earthly masculine scent, and it was intoxicating! *This guy smells damn good!*

"Are you alright?" His deep baritone voice even sounded soothing. Did she feel this way because he seemed the only one who knew the current heart turmoil she was going through? Did he know what happened earlier?

She nodded weakly. "Yeah, I'm fine."

"I know you and Chandra are old mates," he spoke to her ear. As his breath fanned her ear, there was a ticklish warm feeling within her. "And I know you like him more than just a friend. However, he does not seem to think that way."

She chuckled bitterly. How could he see it, but she could not? How stupid was she for being so blind?

"Don't get me wrong. That's because I know something that you don't seem to know yet," he continued.

She lifted up her head so their eyes met. Gazing at his gorgeous eyes was like swimming in a pool of calamity. Still, his words somehow struck her.

"What do you mean?"

He broke the trance and put his lips closer again to her ear. "if you look in the direction of two o'clock, you'll see the only room with the lights on, on the top level. That's Chandra's room."

Cassie squished her eyebrows while digesting his words carefully. She looked up to find some of the hotel rooms' windows overlooking where they were now. Since it was not the peak holiday season, the hotels were probably only 60% occupied. Most of the rooms were dark, indicating either unoccupied or perhaps the occupier was out. Therefore it was easy to locate the room mentioned. Even though it was probably about twenty metres away, she held her breath as she recognised Chandra's silhouette in the room. And he was not alone. She recognised the tall skinny figure of the other outline was Tom. Since both of them had not joined them yet, it made sense to conclude that those two people were Tom and Chandra.

"I'm not going to turn you around, so we just stick this way. Whatever you see, please stay calm. Please remember we are not in Melbourne. Things are different here."

She complied with the instruction, trying to understand his meaning. They were swinging in their spot, making her giggle inwardly, thinking how silly their dancing was. Luckily, no one noticed, as the music was still playing along soothingly. Her eyes flew back to the window of Chandra's room. She watched as it seemed both men were arguing. Chandra looked upset as he kept shoving his dishevelled hair while Tom kept yelling at him.

What are they arguing about? Is it about work? Can't Tom leave Chandra alone? It's the weekend!

After their incident and recalling Chandra's distressing look when she left them, she felt pity to see Chandra also had to bear with Tom's anger. She wondered whether she should stop them, but Brad's sudden squeeze on her hand put her to a halt.

"Don't move. Just stay this way," he whispered.

"What the hell is Tom doing?" she hissed agitatedly.

"Ssshhh... Just watch. I'll explain later."

Cassie huffed and felt annoyed as she had no idea how long she had to watch this. This time both men looked like they had calmed down from their argument, whatever it was. Tom's hand fell on Chandra's shoulder as their foreheads slowly met. She quietly took a relieved breath that at least there was no sign of a physical fight would happen. However, what unfolded a few minutes later, made her breath hitched, and a soft gasp sneaked out from her lips. Another hard squeeze on her hand reminded her to stay unmoved. Slowly comprehension dawned on her, and she understood the meaning of Brad's words.

Brad gently turned her body around at the right time as the music reached its ending. While holding her hand, he took her back to their seat. Nina, Helda and Tita excused themselves to return to their room as the night was getting deep. Once they left, Cassie felt her emotional wall finally collapse as she buried her face with both hands. Brad's hands gently rubbed her back, comforting her.

It was definitely a hell of a night.

Chapter Eleven

"Dimana bumi dipijak, disitu langit dijunjung" – an Indonesian proverb.

"When in Rome, do as the Romans do"

It was a sleepless night for Cassie. When the morning sun started peeping in from the edge of the blackout curtain, she rolled herself out of bed despite her body screaming, commanding her to return to the comfy and cozy bed. However, she knew she had to get up. It was another day that she had to face.

The scenes she watched last night were replaying before her eyes. It was not Chandra's rejection that upset her anymore, but something else caused the aches in her chest. After the restless night, tossing herself back and forth on the bed, comprehension dawned on her. The heartache she felt was for Chandra because she cared for him as a friend. She finally understood what he had been struggling with. Her advance on him only made things worse. She was the one now filled with self-loathing.

Last night, she was sitting with a vacant stare in the outdoor lounge, listening to live music until the end when the time reached midnight. Despite no words uttered between them, Brad was on her side all the time. Finally, when the last song was played, and the band singer was dispersed, she felt awakened by her deep thoughts. Brad gripped her forearm gently, motioning her to the lift and taking it to her room. Only the words 'good night' were exchanged before they disappeared into their rooms.

She owed Brad, in a way, at least gratitude for being such a good friend accompanying her last night when she was not fully herself. But this morning, she knew for sure what she had to do.

She did all her morning routine, wore her dress, combed her hair and for a moment, caught her reflection in the mirror again. She tried to draw a thin smile on her lips, took a heavy breath and convinced herself that she would be fine. Although things never go according to plan, at the end of the day, she always managed to find a positive side of it. This would be one of them.

The crisp morning air and mist greeted her when she stepped into the lobby and strolled into the back garden of the hotel resort. The resort was located behind a mountain, which was the winning point of this place. It was definitely the best place for a weekend getaway from the hustle-bustle of city life. In addition, the surrounding greenery forest gave a sense of freshness and life serenity.

She inhaled deeply, closed her eyes briefly, and filled her lungs with fresh air. It somehow made her light and free, and all the muddle in her mind became clear. When she finally opened her eyes, a shadow of a man from the reflection of the infinity pool of blue water emerged. She straightened her head and smiled warmly at the person.

He was definitely someone who would always fill a special place in her heart in a way. Twenty years of knowing him, even though only as a friend, she would never regret it as their friendship had been a great blessing.

"Good day," she greeted.

"Good morning," Chandra replied. There was a meekness from his eyes behind the spectacles. It reminded Cassie of the first day they met when he attended his first class session at the university.

She spent perhaps a good half an hour composing a text message to him to meet her in this place last night. It was only a short sentence, but she was so indecisive. Typing, deleting and typing that bloody short sentence; *Can we have a chat tomorrow morning, please? I'll be waiting by the pool at 8 am.*

His only reply was 'Yes', which was all she needed.

"Thank you for coming."

"Thank you for asking me to come here." He shook his head with a pinched expression. "I'm sorry about last night."

"No," she quickly interrupted, lifting her finger to his lips to stop talking. But her hand stopped mid-air as she realised what she was about to do. "I'm the one who should apologise. I have no idea. I did not expect my presence put both of you in a difficult position."

He took a heavy breath, and his grave look returned. It made her heart feel like being sliced too, and without realising it, her face was also screwed. While rubbing his puffy face, suddenly, something struck him. His eyes opened widely, and his mouth fell open.

"How do you know?"

"I saw you both last night. Well, it was Brad who was trying to tell me."

He let out a shuddered breath. "Right."

A momentary pause descended. It somehow gave both of them the time to fall into their own thoughts for a brief.

"You're a wonderful person, Cass." His voice finally broke, cracked with emotion. "I want you to know that I am seriously saying this. You deserve a better person."

Cassie drew the best assurance smile on her lips. "Thank you, Chandra. I know you mean it. Please don't worry about me. I'll be fine."

"I know you will, Cass. You are always strong for the people you care."

"And I want you to know that I care for you."

His eyes welled in tears. "Thank you, Cass. I know you do. That's why I feel I am a useless friend to you."

"How could you say that?" She could not restrain herself anymore. Her hand extended to him, and they hugged like buddies, which made him sob on her shoulders.

"I should have told you about us," he sniffled.

"Yeah, perhaps you should," she chuckled. "But, it is not your fault. I guess it is only about time. I know what you've been going

108

through. It must be hard to keep this to yourself while all your family puts you under pressure."

"I did not mean to use you to give my family the wrong impression."

She released their hug and pressed both her palms on his cheeks. "I understand, Chandra. It's okay. Really, it's okay. I don't blame you. Or Helda or your family. I know why you keep it from them." She lowered her voice, almost above a whisper. "For your sanity, you must find a time to tell them about you and Tom. And for your safety, I guess it's best you stay in Melbourne."

He nodded his head between her palms. "I know."

"I should speak with Tom, too. I must apologise to him for what happened. I have made him mad, I guess."

He shook his head. "No, I have explained to him. He has no right to be angry at you."

"It is a misunderstanding that we need to clear. Besides, I'm your friend. I want him to know that he should understand your position too."

"Yes, I know he's trying. Though I guess it's hard for him. Since we come here, we cannot show our relationship openly."

"Then, there was me who made things even worse," she added, shaking her head. "I'm so insensitive. I understand why he hates me."

"It's not your fault."

They ended their conversation with another tight hug, and Cassie felt a huge stone just being lifted from her chest. She could not wait to find a time to speak with Tom too.

They continued to meet with the rest for breakfast before joining the team activities planned for the day. Cassie noticed that Tom's facial expression relaxed, and when their eyes met, she could see a hint of a smile from him.

Because of the restless sleep last night, Cassie started to feel tired in the afternoon after completing the flying fox and tea walk in the morning. While they were in their vehicle for the trip back to the hotel, Tom took a seat beside her that was coincidentally empty. But he only rubbed his hands nervously without uttering any word.

Cassie felt that she should be the one that initiated the conversation first, but she was fully aware that Helda, Nina and Tita were also around. She gently touched Tom's shoulder with her sleepy eyes, which startled him.

"Can I have your shoulder to sleep on?"

He chuckled sheepishly and nodded his head. As their eyes met, they seemed to understand each other. She leaned closer to him, placed her heavy head on his shoulder, and drifted to sleep for a good thirty minutes until they reached the hotel.

Chapter Twelve

Enjoying the remaining of Melbourne's summer and daylight savings would be Cassie's main priority since she returned from Jakarta last week. Her flight reached Melbourne on Saturday. She took the rest of the weekend to relax at her apartment as strictly instructed by Erin and Kieran. It seemed her brother and her housemate had worked together pretty well, including to ensure she did not need to do any errands for Ashleigh and Alicia for the first week after her return. She was glad that at least she was allowed to visit them on Sunday for lunch.

She felt much more refreshed returning to work and felt vigorous to resume her usual role. All her colleagues and manager welcomed her warmly. They immediately updated her with the latest changes in their business unit, which was not exactly much. On the other hand, there was more of the latest gossip about staff and management movements and the scandalous love affairs of the executive team. It somehow made her miss her routine life, despite the fact she used to be sick hearing about it too.

It was the last week of March before daylight savings would end by the end of the week. She took the opportunity to have her routine running exercise after work. Despite Kieran telling her it was unnecessary, she still planned to drop by her brother's place for dinner afterwards. She understood Kieran and Erin were not trying to keep her from seeing the girls. Instead, they tried to ease her burden, so she could hopefully focus on her life to find someone while her biological clock kept ticking.

Obviously, they were worried about her after she told them what had happened in Indonesia. She recalled their disappointment and concerned looks, to which she responded with a genuine assurance smile that she was absolutely fine.

She was indeed fine. She was unsure why. Should she cry? Was there something wrong with her if she did not cry? Was she broken-hearted? She remembered Erin had asked her that question. Her answer was vague. Perhaps she was brokenhearted. Without a doubt, she was disappointed that Chandra had been taken. However, she was genuinely happy for him. Instead, she was worried that his culture and family background put a lot of pressure on his relationship with Tom. She hoped in the end they could work it out.

Flagstaff park was busy as usual, and fortunately, the warm weather still stayed. Cassie took a few rounds of running before she cooled herself down by walking toward the tram stop. She passed by the usual basketball court and was surprised to recognise the only person playing on the court.

His figure became familiar to her, especially after spending time together on their recent trip. It made her think whether he was the same person she helped to return the ball but never uttered a word to her. The more she thought about it, the more she became sure that it was him, especially recalling how he had poor eye contact habits.

Still with her remaining panting breath, she entered the basketball court. He did not realise her presence for the first few minutes until he turned around to catch the ball and was startled to find an uninvited spectator.

"Hi." Cassie waved her hand. "I do not expect to see you here, Brad. How are you?"

Their last meeting was at the airport after they reached Melbourne. They did not sit next to each other on the plane because he was in business class, and she was no longer lucky to have a free upgrade. After collecting their luggage, she bid him goodbye and dashed to the exit without looking back. Her heartbeat was racing erratically. She could not wait to see the friendly faces of Kieran, the girls and Erin, who came to pick her up. Unfortunately, they had never gotten in touch since then. In fact, she had no idea his number. As far as she could remember, she never gave him her contact number too.

"I'm well," Brad replied. "How are you?"

"I'm good, thank you. Do you always play basketball here?"

He nodded. "Yes. Do you always pass by here?"

"I like to have a run in this park and take the tram from that street." She pointed out at the nearby tram stop within their eyesight.

He only nodded his head vaguely as acknowledgement, and they went to unnatural silence, and she cursed inwardly. It seemed they ran out of conversation since they were no longer involved in the same project in Indonesia.

She then remembered that she still owed him gratitude. They did not have a chance to speak much after returning from Bandung. After the Bandung getaway, she returned to her teaching while he was in the head office most of the time. They did not even chat much despite being on the same flight again. Meanwhile, Chandra and Tom stayed back in Jakarta to wrap up the project.

Cassie did not expect she would bump into him again in Melbourne.

"I haven't got a chance to say 'thank you,'" she said.

"For what?" He squinted his eyes as the afternoon sun glared at him.

"For helping me understand what happened between Chandra and Tom. I actually wonder how you know about them."

"I have plenty of meetings with them. I can read it," he answered solemnly.

"But how do you know that night when we danced, I would be able to see them there?"

"Because I know they are such passionate lovers."

Cassie arched her eyebrow while he smirked.

"Tom is an emotional person, and Chandra seems naturally calmer. I guess that's why they belong to each other. It's not only once I watch them quarrelling and ending up with a kiss."

Cassie laughed. She did not expect him to be that observant, analysing people's behaviour. Instead, he seemed like someone who did not give a damn about other people's feelings, and she even accused him of being arrogant.

"Do you live nearby here?" he asked.

"Yeah, not that far. I still need to take a tram. But I work around here." She pointed at the train station's direction. "My office is in Chinatown."

"What do you do?"

She just realised, probably from all their conversations, she never told him what she did for a living.

"I work as IT customer service in a local bank."

"Right. Apparently, your field is also IT."

She laughed. "Yeah, not much different from you." She was taken aback to see a ghost of a smile from him and admiring a faint dimple on his right cheek.

"So, do you always play basketball here alone?" she asked.

"No. I had a game earlier with some friends. I like to stay back and play a bit more by myself."

"Why?"

"Just to cool down, I guess."

"Alright. Shall we do a couple of shots?"

He darted her a dubious look. "Do you play basketball?"

"A bit," laughed Cassie. Basketball was actually one of her favourite sports. Still, as her life was always average, she was also an average player. During school and university time, she usually played with Kieran. However, the habit, unfortunately, died down since Kieran got married and had kids.

"Sure." He threw the ball at her, which she caught at the right time. "Let's go."

Cassie felt the adrenaline rejuvenate within her as she dribbled the ball, aimed the basket and shot it. Although she was still about three metres away, it plunged smoothly to the basket.

He gave her an arched eyebrow. "That was good. I take it as lucky."

She burst into laughter. "Sure! Feel free to fight."

And here they went. He grabbed the ball, and she tried to block him, which he managed to avoid, then shot his ball neatly to the basket. She knew it would be the case, but she did not give up. She took the ball this time, he tried to block her, but she managed to trick him with her swift move, and then made a score. He seemed to realise that she was not a beginner player. Cassie repressed her grin as she focussed back on the game.

She was not sure for how long they were doing that. She had let herself be carried away with the game and forgotten about the time. Towards the end, she started to feel like running out of breath while he was still very much focused. Despite losing a couple of points, she managed to block his ball a couple of times too, which was enough to take him by surprise. The game ended when she snatched the ball from him, dribbled it but unfortunately too far away from the basket, and shot it. Unfortunately, he blocked it easily and shot the ball for himself instead. She made an exaggerated disappointed groan while bending her body down as a sign of giving up.

Their eyes met when she straightened up her body. Seeing his captivating brown eyes again somehow made her heart stir slightly.

"That was a good fight," he murmured.

Cassie felt a swell of pride within her. A compliment was not something she used to get. "Never underestimate your opponent," she grinned.

And their eyes locked for a second, down for another second, up and locked again, which made her chuckle as if he was gauging her next move.

"Alright, I'm thirsty." She was panting while her head spun around, searching for any drinking fountain nearby.

"Would you like to get some drinks from my apartment?"

She turned back to him with a knitted brow. "Do you live nearby?"

He gestured to one of the tall grey apartment buildings within their sight, just across the street. "I live there."

She took out her mobile phone and checked at the time. The sunset indicated she was too late to go to Kieran's house for dinner. Kieran was not expecting her anyway, so perhaps she scrapped the plan. So, maybe the drink offer was not a bad idea.

"That's convenient. Sure!"

He seemed taken aback, but his lips drew a thin smile. "Great! Let's go."

It literally took them only a three-minute walk to reach Brad's apartment. It was a newly built modern building, far in contrast with Cassie's old Victorian heritage-style property that she shared with Erin. The lobby was brightly lit, with modern contemporary wallpaper and shiny gloss tiles. They walked side by side, entering the lift that took them to perhaps the highest floor of the building. Cassie was mentally counting that they were in that lift for almost half a minute before reaching Brad's apartment floor.

There was only silence between them, which somehow made her self-conscious. She was sweaty, still catching her breath, and likewise for him. Once the lift door opened, she let him walk ahead of her to lead the way. It was a long corridor as Brad's apartment was at the end. Seeing the double door of his apartment, Cassie quietly guessed that the inside must be pretty breathtaking.

And she was correct. The moment she stepped in, a full wall-to-wall glass window overseeing Melbourne city first captured her eyes. She sauntered further inside, admiring the view, while Brad went to the kitchen and opened the fridge.

"What would you like to drink?" he asked.

"A glass of water will do," she replied quietly, still mesmerised by the heart-stirring view before her. It was expected that he would be living in such a luxurious place. From what she had heard from Chandra during the project, she would not be surprised that he must have a fantastic career and income. This apartment would be just one of the examples of his lifestyle.

Her trance broke when he approached her and pushed the glass of water towards her.

"Cheers."

She let the water slowly flush her throat, relinquishing her thirst. Her eyes gazed at the distance. The dark sky started creeping in, and the lights from the surrounding tall buildings began to light up. It slowly became a view of beautiful colourful lights. Somehow standing there, watching this, made her feel small. And without realising it, she took a quiet, shuddering breath in awe.

"It must be a great feeling to be at the top of the world, right?" she muttered while glancing at him, who was also sipping his drink with his eyes gazing at the distance. She saw a ghost of a smile on the corner of his lips.

"Yeah," he murmured.

As the sky was getting crimson by the sunset, she felt it was time for her to go. She finished her drink, turned to the kitchen sink, washed the glass with soap and water, and placed it on the kitchen rack. It was a habit that she always did every time she visited someone's house. For her, it was a courtesy to clean up her own mess.

"You don't need to do that," he protested gently.

It was the common words that any host would utter to her.

"I don't wish to trouble you with my dirty dish. Thank you for the drink."

"It was no trouble at all." He strode to the kitchen sink as well and placed his empty glass. That made him stand closer to her.

For a moment, they gazed at each other, wordless. She had to admit that he now seemed to understand the importance of eye contact while communicating. Every time seeing his gorgeous eyes made her breath stall. It was a good one minute that they stared at each other until she could not take it anymore and lowered her eyes.

"I got to go."

His eyes were widening a bit with his curvy lips parting.

"Have a good night," she added while heading to the door. She opened the door and turned around, feeling awkward that he did not say anything and was still unmoved from his place without even looking at her. Was he angry? What had she done? Hadn't she said thank you earlier for the drink?

Hesitantly she raised her hand and said 'bye' before stepping out and closing the door behind her.

"**Y**ou left? You just simply left?" Erin stared at her in incredulity.

After leaving Brad's apartment, Cassie returned to her apartment immediately. Her tummy started grumbling when she smelt a delicious food fragrance from her apartment. Erin was already in the apartment, having dinner on the table with a roast chicken from Red Rooster.

Erin asked her where she went, and she told her about her meeting with Brad.

"Brad? Is he the one who asked you out for breakfast when you were on a video call with us?"

Ah... Erin remembered him! Brad indeed had a striking look, and Erin even labelled him a hunk. It was not a surprise if Erin could remember him.

Cassie nodded. Then she told Erin that she had dropped by his apartment to get some water. While listening to her story, Erin's face, which was initially beaming with excitement slowly became horrified.

"I can't believe you just simply left," gasped Erin, her hand flying to her chest.

Cassie's brows squished together. "Yeah, why? I went there to get a drink. Am I supposed to offer him something in return?" She snapped her finger. "Oh, perhaps I should ask him whether he wants to have dinner together one day. Yeah, you're right. After he helped me find out about Tom and Chandra, I still owe him. Perhaps I'll ask him the next time we meet."

Erin's mouth was still hanging open before finally she burst into huge laughter until her head tipped back.

"I can't believe you don't realise it, Cass!" she squealed in the midst of her laughter. "He's asking you to his apartment! He wants to sleep with you!"

Now it was Cassie who was flabbergasted! *Sleep with him? Did Erin mean...sex?* Her mouth was slackening as she gasped.

"No way! We were sweating like hell! That's gross!"

Erin laughed out loud. "There's a thing called a shower, Cass. Besides, don't you know that sex is one form of exercise? You'll be sweating anyway after glorious sex."

Cassie was lost for words. Was Erin just messing with her, or perhaps she was correct? On the other hand, had she been misreading Brad's intention?

"No, it can't be true," she murmured, shaking her head and throwing herself to the couch.

"Well, Cass. You flirted with him," quipped Erin, still in the remaining laughter that began to subside. She started picking up her chicken again into her mouth.

Cassie turned to her friend, bewildered with bulging eyes. "I did not!" she chastised. "I only played basketball with him. You're thinking this too far!"

Erin shrugged. "Maybe. But let me think. You guys had some moments in Indonesia."

"There was no special moment," Cassie grumbled.

"Well, you went out together a couple of times. In fact, you spent more time with him than Chandra."

"That was because Chandra was with Tom."

"You had a dance with him."

Cassie rolled her eyes. "It was just a dance. There was not even a kiss."

Erin was not giving up. "Oh, you fell on him on the plane!"

"It was a silly accident, and he was furious at the time." Cassie shook her head. "It's ridiculous that we're analysing this."

"But, Cass, he's inviting you to his apartment." Erin shot her a severe look. "It's like a dating rule."

"We're not even dating. It was just a basketball game." Cassie buried her face in her hands and felt frustrated. She wasn't sure what made her upset. Was it because her little heart seemed to knock and tell her that Erin might be right, that she was too naïve, failing to recognise it?

"Alright, alright." Erin threw her hands up in the air. "Let us take a step back. Do you like him?"

Cassie jerked up her head. *Good question!* She probably had no idea. They had an unimpressive first encounter, but when he helped her from standing between Chandra and Tom, there was a tingling warm feeling inside her. However, there was something about Brad that seemed untouchable. She was unsure what, so she had not thought of him beyond a mate.

"Remember, Cass. You know Chandra as a friend first, too. After almost twenty years of friendship, you only realise that you want more than a friend relationship with him," stated Erin.

That's right! Cassie took a sigh. "Well, yeah. But I don't think I'm his type."

"Ah-ha!" Erin leapt out from her seat with her finger pointed at Cassie. "Here you go again! This is probably the problem why you never have a relationship. You always feel you're not good enough. You're underestimating yourself."

Cassie grimaced while tilting her head from side to side. Erin's words perhaps hit some marks, despite not exactly what she had in mind. For the last at least eight years of her life, her focus was helping Kieran and the girls.

"No!" she argued. "It's not that. For someone like him, I can imagine his expectations of women. He's also younger than me. He's about your age. Unquestionably, I'm out of his league." She simply blurted without thinking, as if it would make Erin drop the subject. But it seemed it backfired on her instead.

Erin arched her eyebrow while standing with a crossed arm. "It does not mean you can't sleep with him or have a relationship with him," she challenged with her stern 'don't give me this rubbish' look.

"I don't do casual," muttered Cassie. She swallowed hard while lowering her eyes. *Darn!* Was Erin right about her? Had these been her problem all this time? Did she try to escape from her inferiority by getting herself busy with Ashleigh and Alicia? She took a defeated sigh and buried her face in her hand again.

She knew what was bothering her more with this conversation. Erin might have helped her see what her mistakes had been for the past twenty-five years. She was unable to open her heart to a relationship. Furthermore, her love, slash sex, slash relationship radar obviously needed some repairs. She had misinterpreted Chandra's attention, and now she had missed Brad's real intention if what Erin said was correct.

"It's not the end of the world, Cass." Erin's soothing voice pierced a momentary silence between them. "If you really like him too, you can still chase after him. I know you just got over with Chandra, but there is no harm in giving another go with someone else. I'm not saying this because you seem desperate. I know you are not."

Cassie chuckled bitterly. *Desperate.* Did she need to be desperate? It never crossed her mind that she needed to be with someone by forty, which meant she still had to attend Tiffany's wedding as a spinster. Her only thought was that after Kieran and the girls seemed more independent, it was time for her to look into her life. That was what Kieran had been encouraging her, which was why she made a move toward Chandra. Although things did not work out between them, she was absolutely fine with it. And now, with this misunderstanding with Brad, regardless Erin was correct or not, it was just another lesson she had to take.

Despite this confronting conversation, a cheeky thought slipped into her mind. What was it like to sleep with Brad?

A grin grew on her lips, and thankfully Erin did not see it.

Chapter Thirteen

Melbourne officially entered the autumn season, and the school holiday began for two weeks, coinciding with Easter long weekend. Cassie had made another schedule with Emily's parents to have the girls for a few days during the school holiday. However, she and Kieran agreed to visit their parents in Wonthaggi for Easter.

The temperature started to drop, though sometimes they could be lucky to get some remaining summer heat. The traffic to Wonthaggi was heavy, with most people eager for an Easter getaway. Still, they avoided the traffic jam by starting the journey a day earlier.

Cassie threw her gaze to the outside window while the girls sang along to the music played in the car. She knew Alicia and Ashleigh must be excited about this trip, though they had been in Wonthaggi hundreds of times. They were slightly disappointed that Erin could not join in.

Cassie realised now how the girls were more attached to Erin. She wondered whether her brother also noticed that too. Actually, Erin had nothing much to do for Easter, and she would linger in the apartment. Cassie was about to ask her to come along, but Erin seemed to read her mind and said she would go on day trips with some of her colleagues.

Kieran was the one who looked disappointed instead when Erin broke the news to them that she already had something on for Easter. The girls groaned in disappointment but slowly accepted it. Cassie only observed the whole scene with a furrowed brow. She felt she had missed something.

"Are you disappointed Erin is not coming with us?" Her voice broke a short stillness in the car when the song changed. Her question was directed to her brother.

"I am sad she's not coming along," Ashleigh chimed in instead.

"Yeah! Nun and Pa have not met her before," Alicia added in.

Kieran smirked. "Well, she has something else to do. Besides, she will take you to a museum one day during the school holiday. You will see her again soon."

That was true. Erin now came into the picture of arranging the girls' school holiday schedules. In fact, Erin intentionally adjusted her work schedule to help take the girls to gymnastics class one of the weekdays. Cassie could not believe how her housemate became more involved with her nieces' errands.

"Yeah, but it would be great if she could spend this Easter with us," grumbled Ashleigh.

"Perhaps next time," said Kieran quietly.

Cassie glanced at her brother, trying to read his facial expression. However, Kieran's eyes were hidden behind the sunnies. She wondered whether Kieran was probably interested in Erin. However, she always thought that was impossible.

Erin led a carefree life. That was what Cassie felt. Meanwhile, Kieran, since he got married and had kids and then lost his beloved wife, he became more mature and responsible like any father would, with no breathing space for him to mess around. So if Kieran were looking for a new mother for the girls, Cassie would guess he would try to find someone similar to Emily. As far as Cassie could remember, her late sister-in-law was gentle and soft-spoken, totally different from Erin.

However, Cassie could not deny that Erin had developed a good bond with the girls. Her housemate was probably more fun and energetic than herself. Hence that was the reason the girls loved her. Definitely, Erin could be a great mother too.

"Is Tiff coming?" asked Kieran when the song in the car changed into the upbeat one, and the girls started to sing along and dance.

Cassie shook her head. "I have no idea. She has not replied to our group messages." She scrolled her mobile phone screen and found no new incoming message in their family group messenger, despite their mother had been asking the question since last week. "She must be swamped with work and wedding preps."

"I guess it's not hard to reply to a message. She is always on the phone most of the time anyway."

"You know her, Kieran."

They exchanged a smirk, understanding each other about their little sister.

It was pretty lovely weather when they reached Ferguson's house that afternoon. Janine and Paul welcomed them warmly and immediately were occupied with their grandchildren's non-stop chatter.

"Tiffany just called and apologised for her absence," announced Janine. Cassie could see the disappointment in her mother's wrinkled eyes. "She has some appointments for a wedding cake tasting."

"Sounds fun," commented Kieran while picking a carrot stick on the table and dipping it in avocado lime sauce on the table before it went to his mouth. "Appointments on Easter long weekend?"

The remark was self-explanatory. Obviously, it was just a lame excuse from Tiffany to avoid coming to Wonthagi. Their little sister preferred spending her Easter having fun with her friends rather than seeing them.

Janine took a quiet sigh and pretended not to hear it. "When was the last time you saw your little sister?"

Good question! As far as Cassie remembered, she had not had a chance to see Tiffany since she returned from her volunteer trip. Afterwards, the school holiday began, and she was again busy with the girls' activities.

"I called her to meet up for lunch," answered Kieran. "But she could not make it. I proposed another date. She said she could not make it either. Afterwards, I gave up. I guess she will reach out if she has time."

"She calls, does she, mum?" asked Cassie.

Janine nodded. "She does, but not as often as you guys. I'm worried about her work schedule and wedding plan. She must be swamped."

Kieran scrolled through his mobile phone and showed the screen to his mother. It was Tiffany's Facebook page. There was a picture of her with Joshua with a tall three-tier wedding cake background. "She just posted this an hour ago. She's still alive. Relax, mum. She's a big girl now."

"For me, she's still my little girl," sighed Janine.

Cassie could see her mother's tender eyes when she said those words. There was a glimpse of jealousy that she quickly warded off. Had her mother said the same thing about her before? She doubted so.

"Don't worry about her too much, my dear," consoled Paul while rubbing Janine's back. "She eventually will be here too for the Hens party."

Cassie and Kieran looked at each other with furrowed brows, followed by Paul's laughter.

"Seems she has not told you guys, but Tiff plans to have her Hens party here."

"Here?" exclaimed Cassie and Kieran together.

"And Joshua's two sisters and mother will be joining. So, there will be many things to do in the house to prepare."

"Why here?" Kieran squinted his eyes. "Why not in Melbourne?"

"They want something close to the beach," answered Janine.

"This house is not exactly close to the beach," commented Cassie.

"But it's only two minute walk."

"So, will the party be at the beach or the house?"

"The plan is on the beach if the weather permits. It will be spring at that time. But definitely, they need to use the house."

Kieran and Cassie exchanged glances as if they were communicating through their eyes. That was why Cassie felt sometimes they were like twins. They could use telepathy to understand each other. For sure, they knew why Tiffany did this. Weddings needed huge spending, and using their parent's house for a fun Hens party would be one way to cut some of the wedding costs.

"Yeah, they are going to ransack this house," Paul snickered.

"Don't say that!" scolded Janine. "I'm pretty sure it's going to be a responsible party. The plan is to have everyone sleep here afterwards."

"How many people are coming to the party?" asked Cassie, squeezing her brain with math to calculate the number of bedrooms in her parent's house.

"We have no idea yet." Paul shrugged. "But definitely, I can't stay here when that happens."

"You can come to Melbourne and stay in my house, dad," suggested Kieran.

It seemed Alicia and Ashleigh also heard the conversation. "Pa is coming to our house?"

Paul laughed. "Yes, my dear. Soon."

"Yay!" the girls jumped and laughed together, making the rest of them smile at them.

The conversation about Tiffany's Hens party slowly died down in the afternoon. Even though Janine seemed to mind the idea of the party in her house, Cassie could see that her mother would still do it because it was for Tiffany. She knew her mother would not bear to decline her favourite girl's request. Perhaps, in fact, whatever Tiffany asked from her mother, unquestionably, she would get it.

When Alicia and Ashleigh started getting bored in the house, Cassie took the opportunity to take them to Cape Woolamai to see some sailing boats. She had longed to stroll while listening to the soothing sound of the waves. Kieran seconded the idea.

Cape Woolamai looked busy at the time they reached there. It was still a warm afternoon though the cool breeze blew in. Cassie took the stroll with her cardigan on, enjoying the beautiful scenery while observing some sailing boats. The girls played on the beach and the sand on their feet while their father watched them closely.

While walking along the marina, watching people onboard and offboard from and to the cruise, her eyes caught one of the most luxurious yacht boats Cassie had ever seen. It was probably the biggest yacht parked on the deck. It was double-storey height, and what amazed Cassie more, it was sailing-driven. Growing up in the area was not the first time she had been here. However, somehow this one attracted her, and she approached to have a closer look.

The sailer was on the deck and seemed occupied tidying up his anchor. Cassie found that his figure looked familiar. When he finally straightened up his body and turned around, their eyes met, and both of them were stunned.

He looked neatly casual and striking with his unbuttoned shirts and khakis. Cassie couldn't help feeling her heart stir, admiring his appearance. Erin's words resonated in her head that he could possibly try to sleep with her the last time he invited her to his apartment.

She swallowed hard and cheered inwardly with her ability to regain her wit quickly as she broke her lips into a smile.

"What a coincidence to see you here, Brad," she broke the ice first. "How are you?"

Their last meeting was the day Brad had invited her to his apartment, the day that was still haunting her mind. Her conversation with Erin was still bothering her. Since then, she never came across him anymore, even though she passed by the basketball court almost every day after work. She wondered whether he might be avoiding her. It made sense if Erin's theory was true.

"I'm well, thank you. And you?" He replied lightly. Cassie noticed that he was avoiding her stare. Before he finished his sentence, his gaze was on the timber decking as if searching for something.

Cassie crossed her arms, rubbing her forearm nervously, receiving such a response. "I'm well, thank you. Are you on holiday here?"

"Yeah. You?"

"I am visiting my parents in Wonthaggi."

"Right."

An awkward silence sank in. Cassie squeezed her brain, thinking about what she could say to bring in a conversation.

"Do you still play basketball on the same court near your apartment? I haven't seen you there for a while."

"Yeah, sometimes."

Darn! It was palpable he was not interested in having a conversation with her. However, like Erin had told her before, she should keep trying. But before she opened her mouth, Ashleigh and Alicia's voices were just behind her screaming her name. She turned her head to find the girls and Kieran a few metres behind them. When she turned back to Brad, he looked at the girls before staring down again.

"I'm just thinking whether...."

Again, her sentences were severed. A woman in her translucent beach shirt, sexy and slim with blonde hair, fancy sunnies and a hat, rose from the boat and called him. He turned to the woman's call and nodded at her.

Cassie felt something pierced into her heart, she was unsure what. Her lips were pressed tight, restraining herself from speaking further. He did not seem to realise that she had unfinished sentences as his eyes were again fixed on his feet. He probably wished her to get lost soon from his sight.

Quietly she took a heavy breath, wishing the air could fill in her constricted lung. She took another glance at him, who still did not return her look and seemed not to realise that she was still standing there. Reading that signal, Cassie knew what she had to do.

"Alright, hope you have a good break here, Brad." She tried to make her voice as light as possible, though it sounded dry to her ear. "Have a good Easter."

Somehow she decided to linger a bit longer there, despite half of her body already turned away. She wished he would at least lift his head to wish her 'Happy Easter' back. She could see his lips were moving. However, nothing came out, and his eyes were still down. So she chose to walk away with a bitter smile while quietly taking another deep sigh.

Erin was probably right. He was probably hurt that she indirectly had rejected his intention for her. She was perhaps too naïve, but she could not help it. If they were not meant to be, like Chandra and herself, then it was not meant to be. The door was closed now, and Cassie knew she just had to move on again.

As usual.

Chapter Fourteen

Daylight saving ended, and the sky was getting darker sooner. During this time, Cassie would usually choose to go for an alternative exercise after work. Instead of running in the park, she would prefer an indoor sport. Coincidentally, Ashleigh and Alicia would like a swimming lesson as an additional activity. So Cassie took the opportunity to organise the classes for them while at the same time, she had her exercise too.

The lesson was in one of the biggest aquatic centres in Melbourne. It had a couple of 50-metre lap swimming lanes, plus water play for the children. Cassie knew that the swimming lesson might only take half an hour, however with the girls, it may last for one hour. Fortunately, she organised the class on Friday evening. Since the weekend was approaching, she felt more relaxed about spending more time with her nieces.

Kieran was almost against the idea. He was afraid she might miss Friday night fun if any of her friends asked her out. However, it was something that Cassie did not think about at all. Perhaps that had become her problem all this time. She always put her nieces, and her brother's schedule needs ahead of herself, and without realising it, she missed her social life. That was probably why not many of her friends would ask her out eventually.

Erin also said the same thing to her. Another rebuke from Erin made her think about what she had missed for the past twenty-five years. But she did not regret it, because she was always happy to help her family, especially her brother, who was almost like her twin, except for their huge differences in terms of physical look, which unfortunately was like the earth and sky.

Somehow she did not care anymore if she had to be a spinster for her lifetime. She felt content to dedicate herself to helping Kieran raise Alicia and Ashleigh.

When the lesson began, Cassie took the opportunity to have her lap swim. Swimming had been one of her favourite sports, but again she was just an average swimmer. She had never been selected to be part of the squat team or even won some medals. However, she did not care as she just enjoyed swimming for her relaxation.

The lap swimming pool was quite busy. She noticed that the slow and medium lanes were packed. In contrast, there was only one male swimmer in the fast lane. If she could choose, she would go for the medium lane. However, she was tempted to jump into the fast lane instead. Certainly, the swimmer would not complain if she also swam there. She was confident that she would not swim as slow as a turtle.

There she went. She dived into the pool like a professional. Despite never being in the squat school team, she used to be trained like one. She kept swimming and ensuring that the other swimmer would not be disturbed by her. She had to admit that the other swimmer was probably professionally trained as he kept swimming freestyle back and forth without stopping for the last fifteen minutes. There was one point Cassie chose to wait at the edge of the pool as she ran out of breath and stood at the corner lane as far as possible so he still could do his flip back. However, she did not expect that he also stopped, stood up and took off his goggle.

Then their eyes met.

Cassie sucked in her breath. She recognised those gorgeous pair of eyes, but she was unsure whether he was the person she had in mind. He seemed taken aback seeing her, too, rubbed his face from the water, and squinted his eyes for a moment before his mouth slowly dropped.

"Brad?"

He did not respond, though he stayed unmoved.

Grimacing, Cassie thought that she probably had identified the wrong person.

"I didn't know you're a good swimmer too, Cass."

Cassie was startled and blinked her eyes a couple of times. His deep baritone voice was not foreign to her ear. Upon seeing his face much clearer now, her heart was quivering with relief that she recognised him correctly. At the same time, she was blushing as her eyes inevitably admired his athletic bare wet body.

Feeling warm, she chuckled. "I didn't know that you're into swimming too."

"Do you come here often?" he asked.

"From now on, I will be."

His eyebrows furrowed as if he was trying to understand her answer. Before Cassie opened her mouth again, from her peripheral view, she saw the girls wandering, looking for her.

"Sorry, I have to get them," she muttered and swiftly jumped out from the pool and ran towards her nieces, who immediately broke into relieved grins the moment they saw her. Unfortunately, when she turned around to the pool where Brad was, he was not there anymore. Her eyes roamed around, trying to spot him.

Her eyes finally caught his back. He was walking towards the male changing room without looking back anymore. Cassie could not help but feel a heaviness within her that they had no chance to finish their short chat earlier. Ashleigh and Alicia then pulled her hand to go to the water play, and she had no choice but to follow them.

For the next Fridays, she never reencountered him.

Chapter Fifteen

One of Melbourne's coldest days had arrived. It was raining for the last few days and today's highest temperature was only ten degrees with strong wind. Cassie tightened her jacket, shawl and beanie while jumping into the tram that would take her to Kieran's house. It was one of the days that Kieran needed help to mind the girls while he had an important client meeting in the evening.

The problem was Tiffany also called asking for her help choosing and fitting the wedding dress. Cassie queried why Ruby and Chelsea were not helping. From her last encounters with those bullies, she tried her best to avoid them as much as possible. However, Tiffany said, unfortunately, her friends had something on tonight.

Cassie thought taking the girls along while helping Tiffany at the same time may not be a bad idea after all. Alicia and Ashleigh must be excited to participate in this activity. However, it was Tiffany who seemed displeased. Perhaps for her sister, the presence of her nieces was just nuisances only.

"Can't you ask your housemate to take the girls?" Tiffany suggested when they talked on the phone.

"No," replied Cassie firmly. For Cassie, asking Erin's help for a trivial reason like this was unfair.

"Come on. The girls also love her."

"Ashleigh and Alicia are, in fact, thrilled to see you choosing the wedding dress. Besides, they will be your flower girls."

"Yeah, but I don't want them making a mess later."

"They are good kids, Tiff. Don't worry. They will behave."

"But you need to focus on helping me too."

Cassie took a sigh. This was the time that Tiffany started to be demanding and act childish. "I have no choice. I have to take the girls."

"Alright," Tiffany finally conceded. "Don't be late!"

Cassie managed to reach Kieran's house on time. Ashleigh and Alicia were full of beans when they took the tram to the appointment. The bridal shop was located within the Melbourne city area, but with the hecticness of weekend traffic plus wet weather, it took them longer to reach the place. Cassie could imagine how Tiffany would react when they arrived fifteen minutes late.

"Oh, Cass, I knew you would be late!" groaned Tiffany. "All thanks to you, girls!"

Ashleigh and Alicia were stunned and gave their aunt a guilty look.

"Relax, Tiff. I'm here now. It's Saturday night. The traffic is crazy, and the tram is full," sighed Cassie. She quickly told the girls to take off their jackets and settle. Then she began to take each layer of her attire. From her jacket, shawl and beanie that seemed to have added so much weight to her body. She took a deep, relieved breath, feeling her body much lighter. They were literally running from the tram station to get into this shop earlier.

For the first half an hour, Tiffany was busy coming in and out of the fitting dress room, showing some of the dresses she might consider. Ashleigh and Alicia started to make cheering sounds, praising and commenting about the dress. Tiffany looked irritated instead, as the girls were too loud and did not give Cassie a chance to speak.

"Quiet girls! I only have one hour here!" yelled Tiffany. It was a scolding that made Ashleigh and Alicia immediately fall silent. Cassie quietly sighed and consoled the girls to take out their drawing books instead.

"All the dresses look great on you, Tiff," remarked Cassie after the girls were settled in the corner, colouring their books. "But I like this one." She pointed to the ball gown dress with a high neckline. "It's elegant."

She realised that she had different tastes from Tiffany. Most of Tiffany's chosen dresses were sexy and revealing to the point that Cassie felt it was inappropriate.

"You must be joking, Cass. That dress will make me like an old lady," snickered Tiffany. Then she laughed before picking up another dress and going to the changing room. "Well, yeah, I almost forgot that you're reaching forty on my wedding day."

Right! Cassie only responded with a faint smile. It was one of the nasty words Tiffany would utter to her, which perhaps her sister thought she would take lightly as a joke.

"Where are you going for your honeymoon?" Cassie purposedly diverted the conversation while she sauntered towards the evening dresses hanging shelves and browsed through them. She was considering getting a new dress too for the wedding itself. Perhaps she should discuss it with her mother. They may want to choose similar colours.

"Are you going to buy a dress too, aunt Cassie?" Alicia approached her with beaming eyes. "Can I help you to choose?"

Cassie nodded. "Sure, sweetheart."

"Yay!" Alicia and Ashleigh jumped together and skimmed through the hanging shelves.

Tiffany reappeared from the changing room. This time, she wore a translucent lace white dress that revealed her cleavage, her small back and thighs. Despite the dress was not to Cassie's taste, she had to admit Tiffany looked stunning as her beautiful curvy figure was shown more prominently.

"We are planning to go to the Maldives," answered Tiffany. "I hope Joshua can get three weeks of annual leave for our honeymoon. But it seems his big boss is such a jerk, trying to make it difficult for Joshua to go because it is in the middle of project launching."

"You can go after the conclusion of the project," asserted Cassie. "It's not a big deal, isn't it?"

Tiffany scoffed. "Of course, it's a big deal. A honeymoon should be done immediately after the wedding. Joshua's boss is just jealous. Joshua said he's a workaholic. He doesn't have a girlfriend yet. He's a weird geeky guy. I'm not surprised if no one wants to be with him."

Cassie quietly took a sigh. It was just one of those days that Tiffany would complain about not getting what she wanted and blame someone else.

"So, have you had anyone to go as your partner, Cass?"

Cassie was taken aback by the question. She could see a hint of a mocking smile threatening to appear on Tiffany's lips.

She shook her head weakly. "No. It doesn't matter, does it?"

Tiffany repressed her laughter. "Well, up to you."

"Aunt Cassie, we've found a perfect dress for you!" Ashleigh and Alicia's exciting squeal interrupted. Tiffany rolled her eyes while scoffing. Cassie ignored it while letting the girls pull her hand to the hanging shelves.

"Oh, this dress is for the future bride," said Cassie, seeing the ball gown white dress pointed by the girls.

"But you can still try it, can't you?" asked Ashleigh with her two big, round innocent eyes.

"Well, yeah," murmured Cassie. "But It's not me who's getting married soon. It's aunt Tiffany. Besides, you need to make an appointment before trying on the wedding dress."

"Oh, that's not necessary." One of the shopkeepers in her mid-fifties suddenly appeared between them. "My name is Helen. I am free at the moment to help you out."

Tiffany laughed. "Well, perhaps there is no harm in trying it, Cass. Who knows, you may never have a chance to wear one for the rest of your life."

Right! Another cruel joke. Cassie only lowered her head to hide her wince.

"Come on, aunt Cassie," pleaded Alicia, pulling Cassie's hand to the changing room. "Try it. We want to see it."

"Yeah, Cass. Try it," mocked Tiffany while giggling. "This shop carries one of the best wedding dresses in Melbourne. You don't need to pay to try their dresses."

Cassie took a sigh while taking the dress and letting the girls pull her to the changing dress, followed by Helen.

"They are such gorgeous kids, aren't they? You are a lucky mother," remarked Helen while they were in the changing room. She helped Cassie to zip up the dress and guided her out. "I think you look absolutely stunning in this dress. The girls will love it."

A lucky mother! Cassie chuckled. *Do Alicia and Ashleigh look like her?* Based on her observation, they inherited half of Emily's facial features, like her nose and lips and even Emily's curly hair. However, the girls' eyes were deep blue like Kieran's. Feeling amused, Cassie stepped up to the shallow stage in the middle of the room with the wide mirror background. Tiffany and the girls waited for her expectantly.

Immediately the cheering sounds from the girls echoed. Cassie smiled sheepishly while placing both of her hands on the waist, pretending like a wedding model. Then, she twirled around to see her reflection in the mirror.

It was indeed a beautiful wedding dress. It was a ball gown dress with soft cream tulle and a tube top. If she was getting married, perhaps she would choose this dress. The thought made her chuckle, and she shook her head, feeling ridiculous.

While admiring her reflection in the mirror, she laughed and lifted her chin sternly when Alicia and Ashleigh started acting like her flower girls, bowing to her like the queen. However, her laughter was rather abruptly stopped when her eyes caught someone who had just appeared at the entrance door, a few metres away from where they were.

Perhaps at that second, her heart stopped beating. Was she only dreaming? *Isn't that Brad? What is he doing here?*

Initially, Brad did not see her. But once he turned in her direction, he was stunned. His eyes lingered on her for a while, dragging slowly from her top to bottom. His staring was so intense, without even a second of blink. It made her breathless. Somehow, how he looked at her made the air in the room freeze, sending a spiral of shiver down her spine. It made her feel....*naked.*

"Let us take a picture, aunt Cassie!" Ashleigh's voice that broke their eyes trances. "I want to show it to daddy when we get home!"

Cassie stuttered. "Ah..yes." Her eyes quickly were back to where Brad was. He was not there anymore but walking towards the other room appointment. And he was not alone. A sexy beautiful woman, the same woman that Cassie recognised from last Easter, took his arm and pulled him to enter the other room. It was a sight that somehow made her lung constrict.

With drooping shoulders, she dashed to the changing room once the girls took plenty of pictures of her. She took the last look admiring herself in that wedding dress before she chuckled bitterly. Her fingers reached the zip at the back, and she quickly got herself out of it as if she was disgusted with it.

Chapter Sixteen

It was supposed to be another Friday for Cassie to take Ashleigh and Alica swimming. However, Chandra had invited her to his and Tom's simple engagement party. Chandra sent her a text message informing the time and detail of the party, which Cassie initially doubted whether she could attend. However, Erin was just beside her when she read the message, and immediately Erin offered to take the girls instead.

"You have to go, Cass. He's your best friend."

"Erin, I need to discuss this with Kieran."

"I'll take the girls, Cass. Kieran will not mind. He would be furious if he knew you missed the party because of the girls' swimming lesson."

Cassie sighed. "It was my idea to get the swimming lessons for the girls."

"Which I believe Kieran appreciates," added Erin. "He is not blaming you if you can't go and take the girls. Anyway, I can do it too."

"But it's Friday night, Erin. Don't you usually go out with your colleagues for drinks on Friday night? It's unfair that you miss your social life because of someone else's kids."

Erin's face turned into a pout. "Someone else's kids? You speak as if Ashleigh and Alicia do not mean anything to me. I have taken them as my own nieces too, Cass." Her eyes were protruding. "Or you don't like me, an outsider, interfering with your family life?"

"No, no!" Cassie waved her hand in panic. "That's not what I mean. I am grateful for your help, Erin. I know you love the girls, and they love you too. I just hate to trouble you."

"Don't be," countered Erin with a curled lip. "Because I don't mind at all."

Cassie only took a defeated sigh. And it was settled. Kieran had been informed too of the change of plan that Erin would take the girls so she could go to Chandra's engagement party.

Cassie had to admit she wanted to go. Since the last trip to Jakarta, she did not have much chance to talk with Chandra. This engagement news came as a surprise, and she was delighted to attend it.

She took the tram to the party place. Tom's house was in South Yarra, not far from the city. Once she jumped out of the crowded tram, the cold winter breeze was like fresh air. The place was just another five minutes walk from the tram stop.

The sky was already pitch dark, although the night was still young as the time only showed 6 pm. Cassie hid one hand in the jacket's pocket to fight the chill of the night while the other hand was holding her mobile phone so she could check the navigation, ensuring she walked in the right direction. She did not pay much attention that someone was walking closely behind her.

"Tom's house is the one with the balloon."

She startled and lifted her head to meet with a pair of eyes that immediately made her heart leap.

Darn! She should have known that he would be here as well! *Or not?* She thought Chandra and Tom's acquaintances with Brad were only for work projects.

"Hi." She broke a weak smile.

It was dark on the street, with a dimmed illumination from the street light. Still, she could not deny that Brad looked tall and dashingly handsome with his broad shoulder covered by an expensive dark overcoat. His earthly masculine aftershave cologne somehow reached her senses despite the fact they stood about one metre away from each other.

"How are you?" he asked while continuing his walk, assuming she would follow him. She quickly followed his pace.

"Good, thank you. How are you, Brad?"

"I'm well."

His voice sounded flat, as if he was not interested in further conversation with her. And she was correct as there was only unnatural silence during the walk until they reached the house door and knocked on it.

Soon the door was opened by the host himself, who gave them an arched eyebrow and twitched lips.

"My favourite people," grinned Tom while opening his wide arm, welcoming Cassie to his embrace and planting a light peck on her cheek. He acted formally with Brad by offering him a handshake and greetings only.

A couple of other guests were at the party, but Cassie did not know most of them. Her eyes roamed around to spot Chandra chatting with one of the guests in the living room. However, when he realised her presence, he quickly excused himself and approached her. Cassie could not contain her excitement, and perhaps she was half squealing when she threw herself into Chandra's embrace.

"Congratulations!" She was practically jumping like a little kid when Chandra put her back on the land.

Chandra returned with a sheepish smile. "Thank you, Cass. I'm so glad that you're here."

"Is Helda or any of your family here too?"

Chandra's face pinched as he shook his head weakly. "No."

Cassie could read it and felt terrible for asking about it. Chandra diverted the topic by asking her to help herself with the food and the drink. It was a good escape for her to avoid an awkward conversation, especially when pertaining to this supposed to be a joyful day.

She found herself alone for the next few minutes while observing Tom and Chandra busy with other guests. While grabbing the food and drink, Brad appeared at her side. However, no words were uttered, and somehow it was something that Cassie would expect from Brad. She knew no one else in the room that Brad was familiar with, which was why he approached her instead.

Cassie felt the itch to break the ice. "How are things going with you, Brad?".

"Good," he answered curtly. It made her wonder whether he actually needed any conversation.

"Busy with work?"

"Yeah."

Another silence descended. Cassie felt it was a sign that he did not wish for any conversation with her.

A woman in probably her twenties, young and stunning, suddenly approached him. The woman started introducing herself and asking his name. Obviously, she was hinting at him! But what surprised Cassie was the way he responded. His gaze was on the floor, he did not even bother to lift his eyes to see the woman, and his answers were like murmuring.

It reminded Cassie of the first time they met as well. Perhaps that was just Brad. He was just himself. The woman seemed not to give up and kept lingering at his side, trying to make him talk, while Brad seemed unaffected by her presence.

Cassie decided to move away from them and head towards the alfresco. She felt sick watching them, and she did not know why. A freezing crisp winter air splashed her face, taking the suffocated feeling away. However, she took off her jacket when she arrived and left it in the cloakroom. Indeed there was a reason why no one went out to the outdoor area. Luckily she was still wearing her sweater, so she thought to linger there for a moment.

"Hey, what are you doing there?"

Chandra's friendly smile appeared from the door, which somehow gave her a light feeling that it was him who had found her.

"I just want to get fresh air."

"Sorry if I've been ignoring you," mumbled Chandra with a pinched face.

"No!" she hushed him. "It's not your fault, Chandra. I understand you have other guests to entertain."

"Yeah, but you're my special friend." He gave her that affectionate gaze that used to create a tingling feeling within her. It still had the same effect on her, but knowing where his heart belonged, she took it in a different light.

She smiled. "So, how're things going with you?"

Chandra sighed. "Yeah, good. I've told my family about Tom and me. But you know, their reaction is expected."

"I'm sorry to hear that, Chandra."

Chandra shook his head. "It's alright, Cass. I knew it was coming. But, you're right, I can't stay there too long with Tom. So, I quickly asked my line manager to transfer me back soon to Melbourne."

"Does your family know about your engagement?"

"Yes. I've informed them. I invited them to come over. But obviously, that's not happening." He chuckled bitterly while taking a deep exhale. "I guess they need time."

"That's correct, Chandra." Cassie stretched out her hand to rub his forearm gently. "Just give them some time. The most important thing is you're happy with Tom."

He placed his hand over her. "Thanks, Cass."

"I'm so happy for you and Tom."

Cassie threw her glance to the inside and saw Brad still with the same woman who was trying to get his attention.

"I don't expect you would invite Brad," she remarked. "I thought you only knew him on a professional level."

Chandra followed her eye direction. "Well, yeah, I know him because of the project. I guess through our meetings in Jakarta, I found that he's a quiet person but thoughtful. I appreciate his understanding of my situation with Tom. You have no idea how we were in Jakarta. A couple of times, Brad witnessed our quarrelling but managed to mediate and calm us down." He sipped his drink with an embarrassing chuckle. "We were so childish when we were in love."

"Yeah, right!" Cassie laughed. "I remember Brad told me that you guys are passionate lovers. So take that as a compliment."

Chandra threw his head back, laughing. "Oh, that's actually embarrassing. But I appreciate that he supports us. We were far from being professional at that time."

Their conversation stopped as the door suddenly swung open, and another head popped up.

"Hey, what are you doing here? It's freezing outside."

Tom appeared, then followed by Brad. Each of them brought two bottles of beer. Cassie arched her eyebrow, not expecting Brad to manage to get away from the young woman earlier.

"Shall we have a toast?" asked Tom while giving a bottle to Cassie and Chandra.

"That's right!" exclaimed Cassie. "For the gorgeous couple in Melbourne." She cheered.

A clicking sound from their bottles echoed before silence descended while everyone sipped their drinks. Tom slowly moved to Chandra's side, and he wrapped his arm around Chandra's waist.

"So, what's up with you, Cass?" queried Tom.

Cassie shrugged with a downturn lip. "Nothing much, still the same old. I'm just busy with the kids."

"I don't see any ring on your finger yet," Brad commented, pointing at her hand with his bottle.

Cassie squished her eyebrow, confused by his question. But before she could answer, Chandra interrupted, "When is your sister's wedding again?"

"In Spring. Exactly falls on my 40th birthday."

Chandra whistled. "You must be thrilled."

"Well, people will be cheering for her new life rather than cheering me on having another year of life," she grumbled.

Tom's prominent cheekbones sneaked out. "She must be excited. How is she going with the wedding plan?"

"She's mad like any other bridezilla," muttered Cassie, hiding her smirk through her beer bottle. She checked the alcohol level on the bottle label afterwards, puzzled by her own sarcasm.

"Speaking about bridezilla..." Candra glanced at his fiance.

Tom bulged his eyes. "I AM fine, Chandra!"

Chandra burst into big laughter while kissing his fiance. It was a sight that warmed Cassie's heart, seeing a happy couple in front of her.

"Tom complained because I haven't given him any ring yet," teased Chandra in the remaining of his laughter. "What's your sister's engagement ring like?"

"It is absolutely smashing!" gloated Cassie while describing the huge diamond on Tiffany's ring. "Anything about her has to be spectacular and extravagant." Did she sound jealous? Very much. But somehow, tonight, she did not give a damn care. Before her, were three charming men, and yet she did not feel pressure to keep her wall up.

"Sorry, who's getting married in Spring?" Brad's confused voice interrupted. Cassie just realised that he had been the only one who kept quiet.

"My sister," replied Cassie.

"I saw you in the bridal shop," he stated.

If she looked dumbfounded, perhaps she was. Her lips were parting as she did not expect he still remember that brief encounter a few weeks ago. They even did not exchange greetings at that time.

"Oh, I was accompanying my sister. She was the one fitting for the wedding dress."

"Are you the maid of honour?" asked Tom.

"Nope." Cassie shook her head with pout lips. "The real maid of honour is totally unreliable. So, I'm there just helping my sister. In the end, she was not listening to any of my suggestions. We have different tastes."

"But you were trying on a wedding dress." Brad's stern voice was heard again.

Cassie felt her cheek warm as Chandra's eyebrows danced up, and Tom repressed his smirk. "I know, guys. I look desperate, don't I? The girls forced me to try one, so they could show the picture to their dad. I was acting like a model for the kids' fun time."

Tom and Chandra broke into a huge laughter. "That must be a hell of fun!"

"So, you were trying the dress for the kids to show to their dad, who will be your future husband?" Brad hypothesized, still in a severe manner.

Cassie just realised that he was the only one that was not laughing. But hearing his words made her body quake as she burst into laughter until her body temperature seemed to jump up.

"I wish their father is my future husband! He's like my other half!" she chortled.

Brad flinched with her reaction and jerked his head back. His eyes were blinking a couple of times with a deep furrow.

"The kids are Cassie's nieces, Brad," explained Chandra solemnly. "Their father is Cassie's older brother."

A sudden quietness pierced through as only the sound of grasshoppers filled the air. Brad's eyes dropped, and he fell into his own deep thought. It was something Cassie did not expect. She thought they would laugh together at the end. She glanced at Tom and Chandra, whose adam apples were moving nervously. It seemed they did not expect such a reaction from him either.

"Shall we go inside? It's freezing here," mouthed Tom to break the silence.

"Yeah, we should," followed Chandra.

The couple went inside. Cassie was contemplating whether to go inside or stay. She did not know most of the other guests anyway and still wanted to inhale more fresh air. With the beer accompaniment in her hand, she decided to linger a bit longer outside.

The creaking sound of the door opening echoed. As Cassie stood facing away from the door, she guessed it must be Brad, who also went inside. She sipped her beer again while looking at the sky, appreciating the full moon and some little stars that night. However, a sudden warmness embraced her as a jacket dropped on her shoulder.

"You could get sick."

It was Brad's familiar deep, baritone voice. He stood behind her while his gaze travelled a distance. As he had given her his jacket, Cassie could admire his broad chest covered in a dark grey sweater with the collar of his shirt sneaking out from the sweater's neckline.

"Thank you," she breathed, unsure what to say next. She did not expect such a nice gesture from him.

For a moment, Cassie did not know why, but she was speechless. He did not look at her and did not utter any word either. They stood there gazing at the dark sky, unsure for how long. Chandra's calling finally severed their thoughts, informing them it was speech time. She returned the jacket to him once they were inside.

After the speech, Cassie could sense Brad was following her. She waited for him to initiate a conversation, but he did not. Ultimately she just gave up and formed a conversation with someone nearby.

When the time approached midnight, the guests at the party started to disperse. As if it was her natural habit, she helped clean up the guests' mess, so she became the last person who left.

"There's an extra bedroom upstairs," said Chandra. "It's not safe for a woman like you to walk home alone."

Cassie knew that Chandra had thought about it. His friend knew her too well.

"Thanks, Chandra. But I'll be fine." She took her jacket and put it on.

The sound from the alfresco distracted them as Brad emerged together with Tom. It surprised her as she was not the last guest in the house. Brad had been in the alfresco chatting with Tom while she was cleaning up in the kitchen with Chandra.

"Tom, Cassie doesn't want to stay. But I'm worried about letting her go home alone. Shall we drop her off?" asked Chandra.

"Sure!" Tom immediately answered.

"That's not necessary, mates. I'll be fine," protested Cassie. "I'll order an uber now." Her fingers quickly typed on the mobile phone screen.

"I can take you home. I'm driving." Brad's voice was heard as he passed by her and took his jacket from the cloak hanger.

"Yeah, that would be great!" Chandra beamed.

Cassie squished her eyebrow. She did not recall that Brad came in a car.

"I parked one block away. It's not easy to find parking around this area," explained Brad as he could read her mind.

"Right."

Chandra strode forward and grabbed Brad for a firm handshake. "That's great! Thank you, Brad. I appreciate your help in taking Cassie home. I cannot sleep in peace if she goes home alone."

"You are treating me like a little kid." Cassie showed her pretend scowl with both hands on her waist before she broke into laughter and gave her friend a good night hug.

"I told you, you're my special friend," whispered Chandra to her ear.

The street atmosphere was eerily quiet after they waved goodbye and began their stroll to Brad's car. As Cassie had expected, there was only silence during their walk. She thought it was better that way, so they could be on guard if anyone suspicious came towards them. Perhaps she was too engrossed with her thought that she did not realise she walked quicker than him until he gently grabbed her forearm.

"Here is my car."

"Ah, yeah, right," she chuckled sheepishly. The next second she held her breath, entering his car.

His car was immaculate, spotless, and it had a musky masculine fragrant, probably from his perfume. However, Cassie could not deny that it was one of the most luxurious cars she had ever seen. Upon closer look, she just realised that the car was electric.

Darn! He definitely has a taste! Somehow it was like a reminder that she was not in his league. Erin's theory that he was interested in her was erroneous. But thinking about it more, he might only want to sleep with her, not necessarily because he needed to like her. *Yeah, right! That's not going to happen.* Casual sex was definitely off from her dictionary. It was better for them to stay as friends.

She tried to restrain her tongue from complimenting his car. He might think she was flirting with him. Which male species would not get a big head for innocent flattering praise on his stuff?

"My apartment is near the Royal Exhibition building." She felt her voice sound crisp in her ear. He entered her address on the big navigation screen in the middle of the dashboard.

"Do you live alone?" he asked while pulling out his car.

"No, I have a housemate."

"And your brother and his kids?"

"Their house is in Kew, not far from city."

"Oh, I thought you stayed with them."

"I did live with them for a couple of years after my sister-in-law passed away. But two years ago, since my nieces entered school, my brother insisted I should not live with them anymore. He wants me to have my own life, although he still needs my help to look after the kids."

"I'm sorry to hear about your sister in law," he murmured.

"It's alright." Cassie took a deep exhale. It became her habit every time the passing of Emily was mentioned. "The girls are coping well."

"May I know what happened?"

"Car accident. Five years ago."

"Drunk driving?"

Cassie chuckled bitterly. "No. A twenty-year-old girl was texting on her mobile phone while driving, crossing over the red light and hit my sister in law's car. It was a fatal accident. The girl survived, but not my sister in law. I guess it's ironic how someone could escape death from an irresponsible act at the expense of other people's life."

Throughout the conversation, his eyes were fixed on the road. But somehow, Cassie could catch his soft gaze as if he could feel the pain of losing someone.

"I'm happy for Tom and Chandra." Cassie purposedly changed the topic. She did not wish to be carried out with grieves. Perhaps he had lost someone dear to him too. "They are a great couple."

"I understand that Chandra's family is still against the relationship," he stated.

"Yeah, but at least they are not in Melbourne. They only need time to accept them. And I would like to thank you again for helping me understand his situation. I still can't forgive myself that I almost stood between them."

There was a ghost of a smile on his face. "You had no idea. It was not your fault. Chandra could have told you earlier."

"Regardless, I still owe you. I meant to ask you ..." Suddenly, she felt silly saying these words. What the hell was she thinking? But the idea had been in her head seemed like ages ago since they returned from Jakarta. However, did it sound weird if she wanted to ask him out for dinner? Did it sound like she hinted at him? It was supposed just a friendly dinner, that was her plan. All thanks to Erin's words that somehow clouded her mind.

"Ask me what?"

Cassie's mouth half opened as her mind was racing about how she put the words correctly without giving any wrong signal. She could feel that he was glancing at her curiously. She swallowed and took another breath.

"I'm meaning to ask you out for a meal."

There it goes! She said the words smoothly with no sign of stumbling.

He seemed taken aback. "A meal?"

"Yeah, there's this tapas restaurant in Fed Square." She kept bubbling and made her voice as light as possible. "The food is great. So, since I owe you, let this be my treat."

"Right. When do you want to go?"

She tried to read his facial expression, wishing he did not think this too far. "How about one of the weekdays? I'm busy with the girls on the weekend. I guess you are also busy with work." She remembered the woman that she had seen with him before. He might be seeing someone at the moment. To avoid a misunderstanding, a lunch appointment sounded more like a mateship than a date. "Monday lunchtime, perhaps?"

"Alright."

"Great! Settled then. This coming Monday at twelve noon, I'll see you at Fed Square."

When her apartment building was within their sight, she felt an unexpected release of tension in her limb. This quirky conversation was quite torturing. "That's where I live. You can stop your car here."

He followed her direction but stopped the car at the parking sign, a few metres away from the apartment's entrance.

"Thank you for the lift," said Cassie while taking off her seat belt. She knitted her brow when he switched off the engine, took off his seat belt and stepped out of the car too.

"I'll accompany you to the lift," he said while gently taking her forearm.

"You don't need to."

"You never know that you might meet a bad guy in the lift. I can see that there is no security gate to enter the apartment."

Cassie had to admit that was true. It was a security issue that Kieran also mentioned to her, too. However, she was too comfortable in this apartment and did not bother to find a new one. She did not want to argue, wishing the sooner she got into her place, the sooner he could go.

It was just another awkward silence as they were in the lift. Luckily her building apartment was only about ten levels, and her apartment unit was on the middle level. Within a minute, they finally reached her door. No sign of lights from the bottom of the door indicated Erin probably had gone to bed. She opened the apartment door, turned on the light, and realised he was still behind her.

"Thank you once again," she murmured. As far as she could remember, no one ever accompanied her to her apartment floor, not even Chandra. Perhaps because she never came back home this late. There was a sensation of being flooded with warmth, feeling touched by his kind gestures today.

"No worries. Good night."

For a glimpse, Cassie found his eyes were on her before he strode away. Once he disappeared into the lift, something struck her, realising they had not exchanged a phone number. Would their lunch on Monday still be on?

She slapped her forehead and her shoulder down while closing the door. She would think about how to figure this out later.

Chapter Seventeen

Over the weekend, Cassie contemplated asking for Brad's mobile phone number from Chandra. She wondered whether that would be a peculiar request. She did not breathe a word about her plan to ask Brad for lunch with anyone, not even Erin! And thinking about her housemate, she noticed Erin was not in her room on Friday night. Her guess was correct as Erin entered the apartment on Saturday morning when she had just got up.

"Where have you been?"

Before answering, Erin scrapped her hand through her messy 'just wake up' hair. "I went to my friend's house."

"Right. But you took the girls last night swimming, didn't you?"

"Yes! I went with the girls. I put them to bed around 8 o'clock, then one of my colleagues called asking me out for a drink."

Cassie nodded. "Right." That made sense to her. She was glad that Erin did not miss her social life when her time was occupied with Ashleigh and Alicia. "I'm glad you still had fun last night."

Erin darted her a stern look. "I told you, I love spending time with Ashleigh and Alicia. Being with them was fun."

Then Erin immediately fled into the shower room while Cassie got herself ready for Kieran's house.

The weekend was her usual routine: taking Alicia and Ashleigh to go for groceries together, doing the household chores, helping them with homework, and sometimes having birthday parties and playdates. She knew at least there were two birthday parties for the weekend; one was from Alicia's classmate, while the other one was from Ashleigh's classmate.

There it went her weekend. However, she got used to it. When Monday morning arrived, she somehow felt her heartbeat faster than usual. She had been typing, deleting and retyping a message for Chandra. A message asking for Brad's number. What would

Chandra think about this? She did not want to give the impression that she was hinting at Brad.

In the end, she was distracted by work as there was an urgent service request she needed to attend to. Fortunately, she looked at the clock when the time already showed a quarter to twelve o clock. Without thinking further, she grabbed her jacket and ran out the door.

It was the end of winter, and Melbourne was approaching spring soon. The sun started to shine more, and though the cold air was still staying, it was a lovely day for her for a stroll. However, she was practically running as fast as possible, wishing she would not be late for the appointment.

Once she reached the tapas restaurant, she was too busy catching her breath. But her eyes roamed around, wishing to spot the person that had been occupying her mind over the weekend. Not knowing his number, and he did not know her number, she would not be surprised if he did not turn up. He probably did not remember that she asked him out for this lunch appointment.

After a few minutes, once her breath was stable, she pushed the door to enter the restaurant. Her eyes dragged to every inch of the area, but her mind was still hazy with the remaining adrenaline pumped within her. She did not register anyone that looked like Brad. With a slumping shoulder and a heavy sigh, she turned her body around, ready to exit the place. But a gentle touch landed on her forearm and stopped her.

"I suppose this is the restaurant that you mentioned."

Her lips parted in surprise. Brad stood behind her with his captivating pair of eyes on her, gazing at her with a squished eyebrow.

"Oh, yeah!" she chuckled, feeling her face hot. "This is the one."

"Then, why are you leaving?"

Because I don't' have your number!

"Sorry, I thought you were not coming."

"Why do you think so?"

She waved off her hand. "Never mind. Let's sit down and order. I bet you must be hungry."

They took a table for two near the window. Cassie tried to calm her heart, despite not denying the tingling sensation within her as she admired his dashing appearance as usual. He looked casual, only with a long-sleeved shirt with two top buttons left open and a pair of dark blue jeans. But his expensive dark overcoat somehow made him look stunning. Meanwhile, she was still sweating after the frantic run. She took off her jacket and put it on her chair while getting herself sitting down. Her eyes glanced around, observing other women consumers wearing formal working dresses. The sight made her feel old-fashioned as she only wore a shirt and long pants.

"I'll leave it to you to decide what to order." His deep baritone voice shook her out from her own reverie. "It's your treat anyway."

"Sure," she smiled sheepishly. Luckily she already knew what she wanted to order.

Once their order was placed, they went into silence for a moment, as she would expect. Quietly Cassie took a deep breath, giving her the courage to think of a conversation.

"Is your office far from here?" she asked.

He shook his head. "I'm in the Rialto building. Where's your office?"

"Near Chinatown."

"That's quite a bit of a walk."

Cassie chuckled. She was literally running earlier.

They went into another silence again until their food was served. Cassie observed him eating for a moment, and it reminded her of when they also had a meal together in Jakarta.

"Do you miss Indonesian food?" she asked.

He shrugged. "Sometimes."

"Do you still go to Jakarta for a business trip?"

"Sometimes."

His short answer was vexing. It intrigued her why he would bother to come here but seemed uninterested in conversing with her. Regardless, after this lunch, she was unlikely to see him anymore.

"Chandra took me to a well-known Indonesian restaurant in Melbourne. The food was pretty good," she commented.

He lifted his eyes to her, which she returned with a smirk. No words were uttered, and then he lowered his eyes again. Cassie rapidly blinked her eyes, thinking that she was just dreaming.

"How's your weekend?" she asked again, wishing to keep their conversation alive.

"Good."

Darn! Another short answer.

"Did you go somewhere special?

He munched his food while falling into deep thinking before finally answering, "No. How about you?"

Cassie realised now that she needed to do the talking to fill the stillness of their conversation. She thought perhaps it did not matter if she just kept bubbling.

"Yeah, it was great! I went for groceries with the girls, helped them do their homework, and cooked lunch. Ashleigh had a birthday party invite on Saturday, and Alicia had one on Sunday. I helped to do some laundry in the house, took the girls to the park for a playdate, and finally took them to see their grandparents – their mother's parents."

While talking, her eyes roamed around, thinking he would stare down anyway. However, when her eyes were back at him, their eyes met. It was like a big thud to her chest as, once again, she was mesmerised by them. She restrained herself from moving as he might want to say something. However, his lips were sealed. It was like a good ten seconds that they were only staring at each other until she felt breathless and broke the trance. After managing to gasp some air, she finally managed to gain her wits and started bubbling again, whatever topic she had in her mind; work or the weather, until she finished her food and glanced at the time.

"I hope you enjoy the food, Brad." She clasped her hand and prepared to stand up. "I think I have to go back to work now. My manager will not be happy to see me coming back late from lunch."

He did not respond as he followed her standing up and going to the cashier. Once they were outside, she turned to him, ready to bid him goodbye.

"Thank you for buying me the lunch," he murmured, but his eyes were not on her.

"My pleasure. Bye!" Then she twirled around and took a brisk walk without looking back.

That's it! She promised herself that there were no 'meal' appointments with Brad anymore.

She literally ran back to her office again. Once she settled her breathing at her desk, she realised she had left her jacket behind. A slap on her forehead by her own hand was the only thing she could do.

Chapter Eighteen

It was just another week before the Spring school holiday. Cassie went back to her usual running exercise after work as daylight savings was approaching. But, while running, her critical brain was also working, planning what she should organise for Ashleigh and Alicia's holiday activities. Perhaps a few days with Amanda and John, or she should take a couple of days of leave to take them out, have a playdate with some of her school friends, or enrol them on a holiday program. There were plenty of options. It was only about dividing the time.

The soft chime from her mobile phone broke her reverie. Usually, she would ignore it and check the messages after her run. But a few seconds later, her mobile phone rang, forcing her to stop running. Her brows drew together, seeing the caller ID.

"What's up, bro?" she answered the call.

An exaggerated sigh from the other side. "Have you seen mum's messages? I can't believe it." Then followed by some hissed cursing words.

Cassie put her mobile phone on speaker so she could also check her phone message. Their mother asked them to come on the weekend to clean up the house before Tiffany's Hens party.

"Oh!" That was her first reaction. Tiffany had announced that her Hens party would be two weeks away. It seemed her sister was still sticking to the original plan, having it in their parent's house.

"And do you know what's the best part, Cass? Tiffany will not be there to help out. She claims she's busy with work and other wedding preps, so Mum is asking our help."

Cassie only quietly took a sigh. "Well, I guess we should help, shouldn't we?" That was for sure, she thought. As much as they did not like Tiffany's Hens party's plan, they would not have the heart to refuse their parents' plead for help.

"I am departing to Sydney this weekend for a week's business trip," whined Kieran.

"Yeah, I know." Cassie did remember that Kieran had told her about his business trip, which coincidentally fell during the school holiday. "You know what, I'll take the girls to Mum's and Dad's house. They would love to spend time with their grandpa and nan. Then, one week later, dad could bring the girls back to Melbourne and drop them at Amanda and John's."

"Well, that sounds like a plan." Kieran sounded reluctantly agreed. "It's quite a trip to Mum and Dad's house, Cass."

"You don't trust my driving skill?"

"It's not that." Kieran drew a huge breath and released it. "Damn Tiffany!" he cursed.

Cassie grimaced upon hearing that. "Come on, Bro. It's for her wedding day."

"Your birthday is also coming, but you are not as demanding as her."

"Wedding is once in a lifetime. You can have a birthday every year," asserted Cassie. "Besides, this actually works well. The girls would be thrilled to spend their holiday in Wonthaggi. Then, for the second week of the holiday, I'll organise some playdates for them."

"Thanks, Cass. I don't know what I'll do without you."

"Don't mention it, bro. Love you."

"Love you."

The phone was hung up. Cassie quietly took a long exhale while continuing her exercise with a brisk walk. Somehow the conversation earlier did bother her in a way.

It was not the first time they shared their complaints about Tiffany's spoilt behaviour. Cassie understood that Kieran was upset for being unable to help their parents, not because he cared about Tiffany's Hens party plan. And again, it was not the first time their mother gave in to Tiffany's request, and they were the ones that had to go the extra mile to make it happen.

Kieran's words about her upcoming birthday somehow sliced her heart. It was another reminder that everyone was focusing on Tiffany's wedding, not her birthday. She did not wish to be the centre of attention. However, that negative feeling returned. The feeling of being forgotten.

While walking towards the tram stop, she passed by the basketball court as usual. She should have expected the person she wished she could avoid to be there. And there he was, dribbling his ball, smoothly shooting it to the basket. Watching him playing made her body itch as well to play.

"Can I join in?" She walked in without hesitation.

Brad turned around with furrowed brow seeing her presence. His adam apple bobbed before he answered, "Yeah, sure." He passed her the ball.

Although she was probably three meters away, Cassie took it and shot it smoothly to the basket.

"Impressive," he murmured.

The compliment was like a passing wind for her as she threw the ball back to him, a sign that the game was on. So there they went, moving tactically to avoid the ball snatching, then shooting it to the basket. It went for the next half an hour, and amazingly there was no single body touch throughout.

Cassie was engrossed in her chaotic mind. Her chest seemed tight without her understanding why. She kept running, dribbling and shooting to score some points, wishing it would chase the feeling away. However, nothing changed even when she started running out of breath and lost focus. Unavoidably, Brad snatched her ball effortlessly and slammed it into the basket.

"Are you alright?" he quizzed with a concerned tone.

"Yeah," she lied. She was literally wheezing hard. But she was desperate to get rid of the squeeze within her. She took the ball, dribbling it while focusing on her next move to trick Brad. However, she lost her balance instead. It was a wrong move as her ankles twisted, and she collapsed.

A soft groan escaped from her lips as her eyes welled in tears. *Don't be like this, Cassie.* She cursed under her breath for letting this feeling overcome her. Why did this time she has to shed tears? Was she getting old, and that was why she became more melancholy?

Like a defeated beast, she supported herself into a sitting position with her right hand covering her eyes.

"Are you okay?"

He kneeled beside her, and his hands were in mid-air as he was hesitant to touch her.

"Do you think you can stand up?"

She nodded weakly, still with her hands covering her eyes. She took a deep breath, gathering her courage to face him with teary eyes. He might think that was because of the pain, not the turmoil in her heart.

He helped her to stand up, but the moment she stepped with her injured ankle, her growl reverberated. But she insisted on continuing to walk by limping.

"How about some ice pack? I have some in my apartment," he offered.

The word 'ice pack' sounded tempting. Anyway, she needed some rest before walking again and hailed an Uber to get home. She nodded weakly.

"How about I piggyback you?"

It was another enticing offer. Their eyes met for a brief before he lowered his head down, waiting for her answer. She could read from his eyebrows that drew together that he was genuinely worried for her.

She agreed by nodding her head weekly. At this stage, in her mind, she just wanted to sit down with a cool ice pack. He squatted before her while she conveniently put her arms around his neck before he grabbed her knees and lifted her to his back effortlessly.

Inevitably she breathed in his earthly masculine cologne, mixed with the humidity of his sweat. It reminded her of when they had a dance in Bandung. She admitted she liked it, and somehow the scent gave her a calamity. While laying her heavy head on his back, she closed her eyes as she wanted to savour this moment.

Once they reached his apartment door, he gently put her down to open it. A bereft feeling slipped in without she could understanding it. However, when he supported her in getting on the sofa, her heart became light again.

Carefully she laid herself down on the chaise. It was a perfect spot to recuperate. The massive wall-to-wall window overseeing the city was just in front of her like a cinema screen. While he went to open the fridge to get an ice pack, she was quietly sitting admiring the view. She jerked up when he returned and placed the ice pack wrapped with a towel on her injured ankle.

"Thank you," she breathed while taking the ice pack from him and pressing it by herself.

"Would you like any drink?"

"Water will do. Thanks, Brad."

He went back to the kitchen and returned with a glass of water. When Cassie took the glass from his hand, a sense of Deja Vu knocked.

The last time she was here, she also came for a drink. Erin had a theory that Brad wanted to sleep with her, which was why he invited her to his apartment. Chuckling bitterly, she found how silly that theory was. Would he be interested in sleeping with someone like her, who always appeared messy most of the time, like now?

He sat quietly beside her, sipping his drink as they gazed in the distance at the vast scenery ahead of them. When it seemed like an eternity of silence, her breathing became settled. Her deep exhale filled her constricted lung and broke their quietude.

"My sister's wedding falls on my birthday too." Her voice was almost above a whisper.

He was unmoved, so she assumed he was listening.

"From fifty-two weekends in a year, I don't understand why her wedding day has to be on my 40th birthday," she scoffed. "It's not that I'm going to have a big celebration anyway, but it's just..." She even had no idea how to express her tight feeling. "I guess I'm upset. She always wants to be the centre of attention. Even without her upcoming wedding, she always becomes the centre of attention. She's always the best. Smart, intelligent, and beautiful. And my mother's favourite daughter. She has a fantastic career and a perfect going-to-be husband. I just..." She smiled bitterly. "I don't know...she has everything. I'm not jealous. I'm happy for her. She's my sister. I'm definitely out of her league. I'm always average, anyway. But..."

Once she blinked her eyes, inevitably, her tears started rolling down, and she closed her eyes, hating herself for talking like this. She did not understand why she let herself be vulnerable in front of him. If he was Kieran or perhaps Chandra, she would not be surprised. Strangely, as far as she remembered, she had never had a meltdown over Tiffany like this before! Quickly she rubbed her tears and reminded herself to be strong.

He did not utter any word, and it was just another silence in the room. Cassie felt it was ironic that only this time she appreciated his quietness despite she would take it as ignorance in the past. She knew he was listening, and she was grateful that he was willing to be a listening ear for her.

Somehow venting out her trouble in words was like lifting a heavy stone from her heart. Her muddled mind also became clear.

She took another heavy breath and felt silly for letting herself have this meltdown.

"Thank you for the ice pack and the drink." She put down the ice pack towel and the glass on the coffee table. "I think it's time for me to go." She pushed herself up, and he also stood up as his hands were ready to support her. "I'll be fine," she smiled, slightly embarassed, while limping to the door.

He closely followed behind her. "I'll drive you home."

Cassie did not wish to argue.

No words were exchanged throughout the journey home. He only focused on driving while she only gazed away through the window. To her surprise, he still remembered where she lived when his car stopped outside her apartment building.

He supported her walking to her apartment door. Cassie felt a comfortable warmth with his kind gesture despite only a stillness accompanying them. When he was about to leave, she repeated her gratitude. As usual, he did not respond, and his eyes were on the floor most of the time before finally, he strolled towards the lift.

Chapter Nineteen

It was six o'clock in the evening, and the sky was getting dark. Cassie lazily stood up from her work desk, collecting her stuff, ready to leave the office. Only a couple of employees were still working on her office floor. She waved her hand to them while walking limpingly towards the lift.

Though her ankle was not swollen anymore, she decided to put her exercises on hold. When Kieran knew about her condition, he forbade her to visit them but felt helpless, unable to help her because the girls still had school. Cassie assured him it was a minor injury, not a big deal.

She messaged Erin, asking whether her housemate was at home. She was planning to take away some dumplings for dinner, and perhaps Erin might want some too. However, Erin replied that she was outside. From their conversation, she learned that Erin was going on a business trip next week. She was about to ask Erin to come along to Wonthaggi with the girls. However, now it seemed impossible.

When finally reaching the ground floor, Cassie stepped out of the lift like an old lady as she sauntered like a snail. Once she was out of the building, the cold crisp night air splashed on her face, and in reflex, she put both hands inside her spring jacket. Holding on to her coat reminded her of the jacket she left in the tapas restaurant where she had lunch with Brad. She thought she could go there and check whether they kept it for her.

However, her tummy had already protested while passing her favourite dumpling restaurants. She decided to buy her dinner first. She thought having dinner while sitting lazily on her lounge sofa while watching Netflix seemed appealing.

As usual, she passed through the basketball court while walking towards the tram stop. No sound of the bouncing ball indicated no one was in the court. However, her eyes caught the tall figure leaning on the fence. Her lips parted as she did not expect to see Brad there. He seemed to be waiting for someone, with eyes staring down as usual and both hands inside his dark overcoat. It was a picturesque sight that created a wheeze in her heart. There was something dark and brooding about him, which she admitted she liked.

Is he waiting for me? She quickly warded off that silly thought. After having a meltdown in his apartment two days ago, she felt her whole face warm from blushing. There was a snap in her mind, thinking about how to avoid him. But it was too late as he realised her presence and immediately straightened up.

His eyes noticed the takeaway carrier in her hand. "Is that your dinner?"

Assuming his presence was just a coincidence, she decided to act normal. "Yeah, it's from one of the best dumpling restaurants in Chinatown," she responded.

"Your jacket is still in my apartment," he stated with tight lips. "You left it in the tapas restaurant. The waiter gave it to me."

Her lips drew a tentative smile as comprehension sunk in. "Ah, right! So you have it with you?"

He nodded. "It's in my apartment. You can have your dinner in my apartment, and then you can get your jacket at the same time."

"Alright." Then she cursed inwardly afterwards for answering without thinking. Erin's words resonated again in her head, which she quickly brushed off. She had been in his apartment twice before, and nothing had happened. The way he suggested the idea sounded like a friendly invite only, not a date!

"How's your ankle?" he asked while matching his pace with hers as they entered his apartment building.

"Better."

He opened the apartment door and let her enter first. Since it was her third time in this place, the living room with the window facing the city nightlife was the first area she stepped in. He seemed to read her mind.

"We can sit there having our dinner. I'll get your jacket first."

She contemplated whether she should take the jacket and excuse herself to leave. This could be another awkward meal they could have, like in the tapas restaurant. However, it was probably rude to change her mind now. *Just go with it, Cass!*

He returned with a paper bag containing her jacket, which she accepted with a murmur of 'thank you'. Before joining her in the living room, he prepared his salad in the kitchen.

Start bubbling, Cass, she thought. *It doesn't matter!*

And that was exactly what she did. She talked about her weekend plan to go to her parent's house with the girls while helping her parents prep the house for Tiffany's Hens party.

He had been quietly listening to her until he broke a question. "When is your birthday?"

Cassie just picked up a piece of dumpling into her mouth. It was a big piece, so munching it took her a while before she answered, "It falls on the fourth Saturday in October. Three weeks away."

"So, it's your 40th birthday?"

She did not expect that his eyes were on her. It was not for the first time her heart twitched, bumping into his gorgeous pair of eyes. She lowered her eyes, pretending to focus on the food while trying to debug her pounding heart.

She nodded. "Yes."

She did not care what he thought about her age. She would guess he must be younger than her. Or perhaps it was his fancy clothes that made him look younger?

"If it is not because of your sister's wedding, are you planning anything?"

She shrugged her shoulder. "Not exactly. But not every year you could have a birthday that falls on the weekend. I was actually thinking of celebrating it at my parents' house. All of us! My brother, the girls, and even Tiffany. It is hard to get everyone together when it falls on a weekday."

"That's a thoughtful plan," he murmured.

"In a way..." She paused while gazing distantly at the window and munching her food. "That wish is coming true. So I finally found a silver lining in my forgotten birthday." She chortled at her own silly words. "All of us will gather together because it's my sister's wedding! I guess I have nothing to complain about."

"Where is your sister's wedding?"

"I forgot the name of the place. I think it's in one of the wineries in Yarra Valley."

"Are you going with anyone?"

Somehow she could feel that his eyes had been on her for a while. It was unusual, and it made her heart quiver. She took a glimpse of him before lowering her eyes. "Do you mean a partner?"

"Yeah."

She chuckled. "I'm not expected to have one."

"I can come with you."

She took a shuddering breath as she heard those words, feeling a shiver on her skin, realising his eyes gazed intently at her.

"Thank you." She complimented herself for getting her wit back quickly. "But you don't need to. I'm not desperate." There was a bravado feeling for saying those words while she took the courage to look at him with a lifted chin.

"I know you're not," he murmured, but he never took his eyes off her.

She lowered her eyes down again, pretending to look at her food. Inwardly, she cursed herself for letting her heart bared two days ago. She must look desperate, and he took pity on her.

She lifted her head and looked him directly in the eyes. "I appreciate the offer, Brad. But that's not necessary. I don't want to trouble you. Besides, I'm saving the bride and the groom's money in a way."

"It's your birthday," he insisted. His face looked tense and stiff, but his voice sounded gentle and endearing.

Cassie felt a clench in her chest. His eyes were still on her, which intensified the trembling within her. She chuckled nervously and could not help the rupture in her voice. "Yeah, but the day will be about my sister, not me. I will be unnoticeable."

"That's not true."

As if hypnotised by his soft gaze, she kept still with her mouth hanging open. She hated herself for being pitied, for being seen as weak. Feeling a prick in her eyes, she blinked a couple of times, turning away, wishing he would not see her tears.

"You're not average, Cass." His gentle voice sent a warm shiver down her chest. She released a shuddering breath while her hands were uncontrollably cold, sweating and shaking. This time, she stared at the floor and did not dare to see him in the eyes.

"Not for me," he added. While her brain was still digesting the meaning of those words, he kneeled before her. He pressed his palm on her cheek and lowered his head to capture her lips.

Cassie's brain went freeze, and slowly her hand dropped the chopstick. Inevitably her eyes were shut, inhaling his scent. His tongue licked on her lips, asking for permission to taste her deeper, and willingly she let him in.

It was probably an unforgettable kiss. Mixed with the Monosodium glutamate, a.k.a MSG of pork dumplings and chilli oil. But as his tongue and lips explored her mouth profoundly, her soul was like being sucked in. Her body was weightless, and he seemed to know it as he wrapped her with his arm and pulled her against his broad chest.

Cassie had no idea how long the kiss was. She softly gasped when he pulled back, and cold air splashed on her. Their foreheads met, and his breath was on her cheek while her mind was still deliriously hazy. Their eyes were still shut for a moment before she took the courage to open them and fell into his spell. Having those eyes in such proximity was like swimming into a pool of calamity that she miserably needed at this moment.

There was something in the way he looked at her. She felt desperately wanted. Needed. And special. Her heart was flooded with a warm feeling that made her body seem to float. As his hand slipped into the back of her neck, he closed the space between them with a kiss that inflamed desire within her and burned every cell in her brain.

Chapter Twenty

The warm morning sunshine sneaking from the heavy blackout forced Cassie to pinch her eyes open. Initially, she wanted to continue her sleep, but her mind slowly cleared, realising that she was not in her room. Her room would not be this big and spacious, and not with wall-to-wall windows covered with heavy dark grey drapes. The bed she slept on was bigger and much more comfortable than hers. Her lips drew a content smile, recalling where she was now.

Brad's room.

Rolling herself to the side, she anticipated finding him there and feeling the well-toned of his body under her palm. But she was alone on that bed. She pushed herself up, put her ears up like a bunny, and tried to catch any noise from the ensuite bathroom. But there was only stillness. When her hands were smoothing the bedsheet, her fingers touched a piece of paper on Brad's pillow. She smiled, reading the notes.

You sleep like a baby, and I do not wish to wake you up. Sorry, I have to go. I have an important meeting to attend.

As he wrote 'meeting', her brain woke up. Today was still Thursday, meaning she still had to work. The time had shown 8 o'clock in the morning. She still had a bit of time to get ready. The only thing that made her laugh inwardly was wearing the same clothes as yesterday.

As she dressed and looked at her reflection in the mirror, she felt over the moon. She was still in disbelief at what happened last night, but it was something she would not mind repeating. Her eyes roamed around, observing the detailed grey, black and cream-coloured interior of the modern luxury of the spacious ensuite. Another smile appeared on her lips, recalling what they had done last night.

It was her first sex, but Brad made it effortless. There was a point she wanted to tell him to take it slow because it was her first, but her little pride held her up. However, he seemed could read her mind. Despite hearing his rushed breath as he caressed her bare skin with his lips, his restrained desire eyes kept asking for her permission to continue. Her pleasure moaning and shaky breath was her only answer.

The moment he was inside her, an electrical shock jabbed her head. Her hand squeezed the bedsheet with a mixture of pain and pleasure whining from her throat. However, as she got used to his rhythm, their eyes latched, their hands held each other, and they became like one.

It was beautiful lovemaking. That was what she felt.

The urge to wee woke her up in the middle of the night. Having no idea of the time except noticing that it was dark outside, she tried to catch her balance while tiptoeing towards the ensuite bathroom. While emptying her bladder, her vision adjusted to the light, and she began surveying her surroundings. It made her chuckle when the realisation hit her where she was.

Her eyes caught the shower room with the massive ceiling-mounted rainfall shower head she had ever seen in an apartment. The cold shower could probably be what she needed to wake her up from her dream. While soaking herself for a few minutes, she was wrapped under his sturdy arm instead. Her shoulder blade gently pressed against the cold tiles room as his lips hungrily tasted hers. Their pleasure cries and groans reverberated, with the sound of water flowing as their musical accompaniment while the wave of passion swayed them.

The next time she opened her eyes, he slept beside her peacefully. That was the moment she could observe his face. The falling fringe on his forehead made him look young, like a boy. Irresistibly she moved forward, brushing and nibbling his lips. It was an act of waking up a beast as he opened his eyes and shot her with an ardent, yearning gaze that made her heart tremble. He pulled her closer to him and dragged her into another passionate lovemaking.

Cassie looked at her reflection again in the mirror and chuckled at herself as she shoved her hair. Realising that the time was ticking, she quickly grabbed her bags and stepped out of the room. Her tummy grumbled, demanding some food, and the only thing she could find in the pantry was some nut bars and cereals. She grabbed a bowl, poured the cereal with a few drops of milk from the fridge and ate them in a rush. A magnetic notepad and pen stuck on the fridge gave her the idea to leave a note.

Sorry, I have used up your milk. I'll get some for you later after work.

She hated leaving the dirty dish in the kitchen sink as usual, so she quickly washed them before flying to the door.

As the lift took her down, one thing struck her mind that made her feel crazy. Until now, she still did not have his number.

In the evening, she dropped by again to the apartment with a bottle of milk after work. However, Brad was not there. He was not on the basketball court either.

Chapter Twenty-One

It was only two hours drive to her parent's house, but Cassie felt it like taking her ages. She tried to focus on her driving as much as possible since Ashleigh and Alicia were in the car. Their happy chatters in the back seat were her constant reminder not to let her mind drift away. She let out a long exhale. However, it could not chase away the hollowness in her chest.

Two days ago, she had her first sex with someone that seemed real, but she had not seen or heard anything from Brad since then. Every day after work, she went to the basketball court but could not find him there, and finally decided to leave a note with her mobile phone number and slipped it through his apartment door. However, it had been more than twenty-four hours since she left the note, and yet nothing from him.

The first thing that came into her mind was that probably something terrible had happened to him, perhaps an accident or family emergency. She wished that was not the case. So she asked the apartment concierge about his whereabouts. The man on duty could not reveal much except that they did not receive any concerning news about Brad.

Then why did he simply leave like that? She was disappointed for sure. She thought they had a great time. Perhaps it was fantastic for her, not necessarily for him. Perhaps he found her lousy in bed. But couldn't they talk about it as proper adults and try to work it out? She might be inexperienced, but she still could learn. Wasn't a solid relationship based on not only great sex but also communication?

Unless she was completely wrong about him. All his words about her when they kissed were just a lie. He only wanted to bed her, and that was all. She was only perhaps a hundredth woman whom he had slept with.

Having that theory in mind was enough to let tears well in her eyes. She reminded herself she was driving with the girls and had to stay safe. Quickly she blinked her eyes, wishing the tears would not affect her vision.

It was ironic. She did not believe in casual sex or a one-night stand, understanding how physical sex could involve a more profound feeling. Some people might take it lightly and move on, but not her. That was the reason she had been against it. And yet, she had fallen into one.

The moment their car entered her parent's house front yard, she let out a relieved sigh that she had safely brought the girls intact. Their arrival had been very much anticipated. After the first hour of settling down and short chatting, her mother started to call her to get to work.

It was practically a spring cleaning. Despite she, Kieran and Tiffany having grown up and lived in Melbourne most of the time, their parents still kept their rooms as they were. Every time they came to visit, they would sleep in their rooms. However, many of the old stuff was left behind, and now it was time to clean them up, to give more space for Tiffany's friends for the Hens party. Janine planned to put some extra mattresses on the floors, so everyone had a bed to sleep on.

The activity gave Cassie some space to distract her mind away from Brad. It took them the whole afternoon to pack and split the unwanted goods accordingly. The old books would go to the library, some toys for the toy library, kindergarten and child care centres, and some clothes for recycling. Janine was not interested in organising a garage sale as it would take too much time, while the Hens party would happen in a week.

Once everything was packed up, Cassie moved to the kitchen to prepare dinner as if it was just a habit. However, she was not herself. She burnt the sausages and the bread, cut herself while slicing some veggies for salad, and overcooked the pasta until they were soggy. Paul came to the kitchen and gently squeezed her shoulder.

"Let's go out and get some fish and chips," he smiled. "The girls would love it."

That was for sure! The moment Paul announced it, Ashleigh and Alicia jumped excitedly. Cassie threw all the unedible stuff into the garbage with her mother's complaining voice in the background.

They went to their favourite fish and chips restaurant, the best one in town, with outdoor decking facing the beautiful scenery of the beach. Ashleigh and Alicia finished their dinner almost instantly, then played on the decking harbour, giving some of their chips to the seagulls. Spring was approaching, but the night wind was quite chilly. Cassie was glad she and the girls wore jumpers.

"Are you alright, Cass?" quizzed Paul.

"I'm alright," Cassie answered weakly.

"What's bothering your mind? I have never seen you like this before," commented Janine.

Cassie blinked rapidly, did not expect her mother to pay that much attention to her behaviour. She always thought she would be 'invisible' in her mother's eyes.

She shook her head weakly. "Nothing," and continued munching her chips.

"Thank you for coming and helping, sweetheart. We appreciate your help." Her dad gave her a warm squeeze on her hand.

"Yeah, Cass. I can't imagine what we will do if you're not coming today," added her mother.

Cassie felt giddy hearing the compliment as her mother gazed at her tenderly. It seemed the last time she was showered with her mother's endearing eyes was ages ago. All this time, if not Kieran, perhaps only Tiffany would be the lucky recipient of it.

"It's alright, Mum, Dad. I'm happy to help."

"You're such a reliable person, Cass." Janine inhaled a deep breath. "You're always around when help is needed. I could not imagine how wrecked your brother was when Emily was gone, leaving him behind with two toddlers. If it were not because of you, I would not be able to sleep in peace. Somehow, knowing that you are also in Melbourne, I know Kieran would be able to pull this out. And it's proven even now. Thank you for taking the girls to see us."

Cassie did not expect the compliment. Her lips were parting as she gazed vacantly at the wooden decking.

"Now, perhaps it is a time to think about yourself, Cass," continued Janine. Cassie flicked her head up. "Alicia and Ashleigh are growing up and are in school now. I think Kieran can manage them better by now. Meanwhile, you're reaching forty soon. You're not a young girl anymore. So perhaps it's time that you think to find someone who could make you happy and build your own family."

As her breath stalled, Cassie looked down to hide her surprise. Never crossed her mind that her mother would say those words to her, an endearing mother gesture. She always thought her mother never cared about her, which she could understand because she was not her favourite. However, only now that she finally realise. Despite her mother being disgruntled about her spinsterhood, but in the inside , she had the biggest concern for her as a mother. The knowledge made Cassie's chest feel expanded, alleviating her current heart wound.

"Thanks, mum." Her voice was rich with emotion as tears pricked her eyes.

"Are you alright, my dear?" Paul squeezed her arm again.

The tone's genuine concern made her unable to control the ache that had been bottled in her chest. Cassie ducked her head, and buried her face in her palms.

"Oh, come here, Cass. Let me hug you." Janine opened her arm wide, letting Cassie crush herself into it. The warmth of her mother's arm induced her to sob even louder. But it had helped to lift the rock from her chest. At this point, she only felt blessed.

"Would you like to tell us what's bothering you?" asked Janine after the hug was released and her wrinkled palm wiped Cassie's wet cheek.

Cassie shook her head weakly with a smile that slowly built. "Nothing, mum. Nothing is bothering me. Trust me. I'm alright." And she said it with solid conviction.

"I know you'll be alright, Cass." Janine hugged her again. "I know you will be."

That night they all had a little camping in the house's backyard, where they all slept in a tent. It was a moment that Cassie would never stop being grateful about. It gave her strength that she would be able to face the truth about Brad, whatever it was.

Chapter Twenty-Two

It was a quiet week. Alicia and Ashleigh were in Wonthaggi, Kieran and Erin were away for a business trip. Cassie found herself alone after work most of the time. Her parents told her to take this opportunity to socialise more, perhaps joining drinks with her colleagues or hanging out with friends. She followed the advice, but it did not stop her from passing by the basketball court or going to Brad's apartment daily to check whether she would bump into him. Even her search on social media about him was fruitless. Perhaps he was not into social media, and she had no idea his full name.

There was one person she had in mind that might be able to help her. Chandra. She was sure Chandra or Tom must have Brad's contact number. Otherwise, Brad would not have come to their engagement party last time. Since she had more time for herself, she texted Chandra to meet up for a catch-up dinner. They met up in an Indonesian restaurant that Chandra was proud of for its authenticity.

She arrived at the restaurant before him and got herself seated. Chandra turned up a few minutes later with his glowing face. He gave her a light cheek peck, and they sat down and placed the order.

"Tom sends his apology. He has some work to do," began Chandra.

Speaking about work, Cassie felt it was a good time to mention Brad. "Are you still in the same project with him?"

"Not really. He moves to another humanitarian project in PNG."

"Is Brad involved as well with that project?"

There was a momentary silence as Chandra squished his eyebrow while picking up the chilli bottle on the table and pouring some into his fried rice. "Brad? No, not this one."

Cassie lowered her eyes, stirring around her *mie goreng* inside the plate. She did not wish to share with anyone that she had slept with

Brad, even with Chandra. Not until she understood what actually happened with him.

"Brad is one of the organisation's board members I work for." Chandra's voice made her lift her head. "His father is the chairman of our organisation's Western Australia chapter. Since his son is here, our management invited him to be the board member for our Victoria chapter."

"Right." Cassie nodded with a timid smile as if Chandra had just delivered a piece of news. Brad obviously held a vital role in the charity organisation that Chandra worked for. He must be busy as she knew he also had another job.

"Have you been seeing him lately?" She could not hold her curiosity anymore. Hesitantly she studied Chandra's facial reaction. There was no flinch or any sign of jolt.

"No. Not lately," replied Chandra while munching his food. "I heard he's going to see his parents, though. I guess some family matters come up."

Here it goes! Cassie felt she had just won a jackpot and felt an unexpected release of tension. That was probably her answer to why she had not seen him recently on the basketball court. Perhaps he was trying to contact her too, but his family matter took precedence. She should understand that would be the case.

Her lips were parting as she struggled with her inner turmoil about whether to ask Chandra for Brad's phone number. The words were just on the tip of her tongue before Chandra diverted the topic to upcoming Tiffany's wedding and her birthday. He asked her to pick a date after the wedding, as he offered his place to have a simple birthday celebration for her. It was a question that gave another fullness to her heart and pushed away the unsettledness about Brad.

For the time being.

Chapter Twenty-Three

"Bullies are people who try to shield their insecurity by coercing others whom they perceive as vulnerable. They are equally desperate to be loved and accepted, and they go out of their way to make people feel unaccepted so they are not alone."

The weekend of Tiffany's Hens party finally arrived. Kieran drove Cassie to Wonthaggi, picking up Alicia and Ashleigh back to Melbourne, joined by Paul. It was not a time Cassie would look forward to, but she was expected to be there. Not only by Tiffany but also by her mother, to ensure that the guests were well served with sufficient food and drinks.

Seeing Ruby and Chelsea was another reason that made Cassie drag her feet. However, it seemed she had no choice. Where else could she sleep tonight if not in this house? Also, she knew that she and her mother would be the ones cleaning up the mess the following day.

As she had expected too, it was a crazy wild party. Tiffany had assumed the whole house for herself and her twenty gals. A male stripper was called. With his smoking hot six-pack body and lap dancing on the bride-to-be, he alone was enough to rock the house with hysterical screaming. It was one of the things that Cassie perhaps could never imagine for herself. Tiffany was probably right. She would be an old maid for the rest of her life anyway.

Her bemused expression invited scornful smiles from her sister. Tiffany grabbed her arm and steered her palm to the male stripper's alluring pectoral. She was paralysed instead of resisting or jerking away shyly, like perhaps her sister had expected. The shadow of Brad's well-toned broad chest immediately struck her memory. Her palm lingered for a while before her mind finally returned to the present once her eyes clashed with the stripper's deep blue eyes.

He was not Brad.

Slowly she lowered her hand and looked away.

"You can have him for tonight if you want to," whispered Tiffany before her sister squealed loudly in the room, continuing her seductive dancing to the stripper.

It was a sight that Cassie felt was inappropriate. Janine even looked away, pretending not to see it and did not wish to reprimand.

As the night was getting deeper, the dusk settling in and the moon peeking in, Cassie decided to be alone in the backyard while sipping her beer as her solace. Although her parent's house did not have direct access to the beach, the sound of the beach wave still reached her ear. She threw herself on the three-seater outdoor swing that had been her favourite solitary spot since she was little.

The image of Brad's hazel flickering amber eyes had been haunting her. She could not deny that she had missed him. It had been over a week now, and still, nothing from him. Doubts started creeping in the more she thought about him. If Brad were really into her, he would simply get her contact number from Chandra or Tom. However, he did not. Or he had not.

Another negative thought also slithered in. Someone like Brad, handsome and wealthy, perhaps would usually do casual sex easily. Many women would be in line to taste him on his bed. It was a thought that made her chest tighten. Brad did not seem that kind of person unless she was completely wrong. And if she was, what could she do unless accepting the reality?

However, it did not mean they could not stay as friends.

Her lips drew in a faint smile with the thought. If she were much younger, perhaps still in her twenties or early thirties, if she was ditched without any word like this, she would not even think of staying in touch as friends. However, perhaps because of her ageing, what was the point to remain angry and resentful? Let the past become the past, and they could move on even as friends. Regardless, they had something special. Though it did not mean anything to him, and it hurt, it was still part of her life that she would be grateful for.

She emptied her first beer bottle before opening another one. She had prepared a couple of bottles because she knew she would not be content with only one. The sound of crickets filling the tranquillity of the night became her other company. However, when a shadow blocked the dim garden light, her head snapped up, realising someone was approaching.

"Hi, Koala." The uninvited company grinned at her. "How are you?"

Something in the way Chelsea looked at her sent a chill on her nape. One of Tiffany's best friends, whom she swore to avoid today, sat beside her without hesitation despite her silent cold response. Chelsea looked strikingly sexy with her tank top and shorts. The night wind swayed her over-the-shoulder blonde hair.

Cassie blinked a couple of times, checking her vision as Chelsea's seductive shimmering blue eyes and twitched lips directed at her. Chelsea also leaned closer to her. Too close, in her opinion.

"I'm well, thank you." Cassie shifted uncomfortably, keeping her cool, gazing distant and sipping her beer.

"You look upset. Are you alright?"

A warm palm landed on her knees unexpectedly, which jolted her to turn her head back.

"I'm alright. Thanks for asking," she answered clipped, wishing that hand would move away from her knee.

But it did not.

Despite the cold night air, Cassie was wearing shorts, too. She had her college basketball hoody jumper and the beers in her hand to add the warmth. With Chelsea's hand on her knee, their skins were practically touched. That small hand glided further upward to her thigh a few seconds later. Her breath hitched, but as her head started feeling giddy, she emptied her bottle and looked away.

The blast of the house system amplifier jolted her up. They had requested permission from the nearby neighbours, so at least looking at the time, they still had a couple of hours to have the music on. The upbeat music from Bruno Mars 'Locked out of Heaven' was then cued in, followed by frenzied squeals from the guests.

A sensation touch on her core stalled her breath, and before her brain came around to figure out what caused it, a pleasure moan escaped from Cassie's lips.

"Perhaps I can help you, Koala." A soft sultry voice whispered in her ear. "Just relax and enjoy."

Her head was heavily spinning, and her vision blurred as Bruno Mars's tenor euphonious voice hit in.

Never had much faith in love or miracles (Ooh)
Never wanna put my heart on the line (Ooh)
But swimming in your water's something spiritual (Ooh)
I'm born again every time you spend the night (Ooh)
'Cause your sex takes me to paradise
Yeah, your sex takes me to paradise
And it shows
Yeah, yeah, yeah

Immersed in his dark desire eyes, as breathless as she was, the tingling nerve within her was endless. Stroking himself inside her in a holistic rhythm, his lips tormented her with a passionate kiss and caress that sent buzzing throughout her body.

'Cause you make me feel like
I've been locked out of heaven
For too long, for too long
Yeah, you make me feel like
I've been locked out of heaven
For too long, for too long

Her heart hammered acceleratedly as his thrusts drowned her into a delirious euphoria she had never experienced before. Her fingers clutched to his bare muscled arm as her head flinched backward with a yearning, whimpering voice that she would never imagine slipped from her throat.

Cassie was unaware of the present world. Her ears were nibbled as a heat of breath brushed her neck. The state of ecstasy she was in deepened further as the centre of her thighs tightened.

She could not help but release another wail as the tension intensified. Everything seemed fuzzy, her legs weak, and her breath stalled in her throat. Slowly her eyes fluttered open, and the night sky with its dots of stars lay before her.

Brad's tender gaze was smiling at her. The urge to touch his cheek pushed her to stretch out her hand. However, her palm landed on a lump instead. It was something that tossed her back to the present. She blinked her eyes a couple of times as her mind slowly cleared. Chelsea's face appeared with a sensual twitch on her lips. And before she reacted, her lips were captured.

Cassie flinched and pushed herself away, jumping out of the swing. As her breath suspended within a second, she turned around at her intruder in horror.

"What the hell are you doing?" Her voice sounded hoarse to her ear. As her mind began to clear on what had just happened, the sound of the rushing heartbeat in her chest reached her ear. She tried to get hold of herself with her shaky legs.

"I'm just helping you, Koala." Chelsea stood up from the swing with a smug smile drawn on her lips. " You know, it's not only men who could satisfy your needs."

Sensing danger was still lingering, Cassie took a few steps back, keeping a distance between them. "I don't need your help. Just stay away from me! Go back inside! Tiffany must be looking for you."

Perhaps the way she spoke sounded like a teacher reprimanding a student. Chelsea scoffed and shook her head with both her hands on her waist.

"Come on, Koala. You have to admit that you like it."

The scorn made Cassie's heart boil. "You took advantage of me," she snarled.

"Don't you understand, Koala? You just have to accept it. You are like me! Otherwise, you would be the one in the wedding dress like Tiffany by now. But that's okay. It's not too late yet. We can be great together."

Her head jerked back as her eyes widened. Confusion flooded Cassie's mind. *Like her? What does she mean? Great together with her?*

"I don't understand." She quickly raised her hand when Chelsea gravitated further toward her. "What do you mean by us being together?"

Chelsea's face softened. "I like you, Koala. Don't you understand? What are you waiting for? I can help you realise how great your feeling would be when you let yourself go."

She likes me? Cassie's mouth hung open as her brain tried to digest those words. Her body went stiff as her eyes stared at Chelsea bewilderedly. As Chelsea sauntered towards her and cupped her face, her muscles went rigid. She could feel the warmth of her breath and the flowery fragrance of her perfume. Her vision went blurred as Chelsea lowered her head and sealed her lips again.

Alarmed by the audacity, Cassie shoved her away.

"Hang on, hang on!" Her hand flapped as she tried to catch her balance while stepping backward. She was still in disbelief at what had happened. Chelsea liked her? But all this time, what she heard from this woman was only mocking words for her!

"You're always making fun of me!" she growled.

Chelsea's lips broke into a pretend sweet smile. "Come on, Koala. I am just joking around. I'm teasing you because I like you. I'm trying to get your attention."

Trying to get attention by mocking her? A shock sheathed Cassie's face as she started hypervalent. "I don't like being called Koala," she scoffed.

Chelsea released a soft laugh. "That's my endearing call for you."

"And I hate it," Cassie interjected coldly. "I have asked you to stop it, but you keep doing it."

Chelsea's face coloured. Guilt-ridden eyes started to come to a surface. "Alright, I'll stop calling you Koala. I thought you liked it."

"I appreciate it if you do that."

When Cassie regained her composure, she reminded herself to stay on guard. Still keeping the distance between them, she darted a stern look at the woman before her, who claimed she had been interested in her despite bullying her all this time. Her hands hid behind her back, clenching tightly.

Chelsea's face lit up as her lips broke into another grin. "So, shall we have fun now?"

"No."

As she had expected, a puzzlement immediately hit Chelsea's facade. She quietly took a deep breath while her mind was scrambling for the right words without the intention of hurting anyone's feelings.

"You're a beautiful woman, Chelsea." Her voice pierced through the dreadful silence between them. "But you're my sister's best friend. I always take you as my own sister."

Chelsea scoffed. "Don't treat me like a kid. I'm an adult too, though I'm much younger than you."

"I know." Cassie shut her eyes for a moment, expecting such a reaction. "But I know who I want. And it's not you, Chelsea. I'm sorry, but it's not you."

Chelsea's expression became tight as her lips pursed into a thin line. Cassie had expected this and instinctively took another step back while gripping the hem of her jumper tightly, anticipating the subsequent reaction.

"You don't like me?" growled Chelsea with titled head and flaring nostrils.

How could I like you? What made her think that consistent rude jokes were a way of flirting to get attention?

However, Cassie restrained herself from spitting out those words. She could not deny that it had never crossed her mind to like Chelsea, even as a friend, not after all these years what this young woman did was mocking her. But seeing the sting of rejection in those alluring round blue eyes reminded her how young this woman was. Like Tiffany.

"I do like you. As a sister," she gulped. She hated to lie and purposedly lowered her eyes, avoiding Chelsea's protruding eyes on her. However, her head jerked back as Chelsea suddenly broke into a burst of bark laughter.

"Are you saying you've met someone?" squealed Chelsea while holding her stomach against her shaking laughter. "Who's the idiot?"

It was a reaction that made Cassie take another sigh. This woman was back to her bullying mode. She pursed her lips and did not wish to retaliate against that sentence.

The laughter eventually subsided. As she still stood in her place, watching Chelsea with a pinched expression, a sorry feeling sneaked in.

Bullies were just someone who tried to shield their insecurity by coercing others that they perceived as vulnerable. That was exactly what Chelsea did. Cassie now understood what Chelsea had been struggling to hide -her true sexual orientation.

There was only silence between them while Bruno Mars' music still played in the background. As her laughter finally died down, Chelsea's facial expression darkened. Her lips were pursed tightly as her fist clenched. "You're pathetic!." And with those last words, she twirled her body around and fled the place.

Cassie was quietly relieved, seeing that sexy blonde silhouette fade into the house. Her lungs expanded through a satisfied breath as a sense of pride filled her for calmly handling the earlier drama.

She was anxious that she might need to share her bedroom with Chelsea and Ruby tonight. Fortunately, Janine asked her to sleep in her bedroom together with Tiffany. Her mother said she wanted to reminisce about when all her girls were only girls.

As expected, everyone left the place the following day without helping clean up the mess. Drawing another deep breath, Cassie was quietly grateful she did not bump into Chelsea when that woman left.

Chapter Twenty-Four

Exhausted. That was the only word Cassie had in mind.

After returning from Wonthaggi on Sunday night, she immediately went to bed. However, she woke up the following day feeling fatigued. She forced herself to get up, thinking it was just her Monday blue feeling, and once she got to work, she could return to her routine.

However, she was mistaken. Reaching Wednesday, she decided to take a break. Brad's matter still clouded her mind, plus what Chelsea did to her at Tiffany's Hens Party disturbed her. Plus, maybe because she was reaching 40 years old soon, she felt old and rusty. Although she went to work in the morning, she asked for permission for sick leave after lunchtime.

While strolling through the park on her way home, something jolted her mind. Brad mentioned where his office building was before. Though she had no idea exactly which floor he would be on, perhaps she could try to find out. Recalling Chandra mentioned that Brad was the board member for the charity organisation Chandra worked for, her fingers tapped on her mobile screen, googling the information.

She cursed inwardly for not thinking about this before. Brad's profile was the first in line for the board members section, and only then did she find out his full name and the name of the company he owned. She googled further to confirm that the company's office was indeed at the Rialto tower, complete with its floor level. Her successful research rushed her adrenaline, making her lips tremble as tears rolled down her cheek simultaneously. She giggled, glancing around to feel relieved that no one was watching her.

Half running, half brisk walking, she went to Rialto Tower. She did not bother to check any tram route going in that direction. However, before she entered the building's main rotating door, her eyes caught a familiar black glossy Tesla parked off the street. She was convinced it was Brad's car even though she could not recall his car's plate number. So that could possibly be Brad back in Melbourne!

Her heart leapt with joy. Twirling her body, she was about to enter the building. However, her body went stiff as she saw his tall, broad-shoulder figure a few meters from her and about to enter the building. Instead of running into him, her head turned around frantically, trying to find a hiding spot. She ran to the nearest wall and pressed her body as much as possible as if she could disappear through it. From her peripheral view, she was sure Brad did not see her. As usual, his eyes were staring down. Meanwhile, a gracefully dressed young woman walked beside him, her hands clinging to his sturdy arm.

It was a sight that made her chest tight as she clenched her trembling moist hands. That woman looked familiar, and she recalled that she had seen her before with Brad in the bridal shop and Philip Island. How could she not think about this before? He had been with someone! And yet, they made love.

While seeing him and the woman slowly disappearing into the building, she had probably forgotten to breathe. Her vision was a blur as her fatigue returned. She let out a huge exhale, and with her shoulder down, she sauntered away.

Like a lost person, she had no idea where she was heading for a moment. The hustle-bustle of Melbourne CBD traffic full of car horns, pedestrian crossing signal sound, building construction and people chattering were like an echo sound to her ear. After walking for three blocks aimlessly, her mind slowly cleared. The only thing she needed now was her bed.

Throughout her lifeless walk, the ache within her and throughout her body intensified. Despite what she and Brad had was great, it did not change the fact it was just casual. She was almost forty, and yet she failed to judge someone's character. Or perhaps she was too quick to judge? Would there be a better explanation from Brad? She had no idea if she could give him a chance to explain. Since he was back, that meant he had seen the notes she left for him in his apartment. He could contact her if he wanted to. But he did not. Or perhaps he had not. He was probably just busy. Even too busy for her.

Cassie shook her head, feeling silly with the turmoil in her mind, but could not help the prick in her eyes. In her choked desolation, her mobile phone ringtone startled her. Seeing the incoming caller, she quickly rubbed her tears and cleared her throat before answering.

"Tiff?"

"Cass! You must help me!" Her sister's voice sounded freaked out and desperate. "Chelsea pulled out as my maid of honour."

The words boomed between Cassie's ears. Her lips parted as she felt a stab in her chest. This should have been expected. A bully would not accept defeat easily. Obviously, Chelsea wanted to take revenge on her through Tiffany.

"Why?" Her voice sounded raspy to her own ear. But it was still far from Tiffany's notice as her sister started to rant.

"I don't know! We were having lunch, and she said she was not in the mood to be the maid of honour. She just wanted to quit. She said it took too much of her time!"

"But you're her best friend."

"I know, Cass. I can't believe she is doing this to me. "

Cassie took a sigh while rubbing her temple as dizziness set in. What is a definition of a best friend? It seemed her sister still had no idea what it meant.

"That is very childish," she murmured.

"Well, I still have a wedding to run. I am not letting her ruin it. You must help me, Cass!"

Don't you have any other best friend, Tiff? Aren't you the cool popular chick in school? Cassie complimented herself for holding her tongue, not spitting out the words. Instead, with a defeated sigh, she asked, "What do you want me to do? I have to get myself fitted with the maid of honour's dress?"

"That's not necessary. But you will be the main contact for everything from now on. Chelsea gave me the list of all the vendors. It's about ensuring everything is in place—the final number of guests and the seating arrangement. Oh, speaking of which, please make sure aunt Marie and uncle Bernie sit far away from Mum and Dad. I don't want them to distract Mum too much with their non-stop gossip. Also, please ensure the cake, limousine, and photographer arrive on time. Ruby will still be around helping me with the dress and the bouquet."

Is that all Ruby has to do?

"Alright."

"Great! I am sending you the list now to your email. Please have a look at it tonight, Cass. I still have the last fitting of the wedding gown tomorrow, medi pedi on the next day, and we have the last rehearsal on Friday evening. Don't be late! I've got to back to work now. This has been a crazy day. Bye, Cass!"

The conversation ended, and Cassie only expelled a huge breath while shutting her eyes in pain before dragging her feet again. Hailing an uber would be the next thing she could think of, as much as her body yearned for her bed. She was sure she would collapse if she was still outside in the next half an hour.

When she entered the apartment, she was expecting solitude. Instead, the noises of wall bumping greeted her. She glanced around, seeing no one in the living room or kitchen. However, certainly, there was someone in the bedroom. Immediately she was on guard. Letting the door open, she strode to the kitchen and grabbed a frying pan.

While walking closer to Erin's room, the noise changed into a murmur talking between two people. One voice definitely sounded like Erin, but the other, a male voice, sounded like...

Cassie lowered down her frying pan. It seemed her housemate was also not at work, and she seemed to have fun with someone in this broad light of day. Letting out a relieved breath, she was ready to turn to her room and crash herself there. But suddenly, Erin's room door flew open.

For a couple of seconds, both of them were stunned like statues, eyes widening with blanched faces. Only the sound of a tram bell hovering in the distance filled the air.

It was not the first time Cassie found her housemate brought someone back to the apartment. She never questioned who that person was unless Erin chose to introduce them. But this time, an introduction was unnecessary. Because seeing the person standing behind Erin instantly increased Cassie's headache.

"Kieran?" She could not believe that she still had the energy to speak.

"Oh my..." Erin's hand flew to her mouth before she closed her eyes briefly and opened them again, flooded with guilt.

The scene before her seemed to drain Cassie's energy. With her lips still parting open, blurry vision and dry throat, she dazed hazily at the two people before her. Despite that, her brain was still trying to crack what was happening before her. Her brother and her housemate were in the room together. Looking at their dishevelled appearance, well...Kieran's shirts were still unbuttoned. Thank God he was already in his pants! And Erin was only in her bikini underwear. That meant.....

"Cass..." Kieran's baritone voice pierced the silence as his adam apple bobbed nervously. "Let me explain..."

An unnatural silence fell. It gave time for Cassie to gain her wit back finally. Her agape mouth slowly shut, and as comprehension started to sink in, she finally let out a breath that seemed overdue to escape from her throat. Seeing both her beloved brother and her housemate, whose eyes stared at the floor without any courage to look at her, an amusement tickled within her. She found the two grown-ups before her like two teenagers caught red-handed and ready to be scolded by their parents.

She cleared her throat, folded her arms and gave them an arched eyebrow.

Kieran lifted up his head and swallowed nervously. "We're together," he murmured and lowered his eyes again.

"Until when are you going to hide this from me?" She purposely made her voice sound rigid. She had to admit she was still in disbelief. But somehow, she knew this would happen. Recalling the past, she now understood why Erin was so eager to help with Alicia and Ashleigh's errands. Perhaps her housemate had been eyeing her brother from the beginning.

No answer as both Kieran and Erin pursed their lips.

"Do the girls know?" Cassie asked. This time she received a weak shake of the head.

She shook her head with a huff. "I can't believe that you do this in broad daylight."

Erin swallowed the lump in her throat before finally her eyes lifted to Cassie. "We met during the business trip," she began quietly.

The words somehow struck Cassie instead. "So, you've been together since the business trip?"

The question made the duo nod weakly.

Cassie tilted her head. "Where did you go again for your business trip?" She knew Kieran went to Sydney but never asked the detail from Erin where she went.

"Sydney."

"Were you actually on a business trip or having a holiday together?" shot Cassie with a more fierce tone, despite it took a herculean effort within her not to reveal the smirk that threatened to sneak on her face. It made the atmosphere in the room even more intense. Kieran and Erin lowered their heads even deeper.

"I can't believe you let me take the girls and help mum and dad by myself while you're having fun, bro." Cassie put both hands on her waist while giving her brother a harsh look.

Finally understanding that he had to face this as a man, Kieran lifted up his eyes to her. "Sorry, Cass. I did not mean to neglect you or the girls. Tiffany's Hens party made everything more difficult."

"Don't blame Tiffany," snapped Cassie.

Kieran swallowed nervously. "I know. I'm sorry, Cass. Please let me know how I can make this up."

Bingo! Those were the words that Cassie had been waiting for. With a pretend angry mask, she quietly enjoyed seeing the pair in front of her, who seemed remorseful and willing to do anything to gain her forgiveness. Fortunately, Kieran and Erin were too nervous even to notice her act.

"That's easy." Cassie twirled around to the living room to hide her almost unrestrained laugh. She turned around again, facing the couple, and returned to her stern facial expression. "Chelsea pulled out as a maid of honour. Tiffany passed all her jobs to me."

As she had expected, her housemate and brother lifted their heads with dropped jaws and bewildered eyes.

"What happened?" roared Kieran.

Cassie did not intend to share what Chelsea did at the Hens party. She shrugged lightly with a sigh. "I have no idea. Tiffany said Chelsea is not in the mood anymore."

"Is she for real?" squealed Erin. "In less than a week before the wedding? What kind of friend is she?"

Kieran sighed heavily while shoving his hair. "Well, I hope this gives a lesson to Tiffany in choosing her friends."

"Come on, bro. They've grown up together. Who knows, someone could change?" commented Cassie while throwing herself to the couch in the living room. Her fatigue returned, and she started feeling dizzy. Once her pretend act ended, all her limbs suddenly became weak. However, she was determined not to let them know what was actually bothering her more.

"Of course, Cass. Even without mentioning it, I'll help you too. This is for our little sister, right?" Kieran's voice had a hint of annoyance as he rolled his eyes. "Anytime."

"Good!" Cassie snapped her finger. "So, bro. The first thing you need to do is to add another guest to the wedding invite list."

Kieran frowned as he darted her a blank look. It was a sight that made Cassie could not hide her mischievous grin anymore.

"Erin also needs to redeem herself. So, she has to be added to the guest list as your partner attending the wedding," winked Cassie.

The tease made both Erin and Kieran's expressions become relaxed, followed by a hint of blush on Erin's cheek.

Though finding their relationship had helped to distract Cassie's mind away from Brad for a bit, it still did not prevent her headache from bugging her again. She gathered her strength to get up from the couch and straightened her spine with a lifted chin, walking boldly like a soldier, despite her body screaming, longing for her bed.

However, her slack expression did not escape her brother's notice.

"Are you alright, Cass? Why are you home early too?"

Fortunately, she was already at her room door, with her back on Erin and Kieran. However, she reminded herself to act normal. Quietly taking a deep breath, she turned her head around briefly.

"I'm alright. I have a headache. "

"Are you unwell, Cass?" Erin asked with a concerned tone.

She glanced back briefly again, wishing no one noticed the prick in her eyes that she even could not understand why suddenly itched.

She was not used to being asked such a caring question. She was the one who usually asked the question to the people she cared about. Nevertheless, the question sent a tremble vibe within her, sending another prick of pain in her nose and eyes.

"I'm..." *Darn!* Her voice now started to crack as well. "I'm alright. I just need to sleep." It was such a brusque answer as she rushed to shut the door.

The darkness in the room greeted her, but it was all she needed. Quietly she felt relieved that Erin and Kieran had let her alone. Once her body touched the bed, she drifted to sleep within seconds.

Chapter Twenty-Five

Melbourne was blessed with a perfect Spring cool breeze and warm sunshine at the top of twenty-three degrees celsius. It was a fabulous day for any event and another flawless thing that could happen in Tiffany's life. Since the wedding would mostly be done outdoors, it was like a gamble to play with the weather, though marques had been set up. Although the weather had been on her side, Tiffany was not satisfied.

Cassie now understood the true meaning of bridezilla.

In almost every little thing, Tiffany was frantic. Even for a tiny black spot on her cinderella white glass wedding slipper, which would go unnoticed by anyone or even be captured in her wedding photo, Tiffany was hysterical and asked Ruby to clean it up. Witnessing that, Cassie only shook her head behind her sister's back when she had a chance. Unavoidably, she was also the recipient of her sister's unnecessary yelling.

It was such a relief when Paul, Janine, Kieran, and the girls finally popped their heads at the door to wish the bride personal congratulations. Janine immediately squealed, admiring Tiffany's wedding dress. Her Spanish guitar figure was wrapped in a deep plunge vee neckline on the front and back, making the swell of her side breasts peek. There was also a deep parting on her skirt that revealed her thigh's smooth, silky skin. It was a sight that instead made Paul squish his eyebrow.

"Wow!" Paul swallowed hard. "Tiff, you look like...."

Cassie could see her father's deep frown, trying hard to find the right words.

"Isn't she fabulous?" Janine interjected. But it still did not hide Paul's disagreement with the comment.

"I have no idea there is such a wedding dress," he murmured.

Cassie exchanged glances at her brother as they repressed their smirk together.

The exciting squeal from Alicia and Ashleigh distracted them as her nieces cheered her 'Happy Birthday' and threw themselves at her. With the hecticness in wedding preparation since morning, the birthday wishes were a pleasant surprise that warmed Cassie's heart. In truth, her mind was too focused on Tiffany's wedding that she even had forgotten that today was also her 40th birthday.

"I have a pressie for you later," whispered her father, giving her a tight hug and kisses on both cheeks.

Cassie chuckled. "Thanks, dad. You treat me like a little girl. I am forty years old now."

"You're still my little girl." Paul squeezed her shoulder while planting a kiss on her temple.

Her eyes then turned to Kieran, who was waiting for his turn. Her brother squeezed her hard in his arm until her feet were off the floor for a couple of centimetres.

"Happy birthday, sis. I have prepared something special for you."

With the remaining laughter, Cassie released herself from the hug and found the smirk on her brother's lips. "Thanks, bro. Do you still feel guilty for sneaking with Erin behind me?" she teased.

Kieran blushed. "A bit. The pressie is from all of us."

Alicia chimed in. "Yes, aunt Cassie, you'll love it. You deserve it."

"Psst Alicia!" Ashleigh reprimanded her sister. "It's a surprise. Don't tell aunt Cassie what it is."

Alicia's hands immediately flew to her mouth. It was a scene that warmed Cassie's heart as she laughed at it.

Cassie could sense that her brother and Erin were worried about her since she buried herself in her room after finding out about them. She had assured them they did not cause her lack of vigour, and they knew it. However, she did not wish to tell them the real reason. At this moment, she just wanted to treasure every moment she could have with her family on Tiffany's big day.

The thought of the bride made Cassie steal a glance at her sister, who was talking to her mother. Tiffany looked upset, with a pout spread over her wonderfully done make-up, and her mother seemed to be trying to console her. It made Cassie wonder what other trivial thing that was distressing her sister. However, she ignored it and focused on getting everything in order.

"Where's Erin?" asked Cassie.

"Outside. She has been welcoming and ushering the guests to sit at their designated places," answered Kieran.

Cassie smiled. "Well done."

The very person mentioned suddenly popped up at the door. Erin signalled that it was time for the ceremony to start. It was a piece of news that jolted Tiffany into another panic mode, complaining about her veil. Janine tried calming her down while Kieran quickly pushed his girls to go out and prepare. Cassie only watched the scene while shaking her head.

"Are you going on your honeymoon soon, Tiff?" Ruby's voice piped in when everyone was already out, leaving only three of them in the room.

It was probably a question asked at the wrong time. It only intensified Tiffany's agitation.

"No! Joshua's boss doesn't want to let him go until after the project launch!"

"When is that?" asked Cassie.

"In three weeks."

"Oh, that's not too bad."

Tiffany rolled her eyes and huffed. "You don't understand, Cass. You're not the newlywed. Of course, you don't understand!"

Inevitably Cassie winced, and from her peripheral view, Ruby also flinched. Cassie only took it lightly, understanding that her sister was under the pump. She took a quiet sigh while following Tiffany, who walked impatiently to the mouth of the wedding aisle in a walking style far from elegant.

The ceremony began, and Cassie had to admit that Tiffany had thought about every single item of her wedding pretty well. From the decoration, the flower arrangement, the colour theme for the family's dresses, the wrist corsage, the singer and the band, to the food at the wedding reception itself. When it was time for the dance between the father and the bride, it was such a heartwarming moment that Cassie felt her heart tremble, and she could not help shedding tears.

The wedding speeches from every groom and bride's family member were touching. Cassie felt a swell of pride when hearing her father's address and quietly wished her father would make such a great speech on her wedding day, too one day. Cassie knew that Kieran felt relieved that he was not asked to give any speech, and she was sure Tiffany would not ask him either.

For the rest of the afternoon, the atmosphere became more relaxed. The bride looked glowing and danced happily with her new husband. Cassie took a glass of wine, thinking of mingling with some of their distant relatives. However, just a second after leaving her table, a couple approached her.

"Hi, Cass. Are you alone?"

Chelsea smiled mischievously at her in the arm of a man that looked like one of Joshua's best men. The corsage on his blazer was the indication.

This woman would be the last person Cassie would expect to see in this wedding, especially after her last-minute pull-out stunt from her crucial role as maid of honour. Cassie could not believe Chelsea still had the gut to attend the wedding. Before she recovered from her shock and thought about retorting the question, Ruby joined them with her partner.

"Needs help to find a partner?"

"No, I'm fine!" snapped Cassie, then her eyes narrowed at Chelsea. "Why are you here? Does Tiffany know you're here?"

"Of course." Chelsea lifted her chin arrogantly. "Without me, Tiffany would not be as cool as now, having a handsome husband like Joshua. She owes me. " She walked toward her closer and whispered in her ear. "If you did not refuse me last time, you would not be this pathetic, Cass."

Cassie's lips pressed tightly into a white slash while clutching at the side of her Audrey Hepburn-style soft pink dress. Her neck went stiff as she restrained the spark of anger ignited in her. She did not give a damn about coming here with a partner or not and would not let herself be affected by this. She darted a sharp glare at Chelse with a defiant lifted chin.

Perhaps she would confront this woman if it were not because they were at Tiffany's wedding. They probably needed to talk to settle their scores. She decided to ignore the two bullies like she always used to for the sake of peace on Tiffany's big day. However, before she twirled around to escape the tension, an arm snaked around her waist, and her lips were captured with a firm, masculine lip.

Her breath instantly stalled as her whole body went numb. The sensation on her lips was hot, full of vigour and longing. Her body was pulled closer and tighter as her hand splayed to the broad, solid chest of the kisser. While inhaling the familiarity of his earthly masculine scent, she felt like she was being carried into heaven.

Cassie had no idea how long she was floating in her own paradise. It was a need for air that broke their kiss. Half panting, she could not open her eyes for a moment, wishing she could savour that kiss longer. His gentle deep voice was the one she longed to hear in her dream every night.

"Sorry, I'm late. Happy birthday."

It probably took her a couple of minutes before she finally opened her eyes. The first thing she saw was his chest in a white shirt and dark grey blazer. Her finger fiddled on the button of his shirt as if she fell into some spell. Her mind was hazy. An exclaimed noise cheering sound echoing Tiffany and Joshua's name was the one slapping her back to the present. She lifted up her head, only to be captivated by his gorgeous pair of eyes for an endless time.

What the hell is he doing here?

"Mr Rilley!" A shout coming from a distance made his eyes shift away from her. "I don't know that Joshua is inviting you."

Cassie felt a thud in her chest as her mind slowly cleared. She was still in disbelief, finding herself in Brad's broad chest and arm. In front of hundreds of people, at Tiffany's wedding party! She only stared at Brad's adam's apple as his body tensed, looking at the people who watched them bewilderedly.

"Hi, Ryan." His voice sounded hoarse. "I..." His eyes were back at her, lifted up for a brief moment, and back to her with puzzlement spread across his face.

"This is Joshua's wedding, Mr Rilley," explained Ryan. But before he continued, the groom himself rushed to them with equal astonishment.

"Mr Rilley, I don't expect to see you here!" exclaimed Joshua. His eyebrow was arched when his eyes landed on Brad's arm, circling Cassie's waist. "I don't know that you and Cassie are together."

The words were enough to increase Cassie's heartbeat.

"I don't know..," Brad stuttered. "I don't know that you're related to Cassie."

And I have no idea that you know my new brother-in-law!

Cassie wobbly straightened herself up with her shaky knee. Quietly she felt grateful that Brad's hand was still on her waist to support her. Otherwise, for sure, she would embarrass herself by falling. Realising all eyes were on her, she took a calming breath. She was never the centre of attention, so this was definitely unsettling.

"Well,..." she chuckled nervously as she absolutely had no idea what to say.

"Cassie, Mr Rilley is the Chief IT Director of the organisation I work for," explained Joshua. "Perhaps I have not mentioned where I work, so you can't link our connection. But, anyway, what a small world." He turned to Brad with a solemn, formal smile. "I'm glad that you're here, Mr Rilley. Welcome to my wedding." He came forward and offered a handshake which Brad hesitantly took.

"Thanks, Josh. Congratulations," murmured Brad in return.

Cassie felt her head spin hard. She chose to keep quiet and, without realising it, squeezed her side dress harder. She was giddy, unsure because of the deadly hot kiss or because Brad was Joshua's boss. She was even uncertain whether she was still standing up or falling down. The heat of Brad's body as his arm was still on her waist somehow made her realise she was not on the ground yet.

From her peripheral view, Tiffany rushed toward them with curiosity all over her face.

"Who is he, Cass?"

Fortunately, Joshua promptly answered the question by introducing Tiffany to his boss. Brad murmured another congratulation to Tiffany.

"Oh, you're dating my sister?"

Cassie was unsure how to interpret her sister's bewildered reaction. Was it an amused smirk on Tiffany's lips? However, Joshua pulled his wife's gently as if reprimanding her.

Before she could recover from Tiffany's reaction, Kieran and Erin approached them with furrowed brows. Cassie felt suffocated, and fortunately, Brad was still holding her close. But their intimacy only invited more curiosity instead.

"Cass?" Kieran arched his eyebrow at her as a sign that she had to open her mouth and say something. She could see her brother's hawk-protective eyes on Brad.

"Brad..." Cassie almost could not breathe as her heart was still pounding hard. Her voice was only slightly above a whisper. "This is my brother, Kieran. Kieran, this is Brad, he is..." And she seemed to have no more energy to utter any word as the two men hesitantly did the handshake and exchanged greetings while waiting for her to finish her sentences.

Erin's gleeful voice saved her. She moved forward and extended her hand for a handshake with Brad. "Hi, I'm Erin! I'm Cassie's housemate. Cassie talks a lot about you."

The words were like an electric jab for Cassie as she glared at her housemate. Erin repressed her smirk while Kieran looked at them suspiciously.

And again, before Cassie could regain her regular breathing, Paul also came over, introducing himself to Brad. This time Cassie did not need to say anything as her father took the initiative for polite conversation while she was standing in the middle between two men giddily.

"Cass, why don't you take Brad to enjoy dessert and drinks?" Paul slowly motioned them away from the rest. Quietly Cassie felt grateful for her father's suggestion. She needed some breathing space away from the people who seemed still in disbelief that she had a partner at this wedding. She caught a glimpse of everyone's reaction before walking away.

Kieran's squished eyebrows.

Erin's teasing smile.

Joshua's solemn look.

Tiffany's questionable smirk.

Ruby's half-opened mouth.

And the best of all, Chelsea's cross face.

Erin mouthed 'good luck' before Cassie finally looked around, figuring out where they should find a quiet place to talk.

But definitely, she needed a drink. Rushing back to her table, she grabbed her wine glass and drank it at once. She could sense that Brad was following her. Twirling her body around after catching some breath, she was still in disbelief, finding him here, standing before her, dark, broodingly handsome in his tuxedo. However, his eyes were staring down, which somehow made her agitated.

He must be waiting for her verdict. He knew exactly the mistake he had made to her. In her snap anger, she wanted to challenge him to look her in the eye. However, she realised that could be a dreadful mistake. Seeing his gorgeous eyes might melt everything away, which was something she did not plan. *Don't look at his eyes!*

"What are you doing here? How did you find me?" Her voice was finally out, shaking and raspy as she had expected, while she was still struggling to calm her pounding heart.

His adam apple moved nervously before he replied, " I called all the wineries in Yarra Valley to find this wedding. I recognised your sister's name from your last name."

Oh? How did he know her last name? She had no idea his last name until she googled him.

"I've promised you I'll be your partner for your sister's wedding," he added. He lifted his eyes for a brief before dropping them down again.

"I never asked you to. You know I don't need one." She could not help the sarcastic tone in her voice.

He shut his eyes with a pinched expression. She even winced with her own words. While gazing at his feature, a glimpse of guilt slipped in. She had promised herself there was no point in being angry at him. She accepted what had happened between them and was boldly happy to stay friends. But, still, she was just a human. Of course, she was brokenhearted and disappointed.

Though, she could not deny the thrill of victory, recalling Chelsea's smug face faded when the bully saw her in Brad's arms.

Brad finally lifted up his head and was about to open his mouth before a group of tuxedo men interrupted them.

"Mr Rilley, please have a seat." Joshua patted Brad's shoulder and motioned him to sit down, which Brad followed hesitantly. "You must tell us how you two met each other."

Cassie was unsure whether she had to be thankful for the interruption. Tiffany also came forward, joining her husband. She tried to interpret her sister's giggle. Seeing Kieran and Erin, plus her parents, were also approaching, Cassie felt her head become dizzy.

There were only polite conversations between her family and Brad for the next few minutes. Cassie noticed that Brad's eyes were never engaged with others while talking. Instead, he was staring at the table. It reminded her of their first encounter and how she criticised him. Someone who had just met him for the first time perhaps would judge him as arrogantly rude, but she knew him for quite a while and somehow had expected that. Her breath hitched when his hand seized and squeezed her hand as if he was about to fall. Somehow, she sensed that he was intimidated by her family's interrogation of him, something she did not expect from someone like him.

She returned the squeeze, and his body seemed much more relaxed. Slowly she pulled out her hand and stood up, which invited all eyes to fall upon her.

"I'm going to take a drink from the bar for Brad." It was in her mind all along, but she had momentarily forgotten about it due to the interruption. Perhaps a drink also could help to expel his tension.

"I'll come with you." Tiffany popped up from her seat and gripped Cassie's forearm while they walked together to the bar.

Cassie had a feeling that her sister could not resist her curiosity anymore. The moment they were far within anyone's earshot, Tiffany immediately blurted.

"Well, well, well, Cass. You've caught a big fish. It's a surprise."

Cassie took a quiet sigh. "He's not my boyfriend. It was just a misunderstanding."

"Come on, Cass," scoffed Tiffany. "You had a kiss with him in front of hundreds of people. Though he's a weirdo, which is why he's a good match for you, he's loaded."

Weirdo? So that was the meaning behind her sister's mischievous smile. Brad was Joshua's boss, whom Tiffany had labelled as a weirdo. And her sister was laughing at her for getting a weird guy as her boyfriend.

They reached the bar and ordered a drink from the bartender. Tiffany leaned on the bar and darted her with a severe look.

"Since you're with him, you must tell him to give Joshua a break. I want to go on my honeymoon, Cass. He's the asshole boss who disapproves of Joshua's leave request."

Asshole? Cassie could not believe her hearing. She could not help but be annoyed hearing her sister badmouthing Brad. Whether he was probably a true asshole after what he had done to her, it was childish to label him that for such a trivial matter.

She could not help but sound tight. "That's a matter between him and Joshua."

"But you're his girlfriend. You can persuade him. You must help me. This is for my honeymoon, Cass!"

Cassie grabbed one of the filled glass wines offered by the bar and drank it at once, feeling frustrated with her sister's tone of words. It was not the first time she had heard it, but today it seemed she did not have the patience to face it calmly.

"I told you, Tiff. That is a work matter between him and Joshua. I don't want to interfere. Besides, he's not my boyfriend."

"Come on, Cass. You just kissed him! Everyone saw that. Why is it so hard to admit it?"

Cassie took an exasperated sigh. "Whatever, Tiff. I don't want to talk about this now." She felt warm, and her head started spinning.

"But you must help me! You must talk to him to let Joshua go for our honeymoon."

"I'm not going to do that, Tiff."

"How could you do this to me? What kind of sister are you? Today is my wedding day!"

Cassie felt her head almost explode. Facing Tiffany's scowl increased the boiling heat within her. Clenching her fist, her body was shivering with anger. She could not stand this anymore. It was like a fuse within her brain snapped broken. She looked her sister squarely in the eyes.

"Today is also my birthday." Her voice was low and cold. Perhaps colder than she intended to be. But there was a thrill of satisfaction for being able to spit out those words. "I can do whatever things I like. And I am not doing what you ask me because I don't like it."

Tiffany's reaction was beyond words as her eyes bulged, and her make-up's soft colour seemed drained. Her breathing slowly accelerated as her body became tense.

For a couple of seconds, they stared at each other as if none of them believed the words they had just heard. Then, a glimpse of regret hit Cassie. She could see a flash of pain in her sister's eyes. Before she gathered the strength to utter an apology, the line of her eyes caught Joshua approaching them as the wedding MC announced the bride and the groom's open dance.

As the music cued in, Tiffany seemed back to her senses. Cassie had to admire her sister's ability to regain her composure quickly. Tiffany darted her a sharp look indicating that their conversation had not finished yet. At least, with the dance, she still had a couple of minutes to get herself ready for the next battle of their conversation.

As her eyes sent her sister's lithe body disappearing into the dance floor elegantly as if nothing had happened, Cassie took a deep breath. It never crossed her mind that she finally said those sarcastic words to her sister. She had repressed her resentful feelings toward her sister for far too long. Snapping at her sister earlier was unplanned, and she could not help it. She took a deep breath, wishing she would be more mature handling it if she could rewind the time.

But she was just a human.

A gentle touch on her forearm brought her back to the presence. Brad practically stood close to her. Too close, in her opinion, as his warm masculine breath blew on her cheek and his deep brown eyes gazed at her intensely.

Don't look at his eyes!

But perhaps it was too late.

"Shall we have a dance too?"

Being immersed in his eyes melted her body. If she did not break the trance, moving her eyes away from him to the dance floor, perhaps she would immediately say 'yes' to that question. The dance floor looked lively. All her families were swaying, including Alicia and Ashleigh, with other children from distant relatives.

But she knew they needed to talk. He was not supposed to be here. He could not just simply think there was nothing wrong after what he had done.

She gathered her strength before turning back to him. "Why are you here, Brad?"

She could read a hint of guilt in his eyes.

"I know you're angry at me." He shut his eyes briefly while taking a deep exhale. Since Cassie chose to seal her lips and wait for his explanation, It seemed like an eternity as he stared down before finally lifting his eyes again to her. "I did not mean to avoid you. But this is the first time I feel such strong feelings towards someone. I'm confused...I'm..." His adam apple bobbed. "I need some time away to think."

Cassie must compliment herself for not scoffing at hearing those words. *What a cliché!* Weren't those typical words used by any male species when they were cheating with another woman?

She took a deep sigh. She could not deny that the past two and half weeks had been a nightmare. She lost her appetite for food and perhaps for her life. That was called falling in love, perhaps. She did not recall having a crush on someone until she was devastated. Maybe because they had slept together, which somehow deepened the wound. However, it meant nothing to him, as he already had someone. She had been telling herself that she would not hate him whatever happened. They were two mature adults. If they were not meant together, just dust it off and move on.

What a bold thinking! Anyway, snatching a guy from another fellow woman was not in her dictionary at all!

Cassie's forced herself to draw the bravest smile she could put on. "It's alright, Brad. I understand."

His head snapped up as his eyes widened. "You do?"

"Yes, I do," she nodded weakly. "It's alright. We can still stay as friends." She lifted her chin with a swell of pride in her chest. "I have no grudges against you."

He flinched his head back as his face blanched. "Friends? You mean what we had meant nothing to you?"

Jeeezz....did it mean something to him? Was she just one of his casual?

"It doesn't matter what I think," Cassie huffed. "At the end of the day, I don't wish to complicate things. You cannot always have everything, Brad."

She would expect this. With his career and wealth, a man like him would think he could get whatever he wanted. He possibly still thought she did not mind having a casual sexual relationship with him. She gave him a stern look, although her heart was sliced into pieces. Her hands squeezed tightly to her dress as if it would give her strength.

He tilted his head rapidly, blinking as if her words were beyond belief. Cassie lifted her chin while tossing her hair back, returning his gaze with a quiet, shuddering breath. Perhaps this was his first time being rejected by a woman. She was definitely the wrong target because she was too old to play around with.

With mouth half-opened and a stony expression, it seemed comprehension finally dawned on him. Cassie was unsure whether she caught hurt and disappointment from those gorgeous pair of eyes before they slowly dropped.

"Alright," he took as if his defeated sigh. His hand took out a card-sized envelope from his blazer and then handed it to her. "This is for you. Happy Birthday."

Hesitantly, Cassie took it and stared at it blankly. When she lifted up her head, he had already walked away with shoulders down. From a distance, she could see Joshua and Ryan approaching him. They talked briefly before he finally left the place.

What she felt within her was indescribable. A shrinking feeling. A hollow. Her vacant stare was on the envelope in her hand, but she had no energy to open it. At this stage, she did not wish to think anything about Brad. The day before the wedding, her mind was already set on moving on again with her life, but instead, he came back and rocked her world again. Tears pricked her eyes, and she quickly rubbed them off, hoping they would not ruin her makeup.

It was definitely a birthday to remember.

Chapter Twenty-Six

Cassie lazily opened her eyes when the morning sunshine sneaked through the curtain. She rolled around her body to find herself not in her own bed. Her mind and her vision were getting clearer. While appreciating the high ceiling and contemporary wood luxurious furniture around, it reminded her of where she was. She glanced to the side to find Ashleigh and Alicia sleeping peacefully at her side. Supporting herself with her elbow, her heart felt warmth observing the two beautiful angels before her.

Yesterday was her birthday. It was supposed to be a memorable day. Indeed it was. Tiffany's wedding, her 40th birthday, the drama with Brad and the heated argument with Tiffany. After Brad left, she drowned herself with a few glasses of drinks while watching each guest one by one leaving.

The rest of her birthday was spent uneventfully with her favourite people. Ashleigh and Alicia could not wait to give her the birthday present, a photo frame of the three of them, taken one day during the school holiday in a theme park. Her parents gave her a white gold necklace, while Kieran and Erin gave her shopping and massage gift cards. They were lovely gifts that were enough to make her heart feel content again. Brad's unopened envelope sat in her handbag with the rest of the presents. She would open it when she was ready, even though she was unsure when.

However, nothing from Tiffany. It was not she expected one. Tiffany never gave her any birthday gift as far as she could remember. But the quarrel they had perhaps was enough answer to why her sister was the only one not among them at yesterday's dinner gathering, even though Janine defended that it had been a long day for Tiffany and she was definitely tired. Cassie totally understood it.

But it was another day now. Her birthday was over, as well as Tiffany's wedding day. Today would be just another ordinary day.

They spent a night in the winery accommodation with the bride and groom and planned to meet for breakfast this morning. The girls had requested to sleep with their favourite aunt despite Cassie could see Kieran wishing to speak to her privately after what happened. However, she was exhausted and drifted to sleep with the girls once they touched the bed.

Slowly she pushed herself up, which caused a ripple on the bed, and woke Alicia and Ashleigh up. Soon after, there was a soft knock on the door. Kieran and Erin showed up and helped her get the girls ready. Then, they all went together to the winery restaurant to meet with their parents, Tiffany and Joshua's family for breakfast.

The moment they arrived and were seated, Cassie could not escape Tiffany's pout face at her. Quietly sighing and anticipating something unpleasant, she took two seats away diagonally from her sister.

"My apologies for forgetting to wish you a happy birthday yesterday, Cass," said Joshua with a sheepish smile. He was seated along with Cassie's chairside, next to one of his sisters, whom Cassie knew her name as Isla. Next to herself and opposite Isla was Erin. Obviously, whoever arranged these seating arrangements wished the two families to mingle with one another.

"Thank you, Josh," responded Cassie with a timid smile.

"Oh? Was yesterday your birthday? Happy Birthday," Isla chimed in.

Cassie thanked her as well.

"Was the tall man with you yesterday your boyfriend? I saw both of you were kissing," continued Isla. "You said he's your boss, Josh? Is that right?"

Cassie did not respond, only giving a tight smile while pretending to look at her sausage and bacon.

Joshua cleared his throat. "Yes, that's correct. Mr Rilley is the CEO of the company I work for."

"Yeah, he's the man who is ruining our honeymoon," added Tiffany swiftly in a sarcastic tone.

"Our honeymoon is not ruined, honey," rebuked Joshua gently. "It's just postponed. I told you that I have to finish the project. Unfortunately, this wedding coincides with my project launch. We will go on our honeymoon soon in three weeks."

"Yeah, three weeks is not that long," consoled Isla.

"Well, if my sister cares about me, perhaps at least she should try to talk to that weirdo," scoffed Tiffany.

Cassie pursed her lips. *Here it goes!* Although she was almost rolling her eyes, it was Erin who looked tense. Her housemate clutched the fork tightly. Cassie did not wish to make a scene in front of Joshua's family. That would be a childish thing to do. Whatever Tiffany said, she would ignore it for now and address that later.

"Stop calling him a weirdo, Tiff," reprimanded Joshua gently. "He's my boss, and now he's also your sister's boyfriend."

"No, no, no.." Cassie quickly interrupted, which drew all eyes on her. "We are not in a relationship. It was just a misunderstanding."

Joshua was stunned as his mouth hung open for a few seconds before shutting it and swallowing his food. "Right."

"Why don't you admit you are with that weirdo, Cass?" Tiffany snickered.

Cassie could not help but feel a spark of anger within her ignited. She knew what it felt like to be mocked. And she could not accept how her sister did it to Brad.

"Why do you keep calling him weirdo?" she snapped. "Just because he did not let Joshua leave in the middle of project launching for his honeymoon, you're unhappy with him and labelling him a weirdo?"

"Well, Joshua told me..."

"Tiff.." Joshua quickly grabbed his wife's hand to stop talking, but Tiffany shoved it away.

"Joshua told me that he's the weirdest guy in the office. He never looked people in the eyes, mumbling a lot to himself instead of talking to people, yelling over the slightest disorder thing."

"Tiff..." Joshua let out an exaggerated sigh. "He's the CEO, and regardless, he's a genius. Whatever he is, it has nothing to do with our honeymoon plan."

Cassie took a shuddered breath listening to that. Tiffany's description was exactly what Cassie had known about Brad since they first met. But, after what she had gone through with Brad, his quiet disposition somehow warmed her heart. Either by coincidence or not, he was there when she needed someone to hold unto. She wondered whether her biased opinion was because she had slept with him. Perhaps she had fallen for him.

"A weirdo and an old maid. I guess both of you make up a perfect couple. You're lucky that he's loaded," hissed Tiffany sarcastically.

"Tiff, please..." Joshua took a frustrated sigh.

Cassie only shook her head while burying her face in her hand. This unpleasant conversation seemed unavoidable.

A loud clatter on the table suddenly echoed, which caused everyone to hold their breath. "Yeah!" Erin chimed in while piercing the sausage on her plate with an energy more than necessary. "That weirdo is your husband's big boss and possibly could be your future brother-in-law!" While lifting her food into her mouth, she smirked at Tiffany.

Tiffany's face became red, more furious. But the comment was enough to make her shut her mouth for the whole morning.

Cassie quietly felt relieved that the rest of breakfast went uneventfully. Some of Joshua's family wished her happy birthday once they knew it was also yesterday before finally bidding goodbye.

Tiffany would go with Joshua's family for another of their own family function, which meant they would not see each other soon. Janine hugged her youngest child tightly as if she was about to lose her forever. Then each of them took a turn to bid Tiffany goodbye. Cassie was the last person in line, and she intentionally did it that way, wishing she could speak to her little sister for a bit.

It was obvious Tiffany still could not forgive her. Cassie took the initiative to throw her arms around her sister while whispering another 'congratulation'.

"Will we see you again before you go on your honeymoon?" she asked.

"I don't know," answered Tiffany curtly with a stiff posture like a robot with no intention of returning the hug.

"Alright, Tiff," sighed Cassie. "Hope to see you again before the honeymoon. All the best always."

Cassie stepped back, thinking Tiffany would turn and walk away soon. However, her breath hitched when Tiffany darted a sharp glare instead.

"Why, Cass? Why do you always get the best?"

Cassie looked at her sister, confused. "I don't understand."

"You are always everyone's favourite! And yet, on my special day, my wedding day, you chose to ruin it!"

Cassie sighed quietly, pursed her lips, and lowered her eyes. It seemed this uncomfortable conversation would continue. Tiffany would not be happy until she vented all her anger at her.

Still, with her flinty eyes and flaring nostril, Tiffany continued speaking with gritted teeth. It reminded Cassie of when her sister was still a little girl upset over a toy she could not have.

"Everyone adores you, Cass! Dad, Kieran, Ashleigh and Alicia, and even my friends! All of them! You're always the sensible one! On the other hand, the moment Dad and Kieran see me, they will roll their eyes, always assuming that I will make another trouble. I know you're unhappy my wedding day coincides with your birthday. I knew that you were planning something to ruin it."

Hearing Tiffany mention 'friends' made Cassie wonder whether her sister was aware of Chelsea's advances. Regardless, the following words uttered from Tiffany's lips were like a slap to her face. *Is she for real?*

"And now you have a boyfriend," Tiffany chuckled bitterly. "He's more loaded than Joshua, and he's Joshua's boss. I'm pretty sure you feel on top of the world now, aren't you?"

Cassie glances around, wishing no one heard their conversation. Quietly she felt relieved that Joshua's family were still talking with their parents. Kieran and Erin were with the girls playing near the mantlepiece. It seemed Tiffany also tried to restrain the volume of her voice.

Choosing to seal her own lips while waiting for her sister to finish releasing all her anger at her, Cassie hoped they would easily forget about this afterwards.

However, Cassie did not expect to see tears rolling down Tiffany's cheek despite her sister gazing away from her. It made her realise that it was not only she who had bottled an envious feeling, but likewise, Tiffany even treated her as a competitor. It was ironic and made her realise that nothing and no one was perfect.

After it seemed like an eternity of silence between them, Cassie quietly took a deep breath. "I did not plan to ruin your wedding, Tiff. You had a perfect wedding yesterday. I did not plan to ruin your honeymoon either. How do I know that Brad is Joshua's boss? I only knew it literally just yesterday, Tiff. Regardless, you still have your honeymoon. It's just being postponed."

Tiffany scoffed while rubbing her tears with the back of her hand.

"And you know Dad and Kieran love you, Tiff," added Cassie quickly. She did not want to give a chance for Tiffany even to doubt their family's love. There was no such thing as favouritism. She initially thought that way too, but she realised that their parents loved them equally, perhaps expressed differently. "Otherwise, they would not be here yesterday for your wedding. Each of your family is thrilled for you, even Ashleigh and Alicia. You are blessed, Tiff. You know that. You have Joshua, and you love him. He's smart and handsome, has a perfect career, and he is a nice bloke."

Hesitantly Cassie lifted her hand and squeezed her sister's shoulder. A quiet relieved sigh sneaked in as Tiffany did not shove her away.

"It's not about who has the best, Tiff. We are sisters. You have amazing achievements in your life. You do realise that, Tiff. And I am proud of you."

Another silence fell between them. Cassie was unsure how long they were standing there without uttering any word except the sound of their heavy breaths. She held her little sister to her arm, which seemed to help her calm and dry out her tears.

It was Joshua's voice that startled them. Tiffany straightened her posture and walked away with a single last glance. Cassie only took another deep exhale, watching her sister's silhouette slowly disappear from her sight.

Chapter Twenty-Seven

Three weeks had passed. Tiffany and Joshua just departed for the Maldives for their honeymoon on Sunday evening. They managed to have another family gathering in Wonthaggi a week prior, but Tiffany's cold behaviour towards her remained unchanged. Cassie hoped time would eventually make Tiffany forget about their differences, wishing things between them would improve after the honeymoon.

Cassie strolled at the park as usual after her work, thinking about paying Kieran and her nieces a visit tonight. However, on the other hand, since Erin appeared in their life, she did not wish to be the third wheel, even though they would surely welcome her. She offered to mind the girls so her housemate and brother could go on a date occasionally. However, Kieran and Erin insisted that it was not needed yet. On the other hand, they pushed her to spend more time doing other activities that allowed her to see more people and hopefully someone new.

Kieran and Erin did ask her about Brad. She only told them that Brad was with someone already. Erin did not buy the story and felt she should give Brad a chance to explain his disappearance. The advice bothered Cassie, and somehow it pushed her to take the envelope from Brad in her bag today. She was thinking of opening it and reading his birthday message while having a stroll.

She almost reached the basketball court and thought that he might be there. The court was empty. But the tall building of his apartment was just within her sight. Seeing it made her heart sink, especially reminiscing the night they spent together.

She took a heavy breath and took out the blue envelope from Brad. From the shape, she was certain it must be a birthday card. With a slight tremor in her hands, she opened it. It was indeed a birthday card, with his handwriting and two pieces of rectangular paper that looked like tickets. She examined the papers, which were tickets to NBL games last weekend.

Before readying herself to read the message on the card, she briefly shut her eyes, took another breath and started reading it.

Dear Cassie,

Happy birthday! I want you to know that you're special to me. I bought these two tickets because I know you love basketball too. I hope you will come with me to the game.

Sincerely,

Brad.

It was a short message but beautifully handwritten. However, upon reading it, Cassie could not help but feel something tickling within her as if she was reading young kids' writing. It made her think whether Brad wrote them or this was a joke. Tiffany's words of labelling him as 'weirdo' suddenly came into her mind again. It was a mocking word that somehow sliced her heart, too. She was unsure why, perhaps because she cared about him.

She looked at the tickets for a moment, thinking about what she needed to do with them. Unfortunately, the ticket had expired. The date of the game was last Saturday. She was too late to realise it. Otherwise, she might give it away to some of her friends.

It was such a simple gift, but somehow it meant something. He wanted to spend more time with her. But why did he simply disappear after their first great night together? Ah, right! Because he already had someone. However, why did he write this message to her? Did it mean perhaps he had chosen her over the other person?

Cassie shook her head while chuckling bitterly. She did not want to give herself false hope. Perhaps Erin was right. She should ask and listen to his explanation. Besides, was she even telling herself that they stayed as friends whatever happened?

She took another deep breath, one of the heaviest ones she had been doing recently. The blinking light and vibration from her mobile phone severed her reverie. She smiled to see the caller.

"Hey there. How are you going?" His friendly voice always gave her a warm breeze to her heart.

"I'm well, Chandra. How are you?"

"Very well, thank you. I'm calling you to see whether you're free tonight. I'm sorry this is a bit last minute. It's been a hectic day today in the office."

Cassie shrugged her shoulder and felt silly afterwards, realising that the person on the other line would not see it anyway.

"I am free. What's up?"

"Really? No babysitting duty tonight?" Chandra sounded surprised.

"I haven't told you that my brother has managed to find a new babysitter," laughed Cassie. "And potentially a new mother for the girls."

"Wow! That's awesome! I can hear another wedding bell ringing soon."

Yeah, right! But it was still not her wedding bell.

"I'm calling you because Helda is here."

"Really? That's great! I don't know if she's in Melbourne."

A sigh from the other line. "Only for a few nights. Her destination is actually Sydney to see her friends. But she is here to see me. I believe it's my mother's instructions too."

"I'm pretty sure your mother misses you too, Chandra."

"Yeah, I know. I know she wants to make sure I'm okay." Another deep exhale. "I still hope she's the one coming here. Anyway, since Helda is here, I'm calling you to see whether you're available for dinner tonight. Literally now. In my house."

"Yeah, sure. As I said, I'm free anyway."

"It seems your brother has ditched you once he has a new girlfriend."

"Yeah, he told me to get a life," chortled Cassie. "Alright, I'll see you soon."

"*Righto*! See you soon."

Cassie immediately rushed to the nearest tram stop and hailed the tram going to Chandra's house direction. Within half an hour, she reached her destination, looking forward to the dinner meeting. Helda's visit would be a good distraction. Seeing a familiar friendly face and chatting about what was happening with the school project in Indonesia. It made her think she should probably go back there to volunteer again. She would ask Chandra if she had a chance tonight.

The thought lifted her spirit. She pressed the doorbell enthusiastically and drew the widest smile on her lips. The door flew open, and her eyes bumped into a pair of dark brown eyes that always enchanted her.

It was an utter shock, for sure. She was probably stunned like a statue for a couple of seconds before finally gaining her senses back, blinking and squeezing her brain and figuring out where she was now. Suppose it was not because Chandra's familiar voice burst out behind the person, she could probably twirl around and run away.

"Hey, Cass! Great to see you here!" Realising the unnatural tension between the two persons before him, Chandra chuckled nervously. "I suppose you still remember Brad. He was in the project, too. Remember?" He squished his eyebrow. "Oh, and you met him at my engagement party too. I thought you guys went home together that night?"

Cassie felt her cheek warm. The words reminded her that she and Brad, in fact, did sleep together, though it did not happen exactly after Chandra's engagement party.

"We did not go home together." Somehow she managed to speak, which took her by surprise too. She could catch a pinched expression from Brad while Chandra still furrowed his brow.

"You did not?"

"I mean,.." *Darn! Get hold of yourself, Cass!* "Brad gave me a lift home with his car."

"Yeah, right! That's what I mean," chuckled Chandra. "Brad, you still remember Cassie, don't you?"

Brad replied with a murmured voice. "Yes, of course."

Another awkward silence fell, and thankfully was only for a few seconds, as Helda jumped out and squealed excitedly, seeing her presence. Cassie quietly felt relieved that Helda occupied her with plenty of chats regarding her trip and the school project in Indonesia for the next hour. She noticed that besides Tom and Brad, there was another man, who was Helda's boyfriend- Jaka. However, her heart almost stopped when her eyes caught a slender female figure beside Brad. The woman was wearing a flowery sack dress with her over-the-shoulder blonde wavey hair. Her stunning appearance did not make Cassie breathless only for the first time. However, seeing her now standing close to Brad made her wish she could run away.

This is cruel! Darn! She did not ask for this. First, she did not expect to see Brad in this supposed to be just a simple catch-up with an old friend. And now, seeing him with his girlfriend. Oh! She could not believe that he had brought her here! Was he trying to get back at her?

Chandra's voice invited all of them to the dining table, gave her an opportunity to collect herself. There were only seven of them. She tried acting as naturally as possible while sitting between Helda and Chandra. Unfortunately, her eyes had to be sore for the night as Brad and the dashing woman sat opposite her.

Act mature, Cass! You're 40 years old now! Yes, Cassie promised herself to face this calmly and bravely. Perhaps it would be easier if

Brad kept staring down as he used to, but she drank in his captivating eyes as he stared at her instead. Cassie was unsure whether it was a coincidence, but she could feel the heat of his gaze on her, which tickled her to look at him as well. Perhaps it was a mistake because every time she lifted her eyes at him, their eyes met, creating a ripple in her chest.

She tried to distract herself by joining in the conversation on the table while complimenting some of the Indonesian dishes Chandra had prepared.

"I hope you like the *Gado-Gado*, Cass. I know that's your favourite." Chandra's gleeful voice chimed in.

"Hmm.." She nodded as the mentioned food was the one she was munching. "It's delicious, Chandra. I guess you can open an Indonesian restaurant here with this."

"I wish," laughed Chandra, and then he turned to Brad. "What do you think about the *Gado -Gado*, Brad? I know you also liked to eat this dish when we were in Jakarta."

The question gave Cassie a couple of seconds of breathing opportunity as those dark, captivating brown eyes shifted away from her.

"I agree with Cassie. It is delicious."

Other topics of conversation flowed in. However, Cassie still felt suffocated, feeling the intense gaze of the man sitting opposite her. Jeeezz...was it only her feeling? While lowering her head down and pretending to focus on her food, she thought about how to dare him back, and perhaps he would scurry away.

Inhaling a deep breath, she lifted up her head. As expected, their eyes met again, and this time she returned it with a smirk.

"Aren't you going to introduce us, Brad?" she gestured her head to the woman sitting beside him with a raised eyebrow, but successfully drew a friendly smile to the woman herself.

He blinked. It seemed her question took him off guard.

Chandra swallowed his food quickly while glancing at both of them nervously. "Oh, I thought...."

"My apologies." Brad cleared his throat. "Cass, this is Briana. Briana, this is Cassie."

Cassie waited. There should be more sentences, but Brad simply stopped there. However, this time he lowered his eyes to his food.

Ha! It seemed her trick worked this time. She turned to the irresistible-looking blonde with a slight nod. Briana returned it with a sheepish smile.

"I heard a lot about you, Cass," said Briana.

Did you? From your boyfriend?

Finally, Cassie heard her voice. Jeeezz...this woman seemed flawless, even her voice was pleasant to anyone's ear. Gentle and endearing, which seemed could melt anyone's heart. Perhaps she could not deny her envy, but how could she hate her?

"I heard both of you explored Jakarta's culinary together." Briana glanced at Brad meaningfully. "I can understand now why you like the same food."

"I should be thankful to Brad for taking me around," asserted Cassie. She had to compliment herself for acting composed. "I think he knows more Indonesian food than me. Perhaps you should ask him to take you to Jakarta for a holiday trip one day."

"That has been the plan." Briana threw another glance at Brad. "Perhaps that would be our next family holiday destination."

Nice! Family destination. In her mind, Cassie visualised her heart being sliced, like when she cut the roast chicken she had just taken out of the oven.

"That sounds like a good plan." She applauded herself for responding to it lightly.

"Feel free to let me know when you're there," Helda chimed in. "I'll be more than happy to take you around."

"Sure thing."

Another topic of conversation flowed in, and Cassie started to feel dizzy. She only had a glass of sparkling wine. Couldn't it be because of that? Towards the end of the dinner, Helda and Jaka excused themselves to leave. They would continue with their itinerary tomorrow to explore Philip Island together. Cassie wished Brad and Briana would leave soon. However, instead, Tom and Brad continued their conversations in the lounge while she went to help Chandra clear dirty dishes in the kitchen. Briana also joined in with them.

"Are they working on something together?" asked Cassie out of curiosity while helping to scrap the remaining food from the plate into the bin.

"Yes," answered Chandra while placing the dirty dishes in the dishwasher. "Brad is helping Tom to get another role in another organisation. A sister company of Brad's family business."

"Tom is a talented person," Briana said while taking more dirty plates from the dining table to the kitchen. "My father even agrees with the move. Working in a commercial organisation would help him to grow more."

"I can't thank you and Brad enough for looking after him," said Chandra with a solemn look.

"Don't mention it, Chandra. It's our pleasure." Briana then turned to her. Cassie could see an eagerness in that pretty woman's eyes to speak with her. "I heard from Brad that you also work in IT, Cass. He said your office is just in Chinatown. That's not far from Brad's office. Do you sometimes meet him during lunchtime?"

Cassie's body went stiff. She was sipping a beer bottle when the question reached her ear, and the bottle was like hanging on her lips for a moment while she was trying to digest the question's meaning. *Jeez..is Brad for real? How could he talk so much about another woman to his girlfriend?*

She caught a mischievous smile from Chandra. *This is weird*, she thought. But she was telling herself to face this calmly.

"No, we only met once for lunch," she chuckled. The lunch that she thought was disastrous. "I believe you know that he's a busy man."

"Yeah, I know. He's quite a workaholic," smiled Briana. "I guess it's great if you could ask him once in a while. You know, so he realises he needs to take a break."

Cassie squished her eyebrow. *Me? Why is she asking me to take her boyfriend out for lunch? So Brad told her that she asked him out for lunch?*

"Where do you work, Briana?" She guessed that Briana's workplace was probably too far from Melbourne city. "I suppose you meet Brad every day after work?"

"I have my own business. I am a jewellery designer, and I have a couple of shops. So I move around between shops."

"Nice." Cassie tried to hide her smirk by sipping her beer again. Looking at Briana's fashionable, elegant appearance, her profession was not a surprise. This woman, indeed, looked exquisite and sparkling.

"I don't see Brad every day, I'm afraid. I believe he has his own life," added Briana with a twitch on her lips. Her head turned to the lounge where Brad and Tom were before she continued, "I heard your parents live in the town not far from Philip Island. We have a sailing boat kept in one of the marinas in Cape Woolamai, and we're going there this weekend. I think you should join us."

Cassie went stiff again. *Is she for real?* Perhaps Briana had no idea what she and Brad had and was trying to be friendly with her boyfriend's mates. She glanced at Chandra, who again smiled at her rather mischievously. No single soul knew about her and Brad, except perhaps her family. Could Chandra possibly know about them?

"My brother is a quiet person. He never takes any of his friends there. But I think he will be excited if you could join in," continued Briana as she glanced briefly again to the lounge where Tom and Brad sat and talked in a serious manner.

My brother? Cassie blinked for a couple of seconds. She followed Briana's line of eye direction to the lounge. Then a realisation hit her the similarity between Briana and Tom. Both shared the same wavey blonde hair. Now she understood why Tom and Brad were close. It was not the first time they had a meeting supposedly about work. That was how Brad and Briana were together. How could she not realise that before?

"Oh, I have no idea that Tom likes sailing," she chuckled rather bitterly while glancing at Chandra. "Yeah, I don't mind joining in."

Chandra knitted his brows. "Tom, you said?" His lips broke into a laugh. "Are you drunk, Cass? It's not Tom who has the sailing boat. It's Brad."

Now Cassie got more confused and had to admit that she became dizzy. It was her second bottle. But come on! No one could get drunk because of beer!

"Ah, yeah..." she felt momentarily lost in her own thought. *Who are they talking about again?*

"My brother has the boat, Cass," laughed Briana. "Brad is my brother. Not Tom."

"Ah..."

Cassie was utterly lost, and her dizziness intensified. No, she was not drunk! She was sure she was not. But did she hear this correctly? Brad was Briana's brother?!

Her lips were parting as her brain tried to digest her surrounding. Both Chandra and Briana gave her a look with amusement spread on their face. *Darn!* Did she look stupid?

"Yes!" She snapped her finger as she gained her wit back. "I mean Brad, who has the boat," she grinned.

"Oh, that's great!" squealed Briana, twirling towards the lounge. "Brad! Cassie is joining us this weekend to Cape Woolamai."

Darn! It was like another bang on Cassie's head, especially seeing Brad's stunned expression with the announcement. *What the hell had happened?* She practically supported herself on the kitchen bench while pursing her lips and gathering her courage to meet his eyes. Unsure for how many seconds their eyes were locked until Tom's voice broke in.

"That sounds fun!"

It was the voice that broke the intensity of their exchange look. Brad stared down and turned to Tom.

"You guys could join in as well," he murmured.

"Oh, yeah! Of course!" followed Briana.

"Thank you for the invite," responded Chandra. "We already have a plan this weekend. We are going to visit Tom's parents in Yarrawonga."

"Nice."

The rest of the conversation was like an echo sound to Cassie's ear. She kept quiet while sipping her beer and looked everywhere except at Brad. *Get hold of yourself, Cass!*

The next thing she could hear and digest in her brain was Briana's gleeful voice informing her that she was leaving.

"My fiancé is picking me up," said Briana. Then she threw her arm to Tom and Chandra with a peck on her cheek before turning to her. "It's lovely to meet you, Cassie. I look forward to seeing you at the weekend."

Cassie could not form any word as she only nodded weakly with a chuckle that sounded weird in her ear. Briana bid her brother farewell before finally leaving the four of them into unnatural silence.

Cassie knew that it was a signal for her to go, too. And she could not wait to go as the room seemed to suffocate her. She did not realise that she had only been thinking about her escape in her mind but had not uttered it. She dashed to collect her jacket and wear it.

"Oh, you're leaving too, Cass?" Chandra's puzzlement somehow slapped her back to reality.

"Ah, yeah," she stuttered but managed to draw a smile. Her head was spinning. "Good night, everyone." She twirled around and reached the door before suddenly, her forearms gripped.

"Hey, are you alright?" Chandra looked at her with concern. "You look unwell, Cass. I don't think it's a good idea for you to go home alone. I'll take you home."

Before she could protest the offer, the deep baritone voice she had been missing and crying over for the past weeks finally broke in.

"I can give her a lift."

"Oh, yeah!" Chandra's face became relaxed. "You took her home too last time, Brad. Yeah, Cass, please let Brad take you home."

Cassie chuckled nervously. He was the person she wanted to avoid at this particular moment. Her feeling was indescribable, and she could not think properly. She thought Briana was Brad's girlfriend all this time, but instead, she was his sister only. Had he been with anyone? But why did he disappear after their night? Thinking about it only opened up her old wound that she was still trying to patch.

"I'll take a tram. I don't want to trouble you," she insisted, and this time she gave a stern look to Chandra. "I will be fine, Chandra. Good night." She swiftly gave him and Tom a peck, then waved lightly to Brad. She had given a strong signal that she did not wish to be stopped again.

When the crisp cold night air touched her face, she finally managed to breathe. After walking for a couple of minutes, her mind slowly became clear. The street was quiet but not as dark as she thought because it was already Spring. It was something that she desperately needed at this moment.

She actually had no idea where she was going. After finally her brain was recharged to almost a hundred percent, she finally realised that she had been walking in the wrong direction. Shoving her hair while chuckling bitterly, she twirled around, feeling silly about her mistake. Her breath hitched when her eyes caught a familiar tall figure belonging to the person she wanted to avoid.

Darn! What the hell is he doing here?

"You have been walking in the wrong direction. I believe your tram stop is supposed to be back there."

"Right." She shook her head while taking a deep exhale. She must look stupid, but it did not matter anymore. She walked past through Brad, and this time she was sure she was walking in the right direction.

"Chandra is worried about you. How about I give you a lift?"

His voice was just behind her as the sound of his footsteps followed her. She did not want to turn around and wished her silence would chase him away. *Darn!* How much she wished she could face him maturely like she always had in her mind. But things were not as easy as you thought could be done. She was forty years old now, but how could she act like a teenager? What exactly was she afraid of? Whether he was with someone already or not, Erin was probably right. She had the right to know why he left. Besides, she herself had promised that they could still stay as friends.

"Thank you for your birthday present," she panted in the middle of her brisk walking. With his long stride, he was quickly catching up with her pace. She caught a glimpse of him staring down at his feet.

"You're welcome. Did you use the tickets?"

She did not want to be perceived as unappreciative. Then she lied, "Yes, with my brother."

"You did?" he scoffed. "I checked that your ticket numbers have been indicated as No Show."

Darn! Then why did he ask? Cassie chuckled, feeling embarrassed for lying. Her gaze went straight as she could not wait to reach her tram stop.

"I thought you said we could still stay as friends."

"We are!" She turned to him, and this time their eyes met. Cassie had to be grateful for the minimum illumination on the street. Otherwise, she would be enraptured again by those captivating eyes. "Am I not joining you this weekend for the boat trip?" in her mind, she had already thought a good excuse to pull out at the last minute.

"Then, let me give you a lift home."

"That's unnecessary. I can go home by myself."

"Why are you avoiding me?"

Why? Jeeezz...why did he have to make it so hard? Things between them were different now. She was lying to herself all this time that she could only face him as a friend. Perhaps they should openly talk about this, so they had a mutual understanding of how they should behave toward each other in the future.

Seeing her tram stop was like a sign that she should bravely face him. She took a deep breath, clenched her fist, and turned her body to him with a lifted chin.

"I should ask the same question to you, Brad. Why did you disappear after what we had?"

He blinked and seemed taken aback. "I remember you said you understood why." His voice was hoarse, just above whispers.

Her lips twitch with a bitter chuckle. It seemed her worst nightmare had come true. She had predicted this but could not restrain the strong wave within her chest that made her body tremble. How could she be so blind about him? No, on the other way round, she knew about this but stupidly let herself fall for him. *Darn!* It seemed being fooled in love applied to any age.

"Right." She swallowed hard, and her dizziness returned. Turning her face away from him, she was thinking of checking the tram timetable. While looking at the tram pole, her mind whirled around. She was too upset to even think properly.

"Besides, you said that night did not mean anything to you," he continued. His tone sounded sombre to her ear, which she did not understand. She stared back at him to find something that made her heart stop beating. It was a pain. Was he only pretending?

There was a strong urge within her to retort how untrue those words. "I did not say that. On the contrary, the night seemed to mean nothing to you. That was why you left, wasn't it?" She could not help but draw a sardonic smile. "I'm just one of the women you took back to your apartment for sex."

He jerked back as his face blanched. It was a reaction that Cassie did not expect. Or was this just another of his act?

"What?" His face pinched. "What do you mean by that?" His tone of voice was a high pitch. "You speak as if I've slept with plenty of women."

"Wasn't it the reason you were avoiding me afterwards? You are afraid that I might ask more from you just because we slept together."

"No! That's not true!" His eyes were bulging. "Why do you think I went to find you at your sister's wedding?"

She shrugged, flapping her arms aimlessly. "I don't know! Perhaps because you think I will accept you back and be happy to continue our casual relationship."

He looked flabbergasted. His face crumpled with a flare of breath from his nostril. His chest was up and down with his labouring breath. "Is that what you think of me?"

If it was an act, Cassie perhaps would believe him easily. But she felt a punch in her gut, realising that they had been talking on a different channel. His exasperation was unbearable. She had accused him of something that her little heart was telling her he didn't do.

She took a deep exhale, trying to remind herself to act mature. *You're 40 years old, Cass!* "I thought Briana was your girlfriend. But she is your sister." Her voice successfully out sounded calmer.

He huffed. "Right."

"Both of you don't look like siblings." And it was a fact! Almost every feature of him was different from Briana's. He had dark hair and eyes, while everything about Briana seemed light and glowing. Seeing them standing side by side was like a big contrast, but there was a sense of compatibility and completeness.

A ghost of a smile shadowed his lips. "You don't look like your brother, either. That was the reason I thought you were getting married to the father of the two little girls you were with."

Cassie couldn't help but snort at that statement. He had brought up a valid point. Like she always thought it herself, Kieran and Tiffany carried all the best genes in the family, while she was not.

Her laughter somehow melted the tension between them as the stiffness in his body slowly loosened. With both hands hidden inside his overcoat pockets, he stood watching her trying to control her laughter, still with a remaining smile on his lips.

She could feel the heat of his gaze. While trying to keep her face straight, an apprehension started to creep in. It seemed they had a misunderstanding. But it did not answer the question that still haunted her.

She returned his gaze with a defeated sigh. "Then why did you leave?" Her voice was almost above a whisper. She was preparing herself that he might say something else that made her heart wound open again.

His adam apple bobbed as he briefly shut his eyes and opened them again with determination. "Because I have a strong feeling towards you, Cass."

Though those words sounded beautiful, her heart was restless. Cassie anticipated something negative at the end of it.

"I'm scared you will leave me once you know about me."

Oh, here it goes! Pressing her palms onto her eyes, she tried to gather her strength. She knew she had to hear this either way. Though her heart would be crushed again into pieces, perhaps hearing it directly from him would give a better closure.

"I am..." His heavy breath sounded loud in their quietude. "Different."

Cassie's mouth slacked open. Her hands dropped as she stared eyes wide at him. That was not the word she was expecting.

He took another deep breath. With his slumping shoulders and fidgeting hands, she could read that he was struggling. There was a slip of sympathy feeling that perhaps admitting his – what she believed – potentially a double life was obviously hard for someone like him.

"Has Joshua told you anything about me?"

The change in the direction of the question startled Cassie. How did her brother-in-law have something to do with this?

But Brad pressed on his question. "Or perhaps your sister said anything about me? I saw both of you were talking at the wedding."

She blinked while her mind was racing. How did he know that Tiffany might tell her about him? The only thing she could remember was her sister's mockery of him.

"She..." she could not help but stutter. "She was surprised that, apparently, we know each other."

A self-deprecating chuckle popped from his throat. "I understand if she said something unpleasant about me. Perhaps I deserve it. But I can't help it. Because I'm..." He swallowed hard. "Different."

She furrowed her brow, still unable to figure out the meaning of his words.

"Do you remember when we were in Jakarta, and you told me the importance of looking at the person you are talking with?"

Cassie nodded hesitantly. Of course, she remembered that! She stamped him as arrogant because of his poor eye contact. However, after knowing him for quite a while, she did not bother anymore with that issue.

"That's because I'm different." His lips were pursed. His eyes went to the ground for a brief before lifting at her again. She could read the vulnerability shown in his eyes. "I was born with a problem socialising and communicating, unlike other normal people. They told me I am autistic."

"They?"

"The experts. The teachers, the paediatricians, the speech therapist."

Cassie held her breath as her lips parted. The word 'autistic" was not foreign to her. Perhaps because she was involved with Alicia and Ashleigh's life, she was exposed to this topic between the parents. However, it never crossed her mind that Brad was one of them.

"You look..." she breathed, squeezing her brain to find the right word. "Normal."

His lips formed a slow smile, loosening all the tension on his face. His smile was like a little boy who was just being complimented. Comprehension slowly dawned on her that his words may be true.

"I try to work on it. I'm still seeing a therapist every week. But.... " He let out a huge breath. "I thought you knew it. That was why you said you understood why I left. I thought because Joshua had told you about my issue."

"No!" Cassie shook her head in panic. "I did not speak anything about you with Joshua." She quietly complimented herself for not mentioning Tiffany's mocking words about him.

"After we had that night...." He stole a glance at her in a mere second before looking at the ground again. "I wasn't sure about myself. I never had such a great night before." He shut his eyes while shoving his hair. "Believe me. I did not mean to run away. It is the first time I have had such a feeling, and it's overwhelming. I hid away from you because I was scared that I might hurt you instead. I...."

He dropped his eyes. It was a sight that made her body shiver without realising it.

"I talk with my therapist, with Briana, and everyone, and I realise...that I like you, Cass. I adore you."

Hearing those words combined with his soft, yearning gaze seemed to make her float. His confession seemed pure and genuine, like a little kid. But the person standing before her now was a mature adult, and his confession made sense. Nevertheless, Cassie could not deny the tingling warm feeling that washed over her, making her speechless.

Her mind was hazy, filled with the ecstasy of exhilaration. For a moment, she was motionless, like having a mental blank, as her eyes stared at the ground. Her heartbeat was the only thing she could hear. She was fully aware that he was still rooted at his place, standing an arm away from her, watching her in anxiety spread on his face. The heat of his gaze was sufficient to send the hot swirl in her chest that slowly crept into her neck and her cheek.

Her apprehension intensified as her eyes caught his shadow slowly approaching her. His hand stretched out to her and pulled her closer to him, which paralyzed her more as his earthly masculine scent stifled her senses.

If Cassie denied her own feeling, she would be a good liar. But she was a terrible liar. She always emphasised honesty to Alicia and Ashleigh, wishing the girls would not be afraid to always open up to her or any of their family members.

After a couple of breaths, she finally braced herself to lift up her head. Enthralled by his beautiful pair of eyes for an endless time, Cassie had to admit that she believed him.

"I know it was not an excuse to disappear. I am truly sorry for that, Cass. I hope you can forgive me. And I hope...." There was meekness and plead in his eyes. "I hope you can accept this weirdo."

A chuckle and sniffle at the same time slipped from her throat as tears started to prick her eyes. "You're not a weirdo. Not for me."

He beamed. "Really, Cass? Are you serious?"

"Yes," she nodded. She could not deny that there was some boyish aura from him in the way he looked at her. It was a warm feeling within her that she could not help but adore it.

His lips now broke into a big smile as if he had just won the lottery. Her chest burst into a laugh, but what she did not expect when he suddenly lifted her body and twirled her around.

The moment she finally landed back on the ground, he captured her lips vigorously while pressing his palm on both her cheek. It was a kiss that took her breath away.

Once he finished tormenting her lips, the gap of cold air started filling her lung. They stood still in their position for a moment, with their foreheads grazing at each other, inhaling their warm breath for what seemed an eternity.

A sudden sound of clearing throat startled them. Instead of stepping away, Brad tightened his arm around her, immediately on guard as if anyone would harm her.

"Were you guys just making out?"

From the minimum illumination of the street light, Cassie recognised Tom and Chandra's figures, standing before them, with amusement spread on their facades. However, Chandra obviously did a poor job of repressing his giggle as he turned his face away.

The relieved sigh from both of them, followed by a helpless giggle, was their only answer. But Cassie was perfectly far from content, still finding herself in the warmth of Brad's sturdy arm, hiding her blush on his broad chest.

Epilogue

"No one is perfect until love comes."

"Were you thinking of sleeping with me the first time I came into this apartment?"

Their bare legs tangled as their shirtless bodies pressed against each other. They just completed their first love-making once the morning sun was out. They drifted to sleep for probably an hour afterwards, then sleepily awakened and started cuddling.

It was not the first time they had done this. This was probably their new routine on Saturday morning since they had been together for a month. Brad focussed much on his work on weekdays, and sometimes he was away travelling. Cassie began to understand his habit and temperament. How he could not tolerate any distractions when he was doing his work, and how crucial for him to have everything on the schedule. She gave him space during working days while she sometimes resumed her usual role, babysitting her nieces so Erin and Kieran could have a couple of nights for themselves.

He furrowed his brow and pondered on the timeline she asked.

"Remember when you offered me a drink in your apartment after a basketball game?" Cassie explained with eyes full of mirth. "Do you still remember?"

A light bulb moment finally hit him. "Ah, yes." Then he averted his gaze as if he was admiring her breast instead.

Cassie chuckled as her lips lightly brushed his. "That's okay. I'm just curious. Just assume I never ask this question."

He did not respond for a moment while soothing her forearm with his palm. "If yes, was it the reason you left?"

She jerked up her head, trying to read his impassive expression. She could see that his soft gaze was hiding some curiosity as well.

She swallowed hard as her mind raced, thinking about preparing her answers correctly without offending him. He seemed could read her mind.

"It's alright. Just assume I never ask this question." He chuckled as he sealed her lips with a kiss.

It made her burst into laughter, but he held her head and kept nibbling at her jawline and neck, which made her giggle.

She never imagined her life would be this blissful. Not in someone like Brad. This was simply like a dream.

"I presume I am not your first, Brad," she whispered while sniffing his soft hazelnut hair.

He lifted his head and gave her a knitted brow. "I never had a girlfriend before. I told you , you are the first person I have had such a strong feeling with."

She twitched her lips in disbelief. "Really?"

He seemed displeased with her reaction. "Don't you believe me?"

"You seem..." She took a pregnant pause. "Experienced." She avoided his gaze. "In bed."

His mouth was hanging open.

"I am complimenting you," she quickly added, trying to interpret his astonishment. His face became relaxed a second later, which made her feel relieved.

He chuckled. "I have to thank my dad because he organised something for me when I was twenty-five."

Now it was her turn to have her mouth hanging open before an amused smile threatened to appear. "Right."

"I guess it was one of his effort to make me look 'normal'. But I .." he smiled shyly. It was another side of him that she found cute. "I know I will not do it simply with anyone."

"How old are you?" she asked curiously. She was always sure he must be younger than her, or it was just her problem, feeling old because she was already forty.

"Thirty-five."

"And you're not bothered with my age?"

He squished his eyebrow with a smirk on his face. "Not at all. Are you?"

She shook weakly. She lifted her hand as her fingers caressed his cheek. "No. It's just you're too good to be true, Brad."

His lips broke into a slow smile. "And you are too, Cass." And he captured her lips passionately, sent her into seventh heaven.

If it was a dream, Cassie definitely did not wish to wake up. She had been wandering to find someone and felt her patience had finally paid off. No one and nothing is perfect. She realised that. However, she now understood the heavenly feeling when finally finding someone right.

Acknowledgement

For my family. As always.

Special thanks to Melati. Thank you for your time and help in proofreading this story in the middle of your breastfeeding. LOL!

Also by L D Raylene

A Little Amusement
An Amelia : A Modern Twist Pride and Prejudice
The 40 Year Old Virgin

About the Author

Based on The Big-Five Model (B5M) of five broad personality dimensions described by Dr John A. Johnson, the assessment test conducted in Raylene's workplace, she was identified with a high level of imagination. That means she perceived the real world as often too plain and ordinary, but it does not mean she is ignorant of things that happen around the world and how she is grateful for her life each second.

Since then, Raylene has started expressing her fantasy through writing to create a richer, meaningful world apart from her daily job as a part-time office all-rounder, a baker, a mother of two energetic kids and a wife to her, unfortunately not a bookworm, but factual oriented husband.